SOUTH

of the

BORDER

SOUTH
of the
BORDER

MARLIS · WESSELER

COTEAU BOOKS
WWW.COTEAUBOOKS.COM

Edited by Joanne Gerber.
Cover and book design by Duncan Campbell.
Cover photo, "Two Women on Beach,"/Photonica.
Author photo by Don Hall
Printed and bound in Canada by Marc Veilleux Imprimeur Inc.

National Library of Canada Cataloguing in Publication

Wesseler, Marlis, 1952-
South of the border / Marlis Wesseler.

ISBN 1-55050-298-0
I. Title.

PS8595.E63S69 2004   C813'.54   C2004-904620-9

1 2 3 4 5 6 7 8 9 10

COTEAU BOOKS
401-2206 Dewdney Ave.
Regina, Saskatchewan
Canada   S4R 1H3

Available in the US *and Canada from:*
Fitzhenry & Whiteside
195 Allstate Parkway
Markham, Ontario
Canada   L3R 4T8

The publisher gratefully acknowledges the financial assistance of the Saskatchewan Arts Board, the Canada Council for the Arts, the Government of Canada through the Book Publishing Industry Development Program (BPIDP), the Government of Saskatchewan, through the Cultural Industries Development Fund, and the City of Regina Arts Commission, for its publishing program.

For Joanne Shannon

PART ONE

February, 1972

1. PALENQUE

Arlene struggled through a lush undergrowth of sleep, conscious of a pounding noise that didn't make sense. Was it inside her head? She was half-aware she was still dreaming, that the dense fronds of fern and leafy vines stifling her could easily be banished if only she'd wake up. She was trying to reach a sort of icon, an object so obviously phallic even her dream self wasn't fooled. Then she lost it altogether, and couldn't recall what it was. She heard the noise again but ignored it, trying to remember.

She emerged into foggy consciousness thinking the dream had been so exciting that the noise must be her heart beating. She lay on the lumpy mattress trying to breathe normally. Touching herself, she dozed off again for a second before the pounding intruded once more.

"*Señorita* Nelson!" Someone shouted outside her window and she jumped out of bed, making herself dizzy. "Just a minute!" she called, pulling on her jeans, muttering. Who the hell would pound on her door like that? Had she forgotten to pay today's bill? Even so. She stumbled over her backpack, steadying herself on the warm grey cement of the wall, and opened the door.

1

"*Señorita.*" Two Mexican policemen stood outlined in the doorway, as immobile as if they'd been planted in front of her room. They hesitated only a few seconds, but it was enough to engrave their image on her memory for the rest of her life. A fat man with long dark eyelashes and a mole by his left eye stood behind his companion. The man who spoke to her was already inside the doorway. He was short, thin and wiry, but slouched as if he were tall. He had two golden teeth and an aristocratic nose. He moved toward Arlene with a placating gesture while the other one remained in the hotel courtyard, his grim expression unchanging.

"What is it?" she asked, tamping down a spark of panic. She'd heard stories about Mexican police, seen things. Her T-shirt clung to her with sweat, from her dream and from the damp heat that hung in the air like laundry, and she had to resist the urge to pull it away from her skin. She knew the *policía* didn't arrive at one's hotel room for no reason, but she couldn't imagine why they'd come to see her. Had she done something? She glanced at an empty beer bottle on the windowsill. Maybe the legal drinking age in Mexico was twenty-one. She was only nineteen. Her stomach clenched as she wondered if the remains of a joint were still in the ashtray by her bed. She widened her eyes and tried to look disarming. She moved a fraction of an inch to block his view of the ashtray.

"Please." The thin policeman took her hand and patted it. "Excuse me my poor English. I must tell you very sad thing."

An insect of dread crept up her spine. Sheila. Could she and Manrike have had an accident?

"Your friend, Shella, your young lady *compañera?*" He hesitated, nervousness now shading his expression. He cleared his throat. "Your friend is found dead," he said simply. "In the jungle of snakebite."

A high ringing invaded her ears, and she knew she must have heard wrong. "Sheila? Dead in the jungle?" She repeated this carefully, so now he would correct her and say, no, no I mean Sheila's boyfriend, or, I mean somebody else altogether.

"*Sí.*" He kept a gentle grip on her hand. "Jes," he amended in English.

The floor beneath her seemed to shift; she felt a chasm open in front of her. She moved carefully, with the man's help, and sat down on her bed so she wouldn't fall. The policeman avoided her eyes so she looked at his brimmed cap. She examined the square of cement blocks that made up her hotel room, the floor littered with her things, the tumbled bed she'd just vacated. Though in one way it all looked the same as it had that morning, in her new reality everything was transformed, unrecognizable.

The other man came into the room. He nodded kindly at her. She knew beyond any nightmare that these men were simply here doing their job. They were telling the truth: Sheila was dead. A sound rose in her throat, a keening so desperate that when she understood it to be her own voice, she quit. She sat on her bed searching for a Kleenex. The ringing in her ears dissolved into white noise. It was as if she were holding conch shells against both ears, listening for the sea but hearing only the hollow sound of empty containers. She watched the policemen as they spoke to each other; their motions seemed hindered, as if they were under water. The one who'd spoken to her came over to the bed again. "I come back later. Now I find friend for you, speak English."

"But my friend is dead." Arlene felt dead herself at that moment, stunned into paralysis, though she could still feel tears wetting her face.

"*Sí, sí.* I now find someone, speak *Español* and English. We help you," he assured her. The other one had disappeared.

Walking out of the room, the thin man seemed to personify a last hope, a lifesaver floating away from her. "Wait," she called. She ran after him and grabbed his arm. She hadn't even seen Sheila's body. It might not be absolutely sure. "I want to go with you, I have to see her."

"*Qué?*" He waited.

"I have to see the, uh, I have to see her, make sure it's really

Sheila." Wasn't that how it was done? Someone, a friend or relative, had to identify the body?

He looked down, then quickly met her gaze, as if he were flirting with her. "*Señorita*," he said, "the jungle, it is very hot, *comprendes?* A dead body, it, it must..." He hesitated. "We burn it," he said bluntly. "I bring you, in box, *mañana*, the ehh..." He couldn't think of the word.

"Ashes?" She was shocked, incredulous.

"*Sí*, ashes." He nodded.

This finality stunned her into stillness. The policeman attempted a slight move toward her, but she waved him away. He said again that he would return, and left, closing the door. She sat there, willing herself into numbness. If she moved, she didn't think she'd survive. After a long while, she had to go to the bathroom.

Once there, she undressed and stood under a torrent of cold running water. She wanted to feel frozen, shot with Novocaine. She thought about the fact that she was entirely alone and couldn't afford to let herself down. Still, she couldn't stop crying, and she wondered if she'd ever come out of this, if there could ever be an end. In her room again, she seated herself carefully on the bed, trying for the same position as before.

Later in the day, the Señora, the hotel manager's wife, stopped in, leaving a tray of food and a comforting flow of Spanish. Arlene surprised herself by eating something, though after she'd set the tray on the chair outside, she couldn't remember what it was. She realized at some level she'd understood everything *Señora* Louisa had said to her. "You poor thing. *Povrecita*. Eat something so you'll be strong enough to go home to your family. Then things will be much better. You poor thing." She'd shaken her head. "Your poor little friend." *Povrecita. Povrecita.* Arlene repeated the word like a chant.

Louisa had tears in her eyes, tears of sympathy for her, and Arlene felt she hadn't thanked her properly. Arlene's weeping

4

now contained an element of relief: there were other people here. She continued to watch the cement courtyard outside her window where a couple of hammocks hung empty between palm trees. She knew from the shadows that night was coming and she could do nothing about it.

L ouisa returned to sit with her long before dawn. She acted as hostess when people, neighbouring merchants and other hotel guests, dropped in later to pay their respects to tragedy. Arlene was bewildered and somewhat embarrassed by the visitors. This was not her community, after all. She remembered the time after her uncle's death when her aunt had been swamped by sorrow and visiting neighbours, eventually left to mourn her way through a freezer full of casseroles. Oh god. She had a momentary vision of herself, home with Sheila's ashes, having to endure questions from aunts, uncles, neighbours. Sheila's grandparents. It was too horrific to think about.

These people brought gifts too. Three little girls in pastel dresses with matching plastic sandals and white ankle socks presented her with a bag of puffed bacon rinds and a bottle of Orange Crush. They were quiet and solemn but obviously curious, and excited by carrying out an act of kindness that was their own idea. Arlene sat with them on the bed and drank her pop, passing the spicy piggy puffs around. When the girls stood up to go, they shook hands with her. *"Muchas gracias,"* she said solemnly to each one.

"De nada." They seemed to float out of the room, their dresses the colours of water lilies.

An old lady came to pray for her, or for Sheila. She sat on a chair in a corner saying her rosary, moving her lips silently. She was a slender wisp of a woman. Her hair, the colour of tempered steel, was pulled back into a bun so thick it seemed to represent all her strength. Arlene missed her when, after an hour or so, she silently blessed her and left. Several people left food with Louisa, who carried in one of the dishes for lunch. "You have friends here," she said in English.

"*Sí,*" said Arlene, putting her hand on her chest, "and I am so very grateful in my heart." She knew this came out stilted and mannered, yet she didn't feel false. Why should she? It was exactly what she meant. Heartfelt gratitude for sympathy, all the clichés of surviving grief were there for a purpose, as true and useful in one country as in another.

The thin policeman returned, accompanied this time by an elderly American tourist they'd met on their first night in Palenque. His concerned lined face looked wise and patrician, like the grade nine textbook illustration of an ancient Roman senator.

"I'm so sorry," he said, taking off his Panama hat. "You must be devastated."

She nodded. "Thank you." There was an awkward pause.

"I think we neglected to introduce ourselves. My name is Fred Muckle."

"Arlene Nelson," she said politely.

"I hope I can be of some assistance. Perhaps I can help you contact your family. The phone lines here are sometimes difficult to navigate, especially if you don't speak the language."

"I'm going to need a couple of days here and then I may need help to deal with, well, with the authorities I suppose," she said calmly. She sounded unreal to herself. Someone who didn't know her character very well seemed to be feeding her lines. She glanced at the policeman and suddenly remembered Manrike. He must be devastated too. "Where's Manrike? I must talk to him."

"He is gone. He is found nowhere." The policeman continued, speaking in Spanish to Mr. Muckle.

"He says they all know Manrike here; there's a search party out now." Fred Muckle cleared his throat, glancing surreptitiously at the *policía* and slightly lowering his voice. "Uh, how well did your friend know this Manrike?"

"What? Well, not too long but..." Arlene looked at him in confusion.

"Never mind." He shook his head, obviously changing his mind about this line of questioning.

How well *did* Sheila know Manrike? Arlene looked down blindly at the floor, not seeing the dusty cement, but images of what she should have done. She should have argued with Sheila, insisting she get to know him better before going off with him. She could have gone along with them when she'd been half-heartedly invited.

She resurfaced into the present. Never mind what Fred Muckle might have been insinuating. Simple death was enough for her to handle. The police had found Sheila. A snake had bitten her.

"The *policía* has your friend's ashes with him in the car, but you should come in a day or so to the police station to collect her things. I understand there's a backpack with her papers and personal items. I don't know why he didn't bring those as well."

"Papers?" She tried to recall what papers Sheila would have had with her. Her tourist visa, she supposed, though she'd left her birth certificate and traveller's cheques with Arlene.

"*Momentito.*" The policeman held up his hand in an abrupt gesture and went out to his car. He returned carrying a blue metal box the size of a toffee tin. He held it out to her and when she didn't move to take it, set it on the orange crate which served as her bedside table.

She'd thought the worst shock was over, but the idea of Sheila in that small metal receptacle buckled her knees. She pictured herself delivering it to Sheila's mom and dad, standing awkwardly on the steps of their split-level house. She sank onto the bed and rocked slightly back and forth, an autistic child. She barely heard Fred Muckle say something about the container.

The policeman looked uneasy. Fred repeated his comment in Spanish, something about the tin being too small, and Arlene watched them, curiosity giving her something of a reprieve.

The *policía* mumbled a few words and Fred Muckle looked disgusted and bleakly amused.

"What?" she asked. "What about the box?"

"Some of the ashes are lost. They had them in a larger container that leaked, on the trail back to Palenque."

Then a blank white sheet seemed to descend, shielding her from outrage and further grief. She stared at the men in disbelief. This couldn't be happening, she decided. She wasn't going to phone home even to talk to her own mother, let alone Sheila's. She wasn't going to think of telling Sheila's family anything. This was only a trip to Mexico, it was an adventure, it couldn't possibly affect their real lives. Reality, her and Sheila's real lives, were waiting for them at home, in Saskatchewan.

Fred Muckle winced, and the policeman looked away from her, off into a more comfortable distance.

Arlene felt sorry for both of them, standing there sweating, having to deal with her out of the goodness of their hearts. "Nothing could make it worse than it is. I think I'll lie down for a while." She knew the tone of her voice seemed dry, that she didn't sound as grateful as she'd been feeling. But right then she felt dry. Dried right out, so that she was afraid her lids would scrape her eyeballs if she blinked too often. She'd soon dehydrate into nothing but a wisp that could easily drift off. The men looked almost cheerful at the prospect of getting out of her room.

"You ask for me at police station," the *policía* said. "My name is Angel Delgado."

An-hell, Arlene thought.

The men left. From her place on the bed, she considered the tin box. Fred Muckle. She almost said the name aloud. It sounded like something from a hillbilly comedy. He was so damn distinguished, you'd think he'd at least call himself Frederick. She realized she was talking silently to what was left of Sheila, and she felt again that split second of falling, of having to pull herself back. This was no metaphor: there was real danger here.

An image of Sheila smiling complacently, her brown eyes dreamy and lively at the same time, flashed through her mind. Sheila, skipping out of grade ten math to sit in the Stuart's rec room with Arlene and smoke cigarettes; Sheila, bundled up in a parka navigating the icy Saskatoon sidewalks to Taverna's Pizza; Sheila, sitting in the Apollo Room at the Ritz, smugly announcing their trip to Mexico. Arlene couldn't breathe. The idea of it, of Sheila dying, in pain: the sick horror after being bitten by a snake, the final terror of realizing the other presence slithering through the jungle towards her was death.

Arlene stood up. She had to get out. She walked through the courtyard and made her way out of town, noticing nothing but a sense of herself moving through light, until she reached the road to the ruins, where she started to run.

When her breath began to hurt, coming in ragged gasps, she slowed to a walk. When all she could think about was the sun roasting the top of her head and how thirsty she was, she turned around. By the time she got back to the hotel, it was evening. She drank draught after draught of water straight from the bathroom tap. She didn't feel well. The noise in her head was there again, rising after she lay down as if someone had turned up the volume. She passed out, or slept, until late the next morning.

Some Weeks Earlier

2. SAN BLAS

An old woman holding a rooster in a sack sat down beside Arlene and Sheila, excusing herself politely as they squeezed closer to the bus window. She wore a print dress with blue roses on a black background, and her smile glinted with gold. The rooster glared at them from her lap, its head sticking out of the bag.

"He looks like Rusty from *The Friendly Giant*," Sheila said.

"More like one of those *macho* types hanging around downtown."

"You're right. That roosterlike conceit. But at least this one doesn't hiss."

Arlene laughed. "Not so far, anyway." She glanced around. None of the male passengers seemed interested in her or Sheila at close range, but as soon as they'd arrived in Mexico, an obnoxious hissing sound had begun to follow them incessantly, on every street.

"*Sssssita. Mamacita.*"

"*Sssssssss.*"

"*Sssiiitaaa.*"

Accompanied by whispers or shouts, the hissing seemed constant, ubiquitous. It was as if they were inside a balloon with a slow leak, or being stalked by an invisible serpent.

But the hissing and catcalls, the irritated language and shout- ing of the bus terminal were now transformed into laughter and courteous geniality. Travel seemed to be a gracious, polite activity for which people dressed up, the men in white shirts and dark pants, the women in colourful shifts or traditional outfits. Arlene relaxed against the window, delighted to be in the midst of it.

Uncaged animals, mainly trussed-up chickens, continued to be packed squawking inside the bus along with what was becom- ing an astounding number of people. The woman with the rooster smiled again, and asked them something, straining to compete against the noise. Arlene listened closely, trying to seem attentive though she barely knew two words of Spanish. "Canada," she finally answered, assuming this to be an adequate reply to just about anything.

"Ah." The lines in the woman's face deepened as her smile broadened. "Canada," she repeated, looking playfully at the roos- ter. His expression sank from hostility into dementia, and a ragged croon issued from the back of his throat.

Arlene grinned. She smoothed down the material of the new blouse she'd bought in the Mazatlán market. Raw cotton embroi- dered with thick bright-coloured thread, it was designed particu- larly for tourists, but that was fine with her. She loved being a tourist. She decided she'd like to be a tourist of life in general. A person could spend a whole existence touring, like that woman with her old father, who was it? In *Night of the Iguana*. Except of course, she wouldn't want to be stuck with anybody who was old.

She looked out the window for a last view of the city and froze.

"Sheila. *Look.*"

"Where?"

"At that guy. Isn't he the coolest person you've ever seen?"

He was a tall American, with jeans faded just the way they

should be, his Mexican tourist shirt clinging to broad shoulders, his hair hanging loose down his back. He was darkly tanned, his moustache and beard trimmed to accentuate high cheekbones and intense, sharply intelligent eyes. He reminded Arlene of Cat Stevens: everything about him unquestionably right. She couldn't take her eyes off him. When he looked up at her, sensing something, his face brightened slowly with a stunning smile. They both stayed motionless for several seconds, staring at one another. But the moment he made a move toward the bus door, the bus, backfiring a cloud of black smoke, started off for San Blas.

Arlene encouraged chills to go up and down her spine. It was like Anna Karenina seeing Count Vronsky. That image of his brilliant smile, that gaze so intent on her, could remain for the rest of her days. Instead of becoming the love of her life, he'd be caught suspended in a small bubble of memory. And however long he remembered her, even if it was only a few minutes, at least she'd been looking her best: her sunburn had faded to a tan, her hair was brushed, and she'd been filtered, like a touched-up photograph, through a cloudy bus window. It was, she thought with a sense of satisfaction, sort of tragic they'd never see each other again.

"Did you see that?" she asked Sheila.

"Of course I saw him. Smiling at you." Sheila nodded approvingly.

As the bus left Mazatlán behind, Arlene watched the lush Mexican countryside roll past and felt detached from it, as if she were viewing a travelogue or paging through a *National Geographic*. What if he'd been just a few seconds faster?

Halfway through the trip, they both had to go to the bathroom in spite of the fact they'd had hardly any coffee that morning. Arlene observed a couple of men standing in the ditch, legs apart, shoulders back, arrogantly pissing on the vegetation, and at a stop for more passengers, a woman hopped off the bus and simply crouched by the roadside. But as Sheila pointed out, it was one thing to do that when you had a skirt on, but something else when you were wearing jeans. They decided to wait.

Arlene could never remember having a first impression of San Blas. They bolted off the bus at the station and ran inside, searching frantically past ticket cages and broken lockers, manoeuvring around wooden benches with peeling blue paint until they reached the washroom at last: four cubicles with holes in stained and splattered cement.

Outside again, Sheila stopped short. "Look. There's some guy with our luggage." They quickened their pace until they realized he was a young tourist with no evil intentions, just standing there waiting for the bags' owners. He was tall, nice-looking, with long hair, wire-rimmed glasses, and a moustache.

As they came up to him, he shook his head and smiled. "You shouldn't ever leave stuff unattended," he said with a slight Southern drawl. "If I hadn't been here, it might surely be gone by now."

"We couldn't wait for it to be unloaded," Sheila explained. "We really had to go to the bathroom." She smiled at him, and Arlene could see by the warmth in her eyes and her unusual forwardness that she liked him. "We appreciate you guarding our stuff," she added.

Arlene looked down at their duffel bag, a lumpy stuffed sausage holding up a backpack on either side. At home, deciding what to put in the green canvas packs they'd bought for the trip, they'd ended up with a lot of extras: not only such items as Noxzema, toilet paper, and suntan lotion, but fat beach towels, and their black velvet pants in case they ever went anywhere posh. Then they needed nice shirts to go with the pants, and extra sweaters and jeans. They finally decided to carry more luggage. Unsure exactly how they were going to manage their sleeping bags, they eventually tied them awkwardly to their packs. They hadn't planned on doing all that much walking.

"They were the only tourist bags in the lot," he said, grinning. "I was sort of curious to see who owned them."

"Well, anyway," Arlene said. "Thank you. We would've been up shit creek without our packs." Though he and Sheila had only just made eye contact, she was already feeling left out.

They introduced themselves. He held Sheila's hand a bit longer than he did Arlene's. "My name's Luke," he said. "There's a few of us free-camping on the beach. I'm on my way there, if you want to join us."

"Sounds good to me," Sheila said.

"Yes," Arlene said. "The key word here is *free*." They walked out of the bus depot with Luke carrying their duffel bag.

"So where are you from?" Sheila asked Luke.

"I'm from Texas. I'm travelling with a Mexican named Jorge, a real interesting guy, he'll be happy to meet you. Where are you two from?"

It was *siesta* time. The streets were quiet and almost deserted. They walked through the entire village in twenty minutes, Luke and Sheila chatting, oblivious, Arlene plodding quietly past thatched huts and square cement buildings. Those that housed businesses or restaurants were painted in pinks and blues which may have been shocking some years earlier, but were now faded into crumbling pastels. Even the church was in rough condition. Scaffolding hung like an outer skeleton from one side, but no one was working on it.

After they stopped at a kiosk for an orange pop, Luke helped Sheila with her pack and added her sleeping bag to his own load. Arlene sighed audibly as she shouldered her own baggage. Noticing Sheila flash her usually dreamy brown eyes at Luke, she realized she'd become much prettier. Sun and salt water had dried her oily skin and hair. "I do believe," Arlene said to her, imitating someone British, "that your hair has developed body." It framed Sheila's rosy oval face in a silky brown aureole with copper highlights.

"Yours too." Sheila eyed her critically. "Your shag's growing out pretty nice, and you're already a bit blonder."

Sheila's mom had once told them they could both be quite pretty if only they'd spruce themselves up a bit. "Spruce yourselves up before you pine away," their brothers had teased. They paid no attention. It seemed to Arlene that making an effort to be attractive would be caving in to something, though in reality they were both simply too lethargic to bother. They wore bell-bottomed blue jeans, oversized plaid shirts, Army and Navy workboots, and no makeup. They had decided the year before to give up their virginity before they hit nineteen, and Arlene was mystified when there'd been no takers. She looked on chastity as a burden she was being forced to carry because of her social inadequacy. The older she got, she knew, the heavier the burden would become. She began to identify with old maids in Victorian novels. She believed she and Sheila were part of a tiny world minority.

Luke, who was leading the way, slowed so he could walk with Sheila, and Arlene fell slightly behind when they reached the path leading to the beach. The heat was oppressive and she was hungry. The walk was turning out to be longer than she'd expected, and she was in no mood to appreciate the jungle vegetation along the path, or the few people they met on the way. Since they were accompanied by a man, hissing and catcalls were generally stifled.

"I reckon you two are used to a lot of attention by now," Luke said to Sheila.

Sheila shrugged. "It's like that for any women tourists," she said. "It doesn't matter what you look like."

"Huh." He shook his head. "I doubt that."

But it was true. At first Arlene had felt ambivalent about all the *macho* attention. In Mazatlán, the vocal admiration of her looks had been such a new experience, it had crossed her mind that some of her singular inner beauty might be manifesting itself physically in a foreign setting. Then she noticed a girl walking on the other side of the street getting the same reaction, though she was very plain and about forty pounds overweight; she wore a bright-coloured Mexican blouse that was anything but flattering. Arlene had looked down at the dingy sidewalk, deflated. She should have known there had to be something lacking in a population of men so enamoured with her and Sheila. From then on, the hissing had annoyed her.

They emerged from the jungle onto the palm-tree-lined beach of a small cove, where a tent had been erected on the tawny sand along with a plastic tarp hung precariously on sticks. Beside the tarp, Luke's Mexican friend Jorge was tending a large pot over a campfire. Luke greeted him and introduced the girls. Jorge was, Luke said admiringly, his mentor. He made his living hunting and trapping, doing some tourist guiding and odd jobs. He was teaching Luke about survival in the jungle. He spoke no English at all.

Pointing to the stew he was cooking, he invited them to join him for a meal. "What is it?" Sheila asked. Luke translated.

"Iguana," Jorge said, pleasantly indicating where they should sit. Acting the gracious host, he dished out generous helpings.

Arlene examined her bowlful dubiously, picking at some rice. When she recognized peppers and onions, tomatoes and the odd piece of carrot, she started to eat, looking around for a place she could surreptitiously dump the meat.

"Hey," Sheila said. "This tastes really good Arlene. Try it."

Arlene ate a tiny piece, then nodded and smiled at Jorge. "*Bueno*," she said. It wasn't bad, sort of rubbery but mild, like factory-processed meat or poultry without the salt.

Jorge was wiry with muscular forearms, a huge moustache, and slicked-back hair. Arlene estimated his age as close to thirty, although he could have been younger. He said something to Luke and then found a seat on the sand between Arlene and Sheila.

"How long do you plan to stay in San Blas?" Luke asked, translating.

"Who knows?" Arlene said.

"A week or two, maybe more." Sheila conjured a time period from nowhere.

"*Mañana*," Jorge said, "*yo contruiré una cabañita para ustedes.*" They looked up for Luke's translation. "Tomorrow," he said, "we'll build you a grass hut."

The Mexican night had fallen with the suddenness of a power outage in a school gym, and Arlene was ready to roll out her sleeping bag. "That would be really something," she said, trying to sound enthusiastic.

"Do you want to go into town with us?" Luke invited. "There's a nightclub and all."

Sheila nodded. "Oh yes," she said.

Jorge and Luke muttered earnestly to each other in Spanish. They'd go and score some tequila, Luke translated; they'd be gone for a half-hour and then they'd all head into town. It was still real early, he said.

"The night is young," Arlene agreed blandly.

Sheila didn't seem to notice her tone of voice. "Just think," she said later as they waded into the black waves to bathe, "we'll have our own grass hut on our private beach in Mexico! We've got to write some postcards."

"I'll believe the hut when I see it," Arlene said. With the evening, the waves had smoothed into ripples. She ducked under and rubbed shampoo into her hair, trying unsuccessfully to produce lather with the salt water. "God, we'll likely feel just as sticky after bathing as before."

"At least we won't smell so bad," said Sheila.

The jungle pathway was well used and, with flashlights, not difficult to navigate in the dark. The lights illumined exotic vines and leaves, strange insects buzzed and hissed, night birds sang, and the dim consciousness of snakes and scorpions added zest to the whole excursion. Arlene was astounded at her own courage, at the fact that only a week and a half ago, she'd been sitting in the Apollo Room in Saskatoon.

17

At the side of the jungle path, she noticed one of her mother's houseplants thriving in its natural habitat and stopped short, swaying in amazement. She'd sampled too much tequila and knew it: she stumbled on, bumping lightly into Sheila. "Dr. Livingstone, I presume?" she said. She could feel Sheila smile enigmatically in the dark.

They emerged into a clearing where a thatched cement building, open on one side and lit up with Christmas tree lights, blared Latino pop music. It was impossible not to move to it. They paid the admission and stood watching the dancers, but only for a moment. Though Arlene could see men in jeans or dark pants and white shirts, girls in bright-coloured shifts, the impression was that of a crowd moving in unison: a thing in itself, a giant entity. Not one person stood on the sidelines; tables were used only to hold drinks. On the concrete dance floor, Arlene's new blouse shimmered under the strobe light. She felt herself floating, drifting along with the crowd in an ocean of black light and music that seemed timeless until Jorge handed her a beer. After a couple of sips, the atmosphere became close, muggy. She looked desperately around for a washroom, Santana's "Oye Como Va" pounding somewhere inside her stomach. She ran outside and threw up in a flowering bush, then sat down on the steps, her hands covering her eyes until Sheila came outside looking for her.

Luke and Jorge appeared in the doorway, conferring. The dance pulsed behind them, outlining their bodies off and on in random light. "Jorge will take you home," Luke said. "Don't worry none about him; he's a good guy."

"What about you?" Sheila asked. "Are you a good guy?"

"The best." He smiled and put his arm around her. Arlene felt like throwing up again. Since when had Sheila acquired a talent for flirting? Jorge smiled sympathetically. They started to walk back, the night so full of the scratchy hum of cicadas the sound seemed to come from inside her head. "That was the shortest night out I've had in a long time," she said, making a mild attempt to show Jorge she appreciated his company. He nodded silently. At least he didn't expect her to make conversation.

At the camping place, she took off her sandals and waded into the sea to brush her teeth. Through the foreshadow of a hangover she felt light-headed, not only with tequila and fatigue, but with a startled exhilaration again at being so far from home, at finding herself by the Pacific Ocean on a warm Mexican night, watching the dark waves under the stars. On shore, she dried her feet and rolled into her sleeping bag. "*Buenas noches,*" she said.

She could see Jorge's smile gleaming through the dark and thought of the Cheshire Cat. "*Mañana,*" he said. She was conscious he'd been watching her. She rolled over onto her stomach and tried to mould the soft sand around her body. As she fell asleep, she wondered if "*mañana*" was short for "see you tomorrow," or if he had meant it as a promise.

Morning came much earlier than expected, with an attack of tiny insects. She took a long drink of tepid water from her canteen, put a shirt over her head and tried to go back to sleep, but all she could do was doze. She noticed that Sheila and Luke were still gone, but sometime in the night another couple of tents had appeared on the beach. She lay down again, and finally fell asleep after the sun came up and dispersed the no-see-ums.

"Get up Arlene." Sheila was kicking her lightly. "It's nine o'clock." It was hot. Arlene peeled herself out of her sleeping bag, pulled her jeans on and stumbled into the jungle. The other campers were gone, though their tents were still there. Jorge and Luke were toasting tortillas and making coffee. As she drank her first cup after rinsing her face in the sea, she didn't feel as bad as she'd expected. Sheila couldn't sit still; she was bouncing around, giving off waves of energy so strong that Arlene wanted to raise her hands to fend them off.

Luke, on the other hand, looked a bit morose; he stood with his arms folded, talking in Spanish undertones to Jorge. Arlene stopped chewing her tortilla, as if she'd come across some grit between her teeth. "Sheila," she said. Sheila sat down beside her. "You had sex with him, didn't you?" she whispered. Sheila nodded. Arlene felt left behind in limbo. Sheila had crossed over into new erotic territory. Sheila had done it. "God! What was it like? Did it hurt?"

"Sssh." Sheila glanced at Luke and Jorge.

Arlene lowered her voice again. "Did it hurt?"

"Hardly at all." Sheila sipped her coffee. "It was nice. I didn't tell him I'd never done it before, but then he knew."

"But why him?" Arlene asked.

"Because." She paused. "It was just time. You know. Besides," she added, her eyes widening, slyly mysterious, "he seduced me."

Arlene hadn't realized they'd been having a contest until now, when she'd lost. Jorge came over with slices of fresh pineapple, kneeling beside her, making an offering, or an offer. She stared out at the small waves splashing quietly onto the beach. Jorge wasn't cool, but he was far from bad looking. He was older, dignified and nice. It might be uncomplicated and easy to have sex the first time with someone who might as well be from a different planet, with no history or future together. She looked at him out of the corner of her eye. She bit into the pineapple; it was sweet and warm, and the juice ran down her fingers.

She thought of the guy at the Mazatlán bus terminal. Overnight he'd become an icon, an unattainable ideal: his eyes, shoulders, the way he moved. She felt a surge of irritation with herself, and threw the pineapple rinds in the firepit. God. Thinking about men, worrying about them, being turned on by them, dealing with their teasing or condenscension – just simply reacting to men – took up half her life.

Right now she bitterly, helplessly resented all that time and energy. Sometimes she wished she were thirty-five or even forty.

Then she wouldn't care any more; the insecurity and fear of rejection, her complete ignorance of their thought processes, even the excitement would be far in the past.

Luke had one arm draped carelessly around Sheila's shoulders. With the other he threw pebbles into the sea. "We'll build your hut now," he said, "and then tomorrow we have to go to Tepic for a couple of days."

Jorge said something in Spanish, and Luke agreed. "Jorge says you *señoritas* don't need to help with the hut. He's the expert and I'm the assistant, and all the materials are right here," he waved his hands behind them, "in the jungle."

Arlene hadn't considered the possibility of helping to build anything. "We'll go into the village for awhile," she said. "Or go on the jungle river tour."

"Yes," Sheila agreed. "We met somebody in Mazatlán who said it was really neat."

Jorge got a pen and paper from his pack, wrote something and gave it to Arlene. "Jorge guides that tour sometimes," Luke said. "If you give the guide this note, he'll charge you the Mexican tourist rate instead of the American."

On the path to San Blas, Sheila seemed preoccupied. Arlene decided not to ask her anything more. She didn't want to risk being patronized. She'd find everything out for herself, soon enough.

3.

Several alligators sat, looking literally like bumps on a log, by a cement lagoon. They were so entirely immobile that Marjory, one of the sightseers who'd shared the tour boat, asked if they were real. Marjory was middle-aged and English, short and pasty-looking, as if she needed more time in the oven.

Picking up a stick, the guide reached over the fence and prodded the nearest alligator. As though someone had thrown a switch, its legs began to move and it glided swiftly into the water, where only the top of its head and the sinister flash of a lined yellow eye remained visible.

"Ha!" Arlene shook her head.

Sheila nodded at the guide. "Alligator sightings guaranteed," she quoted the tour's advertising disdainfully, though they hadn't been disappointed. The trip upriver had been well worth the Mexican tourist price. They'd motored past gnarled root systems of mangroves that reminded Arlene of the set of a horror movie, hedged in, shadowed by overhanging branches dense with rubbery green leaves. As the boat passed, colourful birds took off into the sky, turtles splashed in the water. The sky was cloudless, a hot cobalt blue.

Marjory's husband, Clyde, had given them each a turn at his binoculars while Marjory recounted their travel itinerary so far.

"And so then," she went on, "we spent five days in this really very ancient and seedy hotel in Guadalajara, but it was close to the loveliest little shops and, naturally, to the marketplace." She became simultaneously animated and dreamy, much in the way Sheila had been that morning. "The shopping! The lovely wool and leather, the silver jewellery. The pottery! And it's such fun bargaining. I bought this bracelet." She held out a freckled wrist with a pretty silver band. "And these sandals." She held up a pudgy foot featuring ordinary Mexican *huaraches*. "Guess how much I paid for them?"

Now, standing in the sun next to the alligator compound and waiting to be herded with the rest of the group to a rustic restaurant visible through the trees, it seemed to Arlene the jungle was closing in. Sheila was drifting back into her vague languor. Arlene noticed Clyde eyeing Sheila surreptitiously and, mildly disgusted, thought she must be giving off some sort of musk.

"I bet they've finished it already," Sheila said as they plodded toward the beach, tired from the boat ride and the heavy and expensive jungle tour cuisine. Arlene had almost forgotten about Luke and Jorge building their hut. She nodded unenthusiastically, expecting to see a few sticks carelessly covered with palm leaves.

When they got there, though, the two men were still working on the roof. It was a real grass hut, neat and compact and professionally put together. The walls, of grass already turning yellow, were thick, woven, and tied together as only an expert could make them. The palm leaves on the roof were arranged in an overlapping, rainproof pattern. The hut sat, squat and cozy in the sand, outlined against the backdrop of jungle like a prop for Swiss Family Robinson.

"It's so neat!" Sheila exclaimed. "It's beautiful."

"It's taken so much work!" Arlene was astounded. She walked around the hut, examining its details.

"It's all yours," Luke said, pleased.

Jorge bowed, graciously receiving applause for a perfect performance. The two builders worked for another few minutes, weaving the final cords of twisted grass through the walls, literally tying up loose ends. When it was finished, they peeled their clothes off and splashed into the water, only Jorge keeping his shorts on. "Toss out some shampoo, will you?" Luke called. Sheila held up a bottle of hers. "It doesn't suds up in salt water, but it's better than nothing," she called.

"Throw me that bottle from my stuff there," Luke pointed to his pack, where Arlene was standing. His penis hung sausage thick and blunt from a sparse growth of wiry hair. "It makes suds just fine," he said. Arlene found the shampoo, noting it to be an ordinary brand called Halo. She tried not to stare at Luke as she threw the bottle out to him. Penises weren't completely unfamiliar to her. At least she'd felt a couple, here and there. But they'd been straining against shorts or blue jeans, or had at least been hidden in the dark. Shortly before breaking up with him, she'd given her last boyfriend a hand job. She'd seen depictions ranging from nude paintings and statues like Michelangelo's *David*, who was rather unimpressive, to someone called Moby Dick Johnson (a Whale of a Tail), in the centrefold of a magazine. Actual sightings of the real thing, though, were hard to come by. Hard to come by. She should run that one by Sheila. Instead she sat quietly by their new shelter and watched as Luke and Jorge washed their hair and rubbed shampoo under their armpits. They dove underwater, then swam far out to sea and floated on their backs until they were washed back to shore in the waves.

Arlene crawled into the hut, feeling like a kid allowed to set up a pretend shelter in the living room. It smelled of new-mown hay. Light strayed in through the low doorway, giving the inside a cool, dusky look. It was about the size of a two-man tent and she wondered what the sleeping arrangements were supposed to be.

She stuck her head out the doorway and thought how cozy turtles must feel.

"We have to go to Guadalajara today," Luke announced as he got dressed, "instead of Tepic tomorrow." He put his arm casually around Sheila and kissed the side of her head. Some business had come up, he explained. They had to leave right away.

Sheila was silent. Arlene emerged from the hut and looked out at the green and foamy Pacific, relieved.

"We'll be back in a couple of days," he said.

"Well anyway, thank you for building this great hut. I mean, I can't get over how much work you did." Arlene looked at Jorge. *"Muchas gracias,"* she said.

"De nada. De nada." Jorge took her hand. *"Adiós,"* he said. He held up two fingers. *"Dos días."* He and Luke slung their packs onto their backs and headed toward San Blas. They turned and waved just before they disappeared down the jungle path. The suddenness of their departure left Arlene feeling vaguely abandoned. She felt sorry for Sheila, although her sympathy was undermined by a sneaking sense of satisfaction.

She noticed Luke's shampoo bottle forgotten on the beach, and grabbed it, happy at the prospect of being able to wash her hair properly. She undressed and ran into the cool waves, quickly diving under. She loved swimming with no clothes on; her movements felt liquid, liberated, part of the sea. The shampoo lathered normally, and she thought of sending a note to the Halo Company, praising their product and suggesting they use her and Sheila in a TV ad. She struck a model's pose, elaborately enjoying the white foam on her head, the rinsing, dramatically flinging back her clean wet tresses. When she came out, Sheila was sitting at the entrance to the hut, gazing out to sea. She looked as if she might cry. "You look like Penelope," Arlene told her.

"Penelope who?"

"A Greek myth. Remember grade nine social studies? She waited twenty years for her lover to return from a voyage?" She fluffed her hair with her fingers, taking mock advantage of the sun and wind, and grinned at Sheila. "Well, actually Odysseus was her husband. She wasn't a myth, but a mythuth."

Sheila gave her a look. "Those guys will be back, you know," she said.

"Probably." Arlene shrugged, getting into her clothes. "Stranger things have happened." To make up for this unnecessary comment, she walked down the beach to gather firewood for that evening. It came mainly in unmanageable shapes and sizes, so by the time she got back, she carried only a few small pieces. A straggly group of young tourists had arrived, and now surrounded Sheila, examining the hut and exclaiming.

"Wow." A stocky young man stood with his feet planted firmly in the sand. "Is this far out or what!" He wore the wrong kind of glasses, and his hair, cut too short at one time, was now growing out in uneven tufts. Even though he was only in his early twenties, he had a spare tire hiding part of the tooled leather belt holding up his cut-offs. He looked around and beckoned to a small, pretty girl in white with very red hair and silver jewellery. "I'm Murdoch," he introduced himself. "And this," he said solemnly, "is Jeanette."

The other couple was explaining to Sheila that they'd been here off and on for two weeks and knew Luke and Jorge well. After introductions, the woman, whose name was Lexie, said to Arlene, "So. Sheila was with Luke, right?"

"Yes?" Arlene raised her eyebrows.

"So does that mean you were with Jorge?"

"No."

"Oh. I didn't mean to be nosy, I'm just curious about what he's like in the sack."

"I wouldn't know." Arlene shook her head. Americans, she thought. "And where are you from?" she asked.

"I'm from Boston, and Hank here is from Kansas." She put her arm around him. "He's off to see the wizard," she teased.

Tall and dishevelled, Hank seemed appealingly absent-minded. He looked just like a Hank. Arlene smiled politely at him, and wondered if he was in the habit of skinny-dipping. This thought hadn't occurred to her on meeting Murdoch. She glanced over at him. He was intently examining the way the roof was attached to the woven grass walls, his glasses slipping, his open shirt emphasizing a small roll of fat. She couldn't understand why Jeanette would be with someone that uncool. Well, maybe he'd turn out to be interesting in his own way. She could start a sort of mental penis collection for comparing and contrasting later on, back in Canada, when everything was back to normal and she was wondering what to do on a Friday night.

"Hi there," Hank said. He'd already been busy collecting a good pile of driftwood. He began to stack it, adding his more substantial pieces to Arlene's sparse offering, while Lexie went for a swim, wearing a bikini. She had, Arlene noticed, a few slight dimples on her thighs, the only indication she was in her late rather than early twenties.

That evening in town they all chipped in and bought refried beans, tortillas, and fruit for dinner on the beach. Hank and Lexie had a bottle of tequila, which they shared around the campfire. Arlene drank enough to feel mellow, trying not to overdo it. She and Sheila sang "Oh Lord Won't You Buy Me a Mercedes Benz," and Hank and Lexie sang "St. James Infirmary." Jeanette described how an LSD experience in Berkley had changed her life, and Murdoch talked about the mystery of the ancient Mayans. He and Jeanette had only met a couple of weeks ago. He was returning to the Yucatán now to show her the ruins.

"They didn't have graveyards," he said. "Ordinary families buried their dead underneath the floors of their houses."

"Really?" Lexie paused halfway between lime and tequila.

"Only powerful leaders were buried in the tombs, of course. So every dwelling was also a gravesite. Interesting, eh?"

"What did they believe about an afterlife?" Lexie asked as she passed the bottle to Sheila.

"It was sort of a limbo, like in that part of Hades where everybody just hung around and existed forever? Dank, sort of oppressive, probably a lot like the huts became in real life if people weren't buried deep enough."

Fanning herself, Arlene decided the jungle heat and dampness were stifling. Not to mention the insects. She wondered if northern Mexico, with its dry dust and wind, its cacti and ponchos, would be more to her liking. It was calm that evening, and no-see-ums were out in full force. "God," she said, waving her hand. "We'll never get any sleep with all these midges or gnats or whatever they are."

"That's why we move to town every couple of days. They even get in through the mesh on our tent," said Lexie. "We rent a hotel room so we can have a good sleep."

"My tent is almost insect-proof," Murdoch said. "Although it's not as classy as a grass hut."

"Did you see that arena in Palenque where they used to play some kind of ball game?" Hank asked.

"Yes." Murdoch nodded enthusiastically. "Where the losing team was sacrificed to the gods?"

"Now that's what you'd call promoting team spirit." Sheila was sharing a joint with Murdoch and Jeanette, and offered a toke to Arlene.

Arlene was struck by the familiarity of all this, the generic comfort of finding people just like the friends she used to go to the bar with at home. "You know what?" she asked Sheila.

"What?"

"I feel as if they've knocked a couple of walls off the Ritz and transported it here. Like a *Twilight Zone* episode. Like everything is different because it's in a new dimension, but it's all the same, sort of."

Sheila smiled absently and looked around at their new companions. "What an idea," she said.

"The problem is," Arlene said, struggling to articulate an apprehension, a mouldy realization just beginning to sprout on her brain cells, "the problem is, they transplanted me with it. I mean here I am, still me." Back in Saskatoon when they'd planned the trip, she had imagined being transformed by a place as exotic as Mexico: she would become graceful and tanned and charming.

"Yep." Sheila put on her dumb-country-girl voice. "Here we are, still us."

"Wherever you go," Murdoch said, "there you are."

Arlene wondered if this was a quote, but before she summoned the energy to say anything, Hank asked, "Where exactly are you two from?"

"Saskatoon, Saskatchewan," Sheila informed him.

"Oh. Well," he said. "That explains it."

Arlene shot a watermelon seed at his forehead. "Good shot," Lexie noted. "Right between the eyes."

"They're not from S'skatchew'n for nothing," Murdoch said.

Arlene and Sheila both looked at him, noticing he'd pronounced the name of the province like a native son. "Where are *you* from?" Sheila asked.

"Swift Current," Murdoch answered.

"Swift Current!" Sheila laughed.

"I don't believe it," Arlene said.

"I spotted you two for stubble-jumpers right away," Murdoch said.

Arlene gave him a disgusted look. "You did not."

"Oh, yes. I did." He took a swig of tequila and belched. His glasses slipped farther down his nose, giving him a cross-eyed look. Arlene snorted and lifted one of his cigarettes. "Hey," he grabbed the package. "Smoke your own!" She lit the cigarette anyway, holding it away from him. He grinned at her and belched again, pushing his glasses back into place. Breathing deeply, relishing the cheap tobacco smoke sharp at the back of her throat, she became conscious of Jeanette looking at her with alarm, and realized she suspected her of flirting with Murdoch. Arlene wanted to sigh.

They added leaves to the fire so the smoke would keep the bugs at bay. "So how come you know so much about the Mayans?" Sheila asked Murdoch.

"I stumbled upon an excavation site at Palenque," he said. "I got to know a couple of the archaeologists; they were good eggs, they let me hang around and help out."

Good eggs? Arlene hoped for his sake Jeanette was in a sort of ongoing haze from former drug experiences. Imagine waking up one day from a trance and finding yourself with Murdoch.

But Jeanette gazed at him admiringly. With her dangling silver earrings glittering in the firelight, her red hair darkened by the night, and her white Mexican Indian dress, she held the aura of an exotic *señorita* from the past.

Around two in the morning, they all rolled into their sleeping bags. Arlene and Sheila crawled into their hut, proud proprietors of their own home. Arlene snuggled down comfortably, enjoying the pleasant smell of grass walls, and was lulled almost to sleep when she heard the tiny high buzz of the no-see-ums. A horde of them wafted and whined through the doorway and surrounded their heads, not even substantial enough to slap. At dawn the girls moved outside and managed to get some sleep before it became too hot. When they got up, everyone else was gone. They went for a swim, and then into San Blas for breakfast.

Sheila ate her *huevos Mexicana* thoughtfully. "I wonder what business Luke and Jorge have in Guadalajara? Even if it was, you know, drugs or something, they could have told us."

"I'd just as soon not know." Whether or not they were involved with anything criminal, Arlene suspected that Sheila was the real reason they had left. Luke hadn't realized how inexperienced she was. He and Jorge had an agreement: in order to justify taking off whenever one of them felt jumpy, they'd exaggerate minor or imaginary problems into major catastrophes needing immediate attention. "They might not be coming back, you know." She meant this kindly. She thought Sheila would have to face the facts sooner or later.

"Whatever happens, at least they built us a great hut," Sheila said. "And one thing's for sure, at least I'm not a virgin any more."

Annoyed that she would hold that over her, Arlene didn't reply. But then she asked, "How was it? Really?"

Sheila's mood improved. "Like I said it hardly hurt at all. Surprising, maybe. When I felt him inside me all the way, I was...surprised. It's hard to describe. But I didn't, uh, I didn't *come*. I just sort of glimpsed the potential." She looked around, then leaned toward Arlene. "You know what he told me?"

"No. What?"

"That I had the smokiest pussy in San Blas."

Arlene snorted. "I'm jealous," she said. She was, too. She believed it to be a sad but inevitable fact that no one would ever say anything like that to her, no matter how long she lived. "No, I really mean it."

They started to giggle, not stopping until they were weeping and struggling for breath. The waiter came out of the kitchen to watch them, which set them off again. Shaking his head, he made an incomprehensible comment to the cook and came over to clear their table.

Three more days passed with Arlene and Sheila becoming more and more miserable because of the no-see-ums. Each night they ended up sitting by a smoky fire until they crawled into their grass hut and passed out with exhaustion. The bugs eventually drove them out into the sun where they dozed the day away in the heat, waking up to cool off in the water or to grab some lunch. By evening, they became a bit livelier, but everyone else went to bed around midnight. Lexie and Hank had given up on the beach altogether and were renting a room in town. Each night, Murdoch and Jeanette crawled complacently into their tent. Though it was set up at a discreet distance from the hut, murmurs and hoarse breathing, repeated requests and moans of satisfaction buzzed through Arlene's sleepless nights as insistently as the no-see-ums.

Sheila agreed it was time to leave. "I guess Luke and Jorge won't be coming back," she admitted, throwing a damp log on the fire. But she seemed more or less to have recovered. "It doesn't matter any more. Luke was just a, well, a sort of blip on the road."

Arlene didn't quite believe her. "You mean blip on the screen. Or a bump on the road."

Sheila ignored this. "Anyway, we'll go bonkers if we stay here much longer."

"Yes, that's one thing for sure." Arlene sat up decisively to look at the map, beginning to revive at the thought of travelling again. They could go anywhere.

"If we hitchhiked," Sheila said, "we could leave any time we wanted."

"Let's head for somewhere dry, like in all those spaghetti westerns," Arlene suggested. "Let's go toward Monterrey." She examined the map. "Or maybe not. It's quite a detour out of our way, isn't it?"

"How can it be out of our way?" Sheila asked. "We don't even *have* a way. That road north might be more interesting than any other one, for now. We've certainly had enough of jungle heat and bugs."

Sheila was right. Nothing was out of their way. This knowledge struck Arlene as something luminous: a cartoon light bulb inside her head. They could take any path, to anywhere at all. It made no difference to anyone.

Before they took off in the morning, they pummelled the side of Murdoch's tent. "Wakey wakey!" Arlene called.

"What the hell?" Murdoch unzipped the entrance and peered nearsightedly at them. "What do you want?"

"Nothing! We're saying goodbye." She adjusted the strap of

her backpack. "We're off to see the wizard, just like Hank." Deprived of another night's sleep, she felt strung out, high on exhaustion. Jeanette's face appeared alongside Murdoch's, looking pasty and swollen, adding to her exuberance.

"Well." Murdoch fumbled behind him and found his glasses. "Good luck you two. Maybe we'll run into each other again some-where."

"Who knows?"

Sheila seemed happy to go, too, but she'd left a note for Luke in the hut, just in case he came back.

4. ON THE ROAD

"How come you look so pissed off, Arlene?" Sheila asked, half dozing on a bench where they'd been dropped off at a pretty, quiet square that was supposed to be near the bus station. Guadalajara was a big city, exciting compared to anyplace they'd visited so far, and this area had that tourist-brochure atmosphere of Old World charm that Arlene could see but wasn't appreciating.

"That truck driver. Did you see the way he put his hand on my knee, right before we got out?"

Sheila shook her head. "Well, at least he got us here. We'll take a bus again tomorrow."

The ancient truck, loaded down with fruit, had reached a top speed of forty miles per hour and the motor had groaned dismally up mountain inclines, overheating to such an extent Arlene half expected it to blow up. They'd had to hold onto their backpacks with the duffel bag lumped under their feet against the gearbox until it started to smoulder. The smell of scorched cotton had lasted the rest of the trip, while Arlene tried to balance the damaged bag on her knees. By the time they'd reached the city she was hypnotized with fatigue. She'd felt it her duty as a hitchhiker to appear bright and interested in the photos of the driver's family, in his efforts to make stories about his work understandable. Sheila had slept so soundly she snored.

Once in the city, the truck had ground its way slowly and stubbornly down the middle of the street, the driver cheerfully ignoring the honking and the verbal abuse hurled at him from car windows. When he'd stopped near the square to drop them off, Arlene had smiled at him, grateful for the ride, and he'd put his hand on her knee, asking her something, making an obscene gesture with his other hand. His heart hadn't even been in it; he'd been performing some kind of ritual, or duty.

"It's too late to go any further today."

"No kidding." Arlene felt weighted down with granite. "I can hardly move." They sat for another half-hour, neither of them wanting to make the effort to stand up. It was peaceful here, though by no means deserted. People in office clothes walked through with a purpose. Lingerers were well-dressed and seemed to have reasons to be here, too: eating snacks, meeting friends. The plaza was enclosed by a very low wrought iron fence, with lush green lawns and full-grown trees surrounding walkways of cement tile. For some reason, the bottom few feet of each tree trunk had been painted white. Some decorative shrubs had been trimmed into unidentifiable shapes, others left to bloom splendid pink or orange flowers. At the centre, an ornate fountain spouted a trickle of water which eventually reminded Arlene she had to go to the bathroom.

When they spotted a couple of young tourists, they summoned the energy to ask directions to a cheap hotel, where they rented a room with an unusually firm mattress and a ceiling so blue Arlene thought if she woke up confused enough in the morning, she could mistake it for sky. They lay down for a nap before supper, practically ecstatic to have a real bed and no insects, and slept through the night.

After breakfast in the chill of a Guadalajara morning, they went back to the plaza. A white early colonial building that sprawled over a whole block of the adjacent street featured a row of brick and tile archways; one of them led to a bank. They needed to cash a traveller's cheque, and as the day warmed up, they waited in line playing peek-a-boo with a remarkably patient baby who gazed blankly at them over his mother's shoulder. When his expression became suspiciously determined, then uncomfortable, his mother asked Arlene and Sheila to hold her place in line while she changed his diaper on one end of the bank counter. Arlene was interested to observe that the people in the queue found this a pleasant distraction.

She admired the way the woman's hair was cut so that it fell in a perfectly groomed helmet to her chin. Her eye makeup and lipstick looked newly applied, and her tailored skirt and blouse still looked crisp and clean in spite of her baby, who now sat portly and placid again in her arms. His arms and legs were so fat they formed rings, sausage links, at his wrists and ankles, and Arlene wondered how the kid was able to see anything past his own cheeks. "*Muy grande niño,*" she said, attempting conversation.

The mother smiled proudly. "Yes, he is very big baby. You want to hold him?" She gave him to Arlene without waiting for a reply, obviously assuming no one would pass up such an opportunity.

"He's quite an armful." She found him about as appealing as a damp sack of flour. He soon reached out to his mother, whining, and Arlene happily gave him back.

By the time they got to the second-class bus terminal it was noon, and third-class buses were filling up quickly with people, and even in such a big city, livestock. They managed to find room on one heading north and settled in with their packs, the duffel bag piled with other luggage on the roof. An ascetic-looking young man sitting near them gave up his seat to a pregnant woman, who, once she was seated, had trouble holding a cardboard box on what was left of her lap. She looked about their age, with a friendly smile and gold hoop earrings. Her flower-patterned shift was too tight, and must have been uncomfortable. An older woman and a child were crammed in beside her, both holding chickens. Arlene realized there was something alive and literally kicking inside her box. The animal squealed and shoved part of its snout through a hole in the side. Because of the awkward position, it was dangerously close to escaping. Arlene examined the bus ceiling. "Sheila," she whispered, "if I offer to take that pig, will you take a turn holding him when I'm sick of it?"

"Why not?" Sheila said. "What's a pig between friends?" Arlene pointed to the box, then to her own lap. The woman smiled gratefully and handed it over. The piglet immediately quit squealing and snuffled curiously, grunting and making odd contented noises like snores. Among all the smells on the bus ranging from chicken shit to soap and perfume, Arlene hadn't noticed anything piglike, and even at close range nothing but the smell of dusty hay emanated from his box. "He likes me," Arlene said. She and Sheila grinned at each other.

"He thinks he's come home to Mom."

Arlene kicked her ankle. "Remember in *Alice in Wonderland* when that baby turns into a pig?"

Once the bus reached the outskirts, the driver hit the gas, blasting the horn every couple of minutes, not stopping for pedestrians or farm animals, playing chicken with everything else on the road. Fifteen minutes out of the city, he slammed on the brakes to collect more passengers from the roadside. Nobody got off. He had to stop regularly to pick people up, but made up for lost time with spurts of manic speed. The bus careened around a blind curve, narrowly missing a truck loaded with pineapples. But along with everyone else, Arlene and Sheila sat serenely rocking from side to side, giving themselves up to a fate Arlene knew was, for them, nothing but benevolent.

The pig's owner offered candied fruit. A man in a white shirt sitting behind them asked their names and where they were from, and seemed astonished at their answer. "Canada!" he exclaimed to his neighbours, who murmured genuine appreciation. Various people introduced themselves, formally shaking hands, radiating a gracious hospitality that seemed characteristic of all Mexicans, whatever their class. Arlene felt she'd been granted a reprieve from tourism, handed a key to something. She relaxed into the heat emanating from bodies and the sunlight shining through the dusty windows, and felt it as universal warmth. She beamed generously at the ascetic young man, now squatting in the aisle beside her. He was obviously poor, but he looked like an intellectual. She wasn't sure how she could tell this. He must be a student, she thought, as he nodded back. With his narrow shoulders and wide, old-looking eyes he could have been any age from seventeen to thirty. If his ears stuck out more, he'd have looked just like Kafka. El Kafkasito. She smiled. "Do you speak English?" she asked.

"A little. I studied some English at university."

"I knew you were a student," she said, pleased with herself.

"And you?" He said this to include Sheila.

"Students," they both answered. "Except now we've quit," Arlene went on unnecessarily, "and we're travelling. We like Mexico a lot," she added.

"Do you?" His smile was ambiguous. His eyes: alternating with a dark inward awareness, an opaque blankness, as if a candle were flickering. She noticed again how thin he was, not scrawny and wiry like many of the working men, but delicate and unhealthy. She felt uncomfortable, and turned her attention to the piglet, trying to get a glimpse of him through the holes in the box. Then she decided to try again. It wasn't often they ran into a Mexican guy who was shy with female tourists. "What university did you attend?" she asked formally, after re-establishing eye contact.

"Mexico City," he said. "*Universidad de México*, then three years in Lecumberri."

"What did you study?"

"Human behaviour." He snorted quietly to himself.

They were silent for a moment. Arlene sensed a subtext to his words but wasn't sure if she wanted to know. "Where's Lecumberri?" she asked. "Is it another school?"

He straightened and looked right at her. "The Black Palace it is called also. I was a political prisoner." The effort to straighten his spine seemed to tire him out. He looked ill.

"For three *years?*" Sheila asked.

"Yes. After student protests in 1968."

Arlene knew whatever she said would sound inane. "That's terrible." She shook her head, looking away. What were they protesting? She didn't ask. When she looked at him again, she said, "You don't seem very well. Why don't we trade places?" Sheila took the pig and Arlene stood up. She pulled her pack from under the seat so she could sit on it in the aisle. The student nodded politely and traded places. "Thank you," he said. "It is true. I don't feel well." Almost immediately, he fell asleep, his head resting awkwardly on the back of the seat.

After a while, Arlene's neck and shoulders started to ache as she tried to keep her balance on the floor of the bus, which now seemed as if it were hurtling through space, veering from side to side to avoid asteroids. She looked over at Sheila, who was eyeing the box on her lap with disgust. "This pig didn't smell this bad when you had him," she said.

"You want to switch places?" Arlene asked.

"I'm not sure. Do you?"

Arlene didn't answer. The student had shifted in his sleep and his shirt rode up, showing his lower back. Interspersed with small round marks ran a network of long ridged scars, as if a road map began at the base of his spine. She instinctively reached over and pulled his shirt down. She caught Sheila's eye, then the young pregnant woman's; both looked away quickly. Conversation among the people around her died, but their faces remained impassive. In spite of the crowding, several men were smoking and Arlene lit a Fiesta of her own. After a couple of drags, she leaned her forehead against the metal on the side of the seat. She shivered.

Imagine going to classes one day and being imprisoned and tortured the next, for protesting. She and Sheila had been in a student

protest march once, against the war in Vietnam. One of their drinking buddies from the Ritz who called himself an activist had talked
them into going. When they were handed papers with the songs
and lines for them to chant, Arlene got one that said "What do we
want? Better day-care!" and had to read off Sheila's. But because of
Kent State, they'd thought they were being righteous and daring.

She decided to clear her mind of everything but the feel of the
metal on her forehead and the sight of her cigarette burning down
to the filter. She played a game with herself, waiting to see how
long the ash would hold its shape before falling to the floor.

In Zacatecas, they headed first, of course, for the washroom.
They carried their backpacks with them, but when they
returned to claim their duffel bag, it was gone. "Aw shit!" Arlene
looked up and down the street in front of the depot. "It's only been
a couple of minutes!"

"Arlene!" Sheila pointed down a side street. It was El
Kafkasito, climbing casually up the steep cobblestone, hauling
away their bag as if he owned it.

"Hey!" Arlene started after him, then saw it was useless. As
soon as he noticed her, he transferred the weight to his shoulder
and ran off, disappearing into the twilight.

"That fucking little asshole! After I gave him my seat!"

Sheila was calmer, and more philosophical. "At least we don't
have feel so sorry for him now." Since he'd done them a bad turn,
she said, they could write him off as not worthy of any further concern.

Was this true? The memory of his scars clutched at Arlene but
she felt too tired to deal with any of it.

"In a way," said Sheila, "I'm glad to get rid of all that stuff.
Well, except for the Tampax and toilet paper." She stopped, trying to remember something. "There was this Eastern poet."

"Leonard Cohen?"

Sheila made a face. "I remember reading, I guess it's a haiku, it goes something like, *Since my house burnt down/ I have a better view of the rising moon.*"

This was just typical of Sheila, so calm, seeming so smugly practical yet way off topic, right after they'd been robbed for the first time in their lives. Arlene counted on her fingers. "That's only sixteen syllables."

Sheila's shoulders stiffened with irritation and she started to walk quickly. Arlene lagged behind on purpose, watching her forge ahead toward the *zócalo,* where, looking up at the rich dome of Zacatecas's ancient cathedral, she allowed her posture to relax. Arlene watched her move through a crowd, past hissing men, as serenely as if she were by herself on a beach, always staying half a block ahead until she stopped to wait.

5.

The countryside was barren semi-desert featuring the odd cactus, a yucca tree and tufts of dry vegetation Arlene couldn't recognize. The gas station, with its pink stucco, was the only spot of colour. This was the Mexico of the movies. Arlene thought of Clint Eastwood, at a funeral on Boot Hill. Instead of sticking out their thumbs, after being propositioned by all three of the rides they'd had so far, she and Sheila decided to wait until a couple or a woman showed up for gas.

A van obviously owned by American tourists pulled up to the pumps.

"Let's see if they'll give us a ride," Sheila said. "It doesn't matter what direction they're going." It was an expensive vehicle of a type usually driven by middle-aged or retired people, but with a psychedelic logo painted neatly on the sides. A couple in their thirties with long hair, loose Mexican shirts and faded jeans got out and Arlene called to them.

"Excuse me. We were wondering if you'd have room for us."

The man nodded genially. He was balding; what hair he had was tied back with a leather thong. "We're headed to Veracruz, for Carnaval."

The woman was quite fat, and also wore her hair in a ponytail.

"We're stopping at a campground this evening though," she added, not quite as enthusiastic.

"The East Coast sounds good to me," Sheila said, shrugging her shoulders. Arlene agreed.

"You're welcome to join us all the way to Veracruz, if you don't mind sleeping outside," the man offered.

"That wouldn't bother us at all," Sheila said. The woman smiled, deciding to be hospitable, and after the gas station attendant appeared, she opened the side door of the van to invite them in. Sheila and Arlene glanced at each other. The whole interior was luxurious wine-coloured velour. An eight-track tape of Jim Morrison asking someone to light his fire was playing just loudly enough.

The couple introduced themselves as Kerry and Chuck. They seemed oddly determined to be laid-back and easy-going, to seem part of the counterculture in the midst of, or in spite of, their age and obvious affluence. Kerry pointed out the little fridge set neatly between the captains' seats and told the girls to help themselves to anything. "And we mean anything," Chuck smirked as he stepped on the gas, cruising down the narrow highway.

When they opened the fridge, they saw what he meant. Besides various drinks and vegetables, there was a baggie full of marijuana. "Gee," Sheila said appreciatively.

Toward evening, they came to a tourist campground with a large area set up especially for recreational vehicles, electric outlets at every site and a huge centrally located cement bunker with showers and washrooms. There were only a few other vans and a couple of trailers scattered over an expanse of dry grass, semi-arid evergreens, and stunted cacti.

"This could almost be a campground near Kamloops," Sheila said. She and Arlene sat by the fire eating from a bag of sunflower seeds they'd been ecstatic to find under one of the seats in the van.

Chuck and Kerry were in the back folding the seats down, miraculously producing a bed. When they finished, Chuck rolled another joint, and they all helped to cook supper out of cans, buying fresh tortillas from a boy selling them to campers.

They passed around another joint, quietly intent on their food. The sun would soon set. Arlene and Sheila were going to roll out their sleeping bags by the fire and sleep under the stars. "We have extra blankets," Chuck said. "You might need them; it can get cold at night this high up."

"We had warmer sweaters and stuff," Arlene said, "but they were stolen."

Chuck and Kerry nodded. "Yes," Kerry said, "we have to watch the van all the time. And insurance is outrageous." Chuck took a long toke and passed the joint to Sheila. The eight-track was playing J.J. Cale singing "They Call Me the Breeze."

Arlene sat off to the side, admiring the grandeur of the parched countryside. She fell into a state. She became conscious of Being. She recalled the essay she'd been impressed with in Philosophy 102. Being there. Being here, being there, beings, beings everywhere. Mexican jumping beings. She giggled to herself.

"What's so funny?" Sheila asked.

"Remember that Heidegger essay we tried to read, on Being and existence?" Arlene said. "Well here we are. You and me. Just being."

"Who? What?"

"Never mind." The air seemed infused with a golden glow; she felt giddy, hearing J.J. Cale but taking in the intense buzz of insects in the dry grass. Contemplating the golden tan of her own skin, she was reminded of the C.S. Lewis books. "Remember Aslan?" she asked Sheila, looking down at her arm.

Sheila smiled, gazing around her.

"I feel like Aslan has just breathed on me."

"Maybe we've crossed over into Narnia. Maybe we'll become royalty." Sheila's face seemed to float for a second, illuminated.

"It's like we really are there: everything's more real than real. Look at that blade of grass. It's a real blade. It could cut things. Look at that cactus, it looks like a ping-pong paddle. Ping-pong paddle," she repeated slowly.

Arlene was still concentrating on the image of Aslan, the giant Christ-lion. She wanted to hallucinate him, to conjure him; she wanted to fondle thick yellow fur over cat muscles. "One of these days, I'm going to try dropping acid," she said. She wanted intensely, at that moment, to see something magical.

As if answering a request, a monstrous silver bullet slipped past her line of vision, glowing in the late afternoon sun. Another one slid past, then another, each a shimmering blunt cigar with windows. "Are they from outer space?" she asked dazed, only partly facetious. She thought she might have talked herself into seeing things. There were dozens of them, maybe hundreds. They slipped, one after another, through the entrance to the campground, floating past her in sun-tinted silver.

"They're trailers of some kind. Can you imagine?" Sheila sounded awestruck.

"It's a caravan of Airstreams," Kerry said. "God, just our luck."

"What?" Sheila and Arlene asked together.

"Mostly retired Americans, dozens of couples with identical trailers. They travel in big caravans through North America and all over."

The silver trailers continued to flow into the campground until well after dark and all they could see were the headlights of the cars pulling them. Chuck fell asleep. Kerry helped him into the van and stayed there herself.

Arlene was beginning to nod off too. Sheila came back from the washroom. "I need munchies," she said. "Where are the spits?"

Arlene handed her the sunflower seeds and got up. "I'd better go to the bathroom too before I fall asleep. You got the soap?" She gathered up her things and went in search of the cement bunker. She had no trouble finding it, but turned the wrong direction in the dark on the way back, and found herself wandering through a maze of dark roads and pathways, listening to the Airstreamers set up camp.

"Dorothy!" a gravelly voice yelled. "Get yer ass out here and relax. It don't matter if the trailer's clean or not. This here's a vacation."

"It matters to me!" Dorothy called back cheerfully.

Arlene pictured Dorothy mopping a tiny floor with Mr. Clean, scrubbing a spotless sink with Ajax.

"Hey, you Johnsons," somebody else yelled into the night, this time in a nasal mid-western accent. "You got any scotch left?"

"Bourbon," one of the Johnsons yelled back. "If you want any, you better hustle your bustle."

Campfires and yard lamps were lighting up the night. Each silver trailer held one couple. Signs on the bumpers or showing through back windows announced, "Hi! We're Ed and Irene Carson from Michigan," or "Howdy y'all! Tex and Dorothy Wurlitzer from Houston."

Arlene felt as though someone had picked her up by the scruff of her neck and dropped her into Purgatory, into a surreal limbo of American suburbia. She couldn't ask directions: of course nobody would know where the van was. She stopped short. Except they would know where the washrooms were. But was she too stoned to deal with these people? She was. If she were still walking around lost in half an hour, she'd ask somebody. She was coming down, and knew she'd be relatively straight by then. If she could tell when then was. She physically straightened her shoulders to speed up the process, and continued with more confidence down several pathways until, sadly, she found herself back at Tex and Dorothy's. She wondered if Sheila was worried about her and thought likely not. She'd be staring into the fire unaware of time passing. "Can't yew sit down?" she heard Tex saying.

"Don't get your drawers in a knot, now," Dorothy cautioned. "I'm off to take a shower."

Feeling like a private detective keeping well back in the shadows, Arlene decided to follow her. Dorothy turned out to be a quick-moving woman in her sixties with a blonde bouffant hairdo. Arlene trailed what looked at times to be a dandelion head floating on its own past dim yellow camp lights and smoky fires, until she finally spotted the washroom. There. She tried the opposite direction to the path she'd first taken, and found the van.

Sheila was watching the dying embers, her legs crossed under her in yoga position. "What happened to you?" she asked dreamily.

"I got lost among the Airstreams," Arlene said.

"I thought so." Sheila shook her head. "I thought so," she repeated.

"Don't get yer drawers in a knot, now," Arlene drawled. "You're no expert navigator yourself." They got into their sleeping bags and settled in for the night.

"Who *was* an expert navigator?" Sheila suddenly wanted to know. "There was some famous Italian or Spaniard from the Middle Ages. Vasto de Gama or something. I mean, you could say, 'You're no Columbus yourself,' except Columbus thought America was India, so he's not a good example." She sat up for a moment. "*You* know."

"I know what you mean. Now I'm trying to think of the name of that navigator. You're no Vasto de Gama. It has a familiar ring to it."

"I think maybe it was more like Vas*co* de Gama."

"Tabasco de Gramma."

"Ancient family recipe."

"Do you two ever stop giggling?" It was Kerry, from inside the van.

"Oh, sorry." They snorted quietly into their sleeping bags. "She sounds like Mrs. Fulton," Sheila whispered. Mrs. Fulton was their high school home ec teacher, who had eventually insisted Arlene and Sheila find other partners for class cooking projects.

"Psst." Arlene started awake. A shadowed face blocked her view of the stars.

"What...?" she started to say.

"Shhh. It's only me."

"Only who?" She was still half asleep.

"It's me. Chuck," he whispered, glancing furtively back at the van.

"What's the problem?" She lowered her voice and looked over at Sheila, who was snoring.

"Come for a walk with me." He put his hand on her shoulder and started kneading. "Bring your sleeping bag."

"Are you nuts?" She twisted away, but sensing an unhealthy undertow to his frustration, stifled the "Piss off." "Look," she went on carefully. "You and Kerry are doing us a favour here and we're grateful. I'm not about to go off with you behind her back."

"Oh." After a moment of consideration, he stood up slowly and disappeared. A while later she heard him return.

"Psst." He was bending over Sheila.

"Jeez Arlene it's the middle of the night."

"It's me, Chuck."

"What are you *doing?*" Sheila asked, loudly. Chuck crept quietly back to the van.

The next morning they took advantage of the luxury of hot showers and stayed in the washroom for over an hour. They combed their hair in front of the first full-length mirror they'd seen since leaving home, wearing underpants and T-shirts, though that late in the morning most of the Airstreamers were long finished with the facilities. "I've definitely got a fatter ass," Arlene said, eyeing herself critically. "But on the other hand I think my breasts are a tiny bit bigger too."

"Just imagine," Sheila said wistfully, "if we could move fat from one place to another, remould ourselves like we were Plasticine."

"Like Gumby and Pokey." They finished dressing and tried to fluff their hair around their shiny faces.

"We'd better hit the road," Sheila said. "I think we've out-welcomed our stay with old Sleazeball Chuck."

"Outstayed our welcome you nit."

A toilet flushed behind them, and a blonde woman came out to wash her hands and create a new hairdo in the mirror over the sink. She smiled at the girls and said, "Hi, y'all. Lovely day, huh?"

Arlene was startled with recognition. "Dorothy," she said.

Dorothy naturally looked surprised and asked, "Do I know you?"

Arlene blushed and shook her head. "No, uh, I said your name before I thought. This sounds dumb but I sort of had too much to drink last night and I got lost. And so I wandered around and then I heard your husband calling 'Dorothy' and then you came out of your trailer with a towel, so I followed you to the washroom and got my bearings again."

"And you recognized me?" She was smiling, friendly. "I must've made an impression."

"I guess you did."

"Where are y'all from, you girls?" She teased the top of her hair, then folded it swiftly at the back, pinning it expertly together with a comb and bobby pins.

"Canada."

"From Saskatchewan."

"Ooh-whee. You're a long ways from home."

Arlene had never heard a live human being say "Oo-whee" before. She and Sheila glanced at each other. "Yes, I guess so."

Dorothy smiled again and gave her newly constructed beehive a last pat. "Hope you have yourselves a real good time here," she said before she disappeared in a cloud of hairspray.

When they got back to the van, Chuck was sitting in his lawn chair. He waved a joint at the Airstreams surrounding them and announced, "The American Dream."

"Where's Kerry?" Arlene asked.

"Still in bed. She sleeps sometimes till two in the afternoon." He offered a toke to the girls.

"No thanks. We're going back on the road today and we'd better be straight." They didn't look at him as they picked up their packs. "We'll be on our way then. Say 'bye to Kerry."

Chuck held up his fingers in the peace sign. "Peace and good luck," he said. He sat hunched over his cigarette, reminding Arlene of one of the rubbies who drank in the Apollo Room at home.

As they walked through Airstream City with its aging couples all making cheerful breakfasts, she was reminded of her own parents at home on the farm. She thought of them going about their work, shopping from *Eaton's Catalogue,* chatting with Sheila's mom and dad outside the Co-op, tuning in to the *Ed Sullivan Show* on Sunday evenings. She felt a mild pang as she pictured her mother checking their post office box for a letter from her.

She and Sheila had phoned their parents at the last minute so they wouldn't be able to drive to Saskatoon en masse and try to talk them out of their trip to Mexico. Both sets of parents had been horrified and Arlene thought they all overreacted, particularly her father. "You what? You're going to where?" He'd sputtered and started to yell, losing his breath in a coughing fit. He'd turned her over to her mother.

"What on earth can you be thinking?" Her mother had sounded stunned into calmness when she realized everything was settled and that they were actually taking off on the plane that very morning. Arlene said she'd phone from San Diego. She didn't know when they'd be back. They were flying student standby and didn't have return tickets.

Sheila's mom went on for some time, with Sheila looking at the ceiling. Sheila's dad wasn't even able to talk to her. He was already warming up the car, not convinced it was too late to catch them before they left.

After they'd hung up, they agreed it was a good thing they had to rely on summer jobs and student loans. At least they weren't taking off using their parents' money, just the government's.

"How long has it been since we've written our families?"

"I suppose we'd better send another postcard," Sheila said. "So they don't think we've been killed by *banditos* or Montezuma's revenge." They were surrounded by the smell of bacon, eggs and coffee coming from each and every silver trailer. "Maybe we should get out on the road," she said. "Maybe that little guy with the tortillas will be by again."

"Yoo-hoo," someone called. "You girls!" They looked around, bewildered, and saw a woman with a coffee pot in her hand waving at them from one of the trailers. She was dwarfed by a man standing beside her, also beckoning to them. "Come on over here and have a cup of hot coffee." It was Dorothy. She and her husband were tending coffee, bacon and pancakes over an expert, compact fire. Sheila and Arlene grinned at each other and went over. "This here's my hubby, Tex," she said.

They introduced themselves and shook hands with Tex, who was well over six feet tall with a beer gut and, of course, a ten-gallon hat. "Howdy," he said, right on cue. "Mighty pleased to meet y'all."

Dorothy soon had them loaded down with plates of food and huge mugs of coffee. With her mouth full, Arlene contemplated the fact that though everything they said sounded as if it had been written for the Beverly Hillbillies, this was cancelled out by the ebullient presence of Tex and Dorothy themselves, genuine, good humoured, beaming on her and Sheila as if they were prodigal nieces. She felt as if she could eat forever.

"It does my heart good to see healthy young appetites," Dorothy said.

"Dad burn it if these ain't the best pancakes you've ever made," Tex commented.

"You say that all the time," Dorothy said. "And you don't need no third helping neither."

"How come you're so taken with healthy young appetites and then y'all give me hell for havin a healthy old one?"

"Huh. Trouble is, your appetite's healthier than you are."

Arlene helped with the dishes. Dorothy was so energetic she felt guilty doing nothing but stuffing herself full of pancakes, and besides, she wanted to see the inside of the Airstream. Sheila had a third cup of coffee and listened to Tex tell stories about the customers in his bar and grill in Houston. Arlene could hear them from the window over the sink.

"Usta have this here regular, he'd be sittin there talking and drinkin when just like that he'd take a big chomp out of his glass. Just as cool as a cucumber, sometimes he'd eat a whole goddamn glass, crunching away there like it was peanuts."

Sheila smiled.

"Don't believe me, huh? But it's the lord's truth, I tell ya. He'd sit there and chew and chew until it was nothin but fine powder and then swallow. And then take another bite. Them that didn't know him would watch quiet-like with their mouths hangin open the whole time. Then he'd belch and order a beer. He got lots of free booze that way. Said his dentist was confounded by his smooth fillings. What a character." Tex shook his head. "Dead now, though."

"Internal injuries?" Sheila asked.

"Yep. Partly." Tex looked mock serious. "Outer injuries too. He was hit by a truck."

Sheila's smile broadened as she took in his expression. Arlene called to her through the window. "Come in and see the trailer, it's so cute you wouldn't believe it." She was interested to note a slight southern lilt in her own voice.

"That story about the glass eater is the real truth," Dorothy said. "I seen him do it lotsa times. He weren't hit by no truck though," she added quietly. "Died of lung cancer."

Sheila came in and was duly shown every nook and cranny, the walnut partitions and cupboards, each neat little appliance.

"Wall, dad burn it, ain't this something," she said, nudging Arlene as they looked at the handy, compact bathroom. Arlene noticed Sheila seemed to have brightened up around Tex. Of course, Luke had been a Texan.

"They're makin fun of us, Tex," Dorothy called through the window.

"I suspected so," Tex shook his head. "They got some nerve too, coming from Saska-toon, Sas-kat-chew-on and all."

"So where are you two headed for?" Dorothy asked.

"We're on our way to Veracruz."

"You can come with us, then," Dorothy said. "We're leavin today and we'll be glad of the company."

"The whole caravan is leaving?"

"Yep. We got a place booked to camp just outside of Veracruz, a big empty field."

"Gee. That's really nice of you to offer. People in trailers and that don't usually give rides to hippies." In reality Arlene considered free meals and rides as natural contributions toward her education as a young woman experiencing the world, an investment in her future. One day when she became middle-aged, she told herself, she would give rides and meals to young travellers. She pictured herself in twenty years, still relatively vigorous, active in a fascinating career of some kind, elegant and well off. Deep down, though, she knew the entire concept of herself at middle age was impossible.

"Hippies?" Tex snorted. "You-all? Why you're just a couple of nice little country gals."

Dorothy, seeing their expressions, laughed. "Don't y'all worry, one day you'll have just the kind of fellows you want, fallin all over you."

Arlene felt as if she were twelve years old visiting one of her aunts. A loudspeaker blared from a car moving slowly through the camp. "Head 'em up, move 'em out," it said, "for Veracruz by nightfall."

They packed up. The girls got into the back of Tex and Dorothy's Cadillac and they floated off, part of a long line of silver trailers snaking their way back onto the road.

Miles later, Tex was describing what it felt like to be stung by a scorpion when he stopped in mid-sentence. He winced, squinting at the trailer ahead of them, and said, "Gol-darned heartburn again." Dorothy looked closely at him. "You stop, right up here now. I'm takin over till lunchtime."

"No sir." Tex gripped the steering wheel. "No sirree-bob. I'm drivin this here outfit as long as I'm still alive and kickin. You cain't steer this thing worth shee-it."

"I can steer a hell of a lot better than some stubborn old ox who's ready to keel over at the wheel."

"For Chrissakes, it's only a bit of heartburn."

"Fine then. Go ahead, just keep drivin away there and kill us all." They both sat back in their seats and straightened their shoulders stubbornly.

"Fine," Arlene mouthed to Sheila, "just kill us all." They both looked intently at their tourist brochures, trying not to go into fits. In spite of Tex's incipient heart attack, Arlene felt as safe in their air-conditioned sedan as she had as a child in her parents' sky blue Chevrolet, a fact that made her antsy, desperate to get away. She pictured Tex slowing down for a yield sign and she and Sheila leaping out of the car, making a narrow escape to freedom.

The floor in the back of the Cadillac was covered with glossy brochures featuring spectacular photos of every major area of the country. She and Sheila had sorted through the literature while Tex and Dorothy meandered through various anecdotes about their travels or their life back home in Texas. Some stories had been more interesting than others.

"Palenque," Arlene read, "is a jungle wonderland, a paradise for the Mayan history buff and the ordinary sightseer alike."

The couple decided they weren't speaking, which Arlene found well worth the slight concern Tex would collapse while negotiating a dangerous curve. "San Cristóbal cannot be described," another pamphlet enthused. "This lovely mountain sanctuary must be experienced."

To combat the silence, Dorothy put a Patsy Cline tape on a cassette deck that seemed rather chintzy after Chuck's fancy eight-track. However, Patsy's determinedly cheerful voice singing "South of the Border" and "Three Cigarettes in an Ashtray" encouraged the girls to sing along with Dorothy, and everyone brightened up a bit.

At one o'clock, the entire caravan stopped in a field for lunch. While Arlene helped Dorothy lay sandwich fixings out on a picnic blanket, Sheila concentrated on yet another of the brochures. "Jalapa," she quoted aloud, "is a city of flowers and gardens on the slopes of the Sierra Madres." She looked up. "Jalapa's not far from here." She indicated a small map included in the pamphlet. "We're at a crossroads right now. The sign's back there; we just passed it."

Arlene was eating a peanut butter sandwich. "Sounds lovely," she said. She ran her tongue over her teeth. Jalapa struck her as supremely desirable, a sort of Garden of Eden.

"Look at the map." Sheila was enthusiastic. "I bet we could get to Jalapa in a couple of hours. In fact," she peered at a group of Mexicans about a hundred yards away standing or squatting along the road, "I bet those people there are waiting for a bus into the mountains."

"I sure do envy you two," Dorothy said. "Nothin to worry about but backpacks, free to go wherever you feel like."

Tex was feeling better. "You don't want to miss the carnival in Veracruz, there," he said. "Y'all could stay in our campground and drive into town with us."

Arlene didn't even have to look at Sheila. "No," she shook her head, trying to seem regretful. "Jalapa sounds too nice to miss. We may never pass this way again."

Other Airstreamers were packing up, ready to get back on the road. "Oh, Dot! Yoo hoo. Dot!" A heavy woman with bluish grey hair was waving and half running towards them from several trailers away. Arlene realized she was calling Dorothy. The woman arrived, panting. For a moment, Arlene thought it might be an emergency. Maybe the god of heart attacks had decided to pass Tex by for today, and had struck down this woman's husband instead. "I need some detergent to clean up with," she said, catching her breath. "I'm plumb out." She offered Dorothy a plastic cup and smiled inquisitively, looking sideways at the girls.

"Just one little minute." Dorothy ducked inside the trailer and dipped the cup in a big plastic tub she kept under the sink. "Laundry detergent." She nodded instructively at Arlene as she handed the cup back. "You can use it for nigh on anything. Dust a bit on a damp sponge and it's better than Comet to clean a sink or tub with."

"Thanks a million," the woman said. She hesitated, hanging around while Dorothy ignored her, shook and folded the picnic blanket. Eventually, exclaiming about the time, she hurried back to her own trailer.

"I would have introduced y'all," Dorothy confided, "but she's so nosy I couldn't bring myself to give her the satisfaction."

"Is she gone?" Tex called from the trailer in a stentorian whisper.

"Yep," Dorothy said. "We'd best get a move on here." She smiled at the girls. "Are you comin or goin?"

"Going," they said, laughing. They used the trailer's pristine and handy little washroom, shouldered their packs and shook hands goodbye. "Thanks a lot for everything."

"You little gals be careful now," Tex called as they walked toward the crossroads.

Sheila turned and smiled at him. "You'd better let Dorothy drive," she said.

He shook his head and waved a last dismissive gesture. He and Dorothy were soon on their way, with him at the wheel.

The girls beamed happily at the few people waiting at the bus stop. "Jalapa?" Sheila asked.

"Sí. Jalapa." A woman in a yellow dress embroidered with orange and red flowers and designs smiled back at them, then looked down again at her needlework, a miniature of her own dress for a little girl.

This seemed to Arlene a final, wonderful, touch to the day. She took a deep breath of the dry atmosphere. "Free at last."

Sheila laughed and sat down on her pack. "How old do you think Tex and Dorothy are?"

"Sixtyish, maybe. Sixty-five."

"I wonder where we'll be at that age? They're pretty adventurous in their own way, you know."

"Yes. You're right. We can only hope to be half that energetic."

"Can you imagine what Dorothy would think of our housekeeping on Fourth Avenue North?" Their basement suite in Saskatoon hadn't been much bigger than an Airstream. It contained a greasy kitchen with an old painted fold-out table, a tiny bathroom off to the side, and a bedroom with enough space for two mattresses. A tie-dyed sheet separated the rooms. Looking back on that twilight existence elevated Arlene's joy. "Imagine if we hadn't come to Mexico. We'd be looking forward to exams."

Sheila grimaced. "God. Just imagine! Just think. Even travelling with Tex and Dorothy would have been better than staying in Saskatoon." The Mexicans stood up expectantly, watching a cloud of dust in the distance. "Say, there's a bus coming already!"

But instead of heading for Jalapa, the bus that arrived was going the opposite direction, to Veracruz. They decided to get on anyway. The Mexican woman touched Arlene's shoulder. "No Jalapa," she said helpfully pointing to the sign on the front.

Arlene nodded. "*Sí, yo sé.*" She hoped this said 'yes I know', but wasn't sure. "*Sí,* Veracruz," she clarified. "*Es bueno.*"

The woman smiled and shook her head as if she thought they were from Mars.

6. VERACRUZ

At the Veracruz bus station, a swarm of young boys accosted them. "Chiclets?" they shouted. "Show you 'roun *Carnaval?*" The boys were rough and ragged and pushy except for one little guy with huge eyes. He hung back shyly from the rest, his voice almost whispering, "You want good restaurant?" He managed to sidle up to Sheila, who looked at Arlene and shrugged. They were hungry, and it was so crowded they couldn't see if the buildings across the street were cafés or not. Revellers, hordes of them, were yelling and laughing, men in white shirts and dark pants, people in traditional dress or costumes, teenage girls walking arm in arm wearing brilliant skirts and dresses. They followed the boy into the crowd as he timidly gestured to the other urchins that they should go away. They all jeered and shook their heads, but eventually disappeared.

"*Como se llama?*" Sheila asked him.

"Pedro." He half-whispered and half-croaked, his voice an appealing miniature of Rod Stewart's. He abused with hoarse obscenities any men who hissed at them as he led them to a hole-in-the-wall establishment with a rough patio. There were, surprisingly, some tables free. "I bet the food's awful," Arlene said to Sheila, giving Pedro a few centavos.

"No, no," he admonished her. "Good food."

Arlene caught the scent of an unrecognizable spice. "I'm sorry," she said to him. She knew she'd been rude, talking as if he weren't there. "I'm sure it's very good." Looking puzzled at her apology, he nodded silently and left them.

They found a table beside a shrub displaying vivid red flowers with petals that looked silken and ungainly. She breathed deeply, enjoying the evening heat, the humid air that had a denser flavour somehow than that of San Blas and was a whole world away from the Sierra Madres. The bus ride down the mountains to sea level seemed to have instilled a singing inside her, an exhilarated keening, and now it rose to the surface again. It was wonderful, she and Sheila here, going out for dinner in the midst of a carnival. She thought how lucky they were to be able to travel, how pleased she was with herself that she'd had the strength of character to go ahead, to do this. "I feel high," she said.

"Me too." Sheila smiled radiantly.

"It must still be the narrow escape from Tex and Dorothy." They watched Pedro swagger over to another group of boys, talking rapidly, gesturing frenetically, while a young waitress took their order.

"Pedro's a little con artist," Arlene said, amused.

"He's not the shrinking violet he let on to us, that's for sure."

As they ate their meal, patrons wandered sporadically onto the patio until most of the outside tables were full. "The food's not bad at all," Arlene said, mopping up sauce with warm tortillas. She watched a few couples disappear through the dark opening in the crumbling stucco of the café. Although the carnival raged only a couple of blocks away, the sounds seemed muted; Arlene felt sheltered here. Then she noticed a young American couple hesitate outside the rusted mock archway. Her mouth became dry; she couldn't swallow, and for a split second, her heart stopped. She abruptly turned away from them. "What's with you?" Sheila asked. "You look like you've caught Tex's heartburn."

Arlene took a drink of beer. "See that American? Don't stare at him. He's that guy who was at the Mazatlán bus depot."

Sheila looked puzzled.

"You likely don't even remember. I saw him through the bus window, and I thought he could have been the love of my life." She shook her head at herself, and started eating again. How could she think her heart had stopped? But it almost had. It was like being in a Harlequin Romance. What were the chances of him turning up again like this? She took another drink.

"Oh yes." Sheila nodded sympathetically.

There he was, in the flesh, the gorgeous guy with the strong features, dark curly hair, and loose-limbed easy way about him she'd seen in her daydreams off and on since he'd caught her eye on the other side of the country. The one she'd imagined in her sleeping bag as she listened to Murdoch and Jeanette and the no-see-ums. He was coming toward her now, close enough to touch. She could see his dark chest hair curling above his shirt; the crotch of his jeans was almost at eye level. She felt his intense dark eyes on her as he gave her a quick glance and kept looking for a table.

God. He didn't even remember her. But why should he?

"At least he's with somebody," Sheila noted, looking appraisingly at his beautiful companion. "You can safely admire him from afar."

Arlene grimaced. His girlfriend looked like one of the Bacardi-girl types they'd seen on the Mazatlán beach: tanned, perfect figure, fine-featured face, sun-bleached streaks in long thick hair. They found seats several tables away, but when there was a lull in the general noise, if Arlene leaned back she could hear him talking.

"We have to go back to San Cristóbal," he was saying. He had some sort of Eastern American accent, Boston or New York. His girlfriend mumbled something, low but impassioned. "Well, it's your decision," he said. "But I'll go back alone then. I have the time. I feel I have unfinished business there that has nothing to do with practicalities. It's important to me in a way I can't quite articulate."

It occurred to her he was out of her league in ways *she* couldn't articulate. Or, to be honest, in ways she didn't want to: looks, sophistication, the way he spoke, even. General coolness. Class. She examined a hangnail, feeling plain and plebian.

His girlfriend shook her head, her perfect mane of hair swirling, shiny. "I won't be travelling by myself for long," she warned. She was wearing a green dress and wild earrings that made her look like a blonde gypsy. Arlene could tell she was one of those women who could look any way she wanted, always emanating an elusive, indefinable chic.

Refraining from licking her fingers, Arlene finished her meal and lit a cigarette, losing the gist of the conversation. She looked at Sheila for a long moment, at her wrinkled T-shirt, her hair pushed messily behind her ears, her shiny forehead, calculating something. She bet the Bacardi girl couldn't pull off their look.

Pedro came in and sat down with them, cockily asking for a cigarette. "You?" She pretended to be surprised. "You want to grow big? *Muy grande?*"

"*Sí.*" He nodded, grinning slyly.

"Then no *cigarros.*"

"I." He pointed to his chest. "Inside me, I very big man."

Sheila nodded solemnly. "I believe it," she said. "How old are you? *Cuántos años?*"

He hesitated, either preparing to lie or searching for the correct English. "Eleven," he said. He could pass, Arlene thought, for seven or eight. She was on the verge of teasing him about too many smokes, then felt sorry for him. Likely he really was eleven. She nodded her head solemnly, taking her cue from Sheila. The three of them sat quietly for a minute. Pedro reached over and took a cigarette from Sheila's pack, which was lying open on the table. "*Por favor,*" he nodded politely.

"Certainly," Sheila replied. They smoked companionably for a few moments. Pedro removed the cap from a bottle of pepper sauce and flicked it into the centre of the table. Sheila and Arlene got their own bottle caps and started a pickup game of crokinole. They played intently for a few minutes until Pedro stopped abruptly. "You have sisters?" he asked. "Brothers?" He seemed to regard them as if they were kids his own age, as if they had something in common against the rest of the world.

For a moment, Arlene felt this was true. "I have one brother," she answered.

"And I have one brother and one sister," Sheila said. "How about you?"

"I have many brothers and sisters. Too many." He grinned, then examined his bottle cap. "Too many," he repeated. They started up the game again, but couldn't seem to regain the spirit of play. He stood up, cadged another cigarette and left them.

"Remember that Christmas holidays your family and mine had a crokinole tournament?"

"God, yes. How uncool is that?"

"We should have bought him something to eat, instead of stunting his growth with more cigarettes." Sheila took a closer look at her package of Fiestas. "Half my Fiestas are gone," she said flatly.

"Jeez. I wonder how he managed that?"

"Oh well." She continued to gaze, fascinated, at the package. "At least he left some for me. I guess I could look on it as an extra tip." They watched the scene beyond the restaurant archway. People were strolling past as if taking a rest from the busier streets, but Pedro and his gang had disappeared.

Arlene checked her bag to make sure her wallet was there. She was no longer high. The carnival now seemed irritating, intrusive. She wanted to find refuge from it and didn't relish the search for a hotel. The guy from Mazatlán and his friend had finished eating. "I'll be there until my visa runs out," he said.

"That's four months!" His girlfriend was obviously upset. They left the restaurant, both grimly silent, without lingering over cigarettes or anything else.

Four months. "Sheila. Where's the map? I have to find where San Cristóbal is."

Sheila raised her eyebrows, amused. "He's way too cool for us Arlene." She was only partly joking.

Arlene lit another cigarette, watching the flame burn down almost to her fingers. "Us? Who's talking about *us?*" The last of her enjoyment seeped out of her, silently and almost unacknowledged, like the quiet farts she and her brother Victor used to perfect in the back row of the United Church. The back pew. For a brief moment in time she felt gloomy on a grand scale, floating alone in a galaxy, the only star not giving off any light.

Confronted by *Carnaval* revellers in bizarre costumes, almost shell-shocked as firecrackers burst near them, she and Sheila wandered through the streets becoming more and more confused. After getting confetti in her eyes for the third time, Arlene put on her glasses. She was so unused to wearing them, she could see the wire frames and feel them heavy on the bridge of her nose, dragging at her ears. The startling clarity made everything seem even more distorted and bizarre. It reminded her of looking through binoculars on the jungle river boat tour. She felt adrift from all the action, floating, gawking at the shore where all the real life and fun were happening.

"I wish I had glasses right now," Sheila said. They stumbled to the doorway of a cantina, wiping away tears. "We can't go in here, it's men only."

"It's filled to capacity anyway." Arlene peered through the clouded window.

"God. Let's get out of here and find a place to stay." They stopped a clown on his way out of the bar, and asked directions to a hotel. He accompanied them to a quieter street, protecting them from confetti attacks, comically threatening every gang of young men they came across. He left them after pointing out several hotels. They passed from one place to another until they'd exhausted all possibilities. Every place was booked solid because of Carnaval.

"Now what?" Arlene said. Her backpack was a dead weight. They couldn't find anywhere to sit down, let alone rest.

Inquiring at any hotel they came across, even those obviously too expensive, they garnered the same answer over and over, *"No hay habitación,"* although one of the desk clerks generously let them use the washroom. They eventually gave up, and sat in a private doorway, exhausted. It was three o'clock in the morning. People were still singing and dancing in the streets, igniting small explosives and shooting fireworks and what Arlene hoped were blanks into the silver sky of the city. They had passed the ability to be startled when the door opened behind them. A young man looked down at them solemnly. "Come in, come in," he said in English. "My house is your house."

Arlene and Sheila peered up at this new provider of hospitality, and then into the interior framed by the open door. Narrow stairs led down to a cubicle with a table, a couple of chairs, and a mattress. It looked familiar to Arlene, somehow, maybe like something out of Dostoevsky. But then, it wasn't all that different from the basement suite they'd left in Saskatoon.

"At least it's away from the street," Sheila said. They helped each other up, went inside and introduced themselves.

The man's name was Ramón. He was dressed simply in a red shirt and black pants, and with his slicked-back hair he looked older than he'd first seemed when haloed by the dim street lamp. His front teeth slanted inward, away from his lips, so that his smile seemed feral. He laughed, almost to himself, and shook his head. "I going out," he said, "and *carumba!* There is you, *señoritas!*" He nodded at them and held his hand to his heart, whether to say they'd almost given him a heart attack or whether he'd fallen in love at first sight, Arlene wasn't sure.

"*Con permiso,*" Sheila said, sitting down on the mattress, and Ramón nodded hospitably.

"*Por supuesto!* Most for certain. My house is your house!" he repeated. "Here," he indicated a chair for Arlene. She sat, gratefully dozing as he recounted in tortured English his plans for the evening. "I must go out, little while," he said, sniffing. "You sleep, help yourselves or so on." He waved his hand in the direction of the mattress, then at the table. Arlene couldn't figure out what he meant by helping themselves; there wasn't any food. Then he pointed out the white lines of powder on a mirror. "You want feel good? Active, no tired?" Using a piece of paper straw, he snorted one, then beckoned to the girls. Cocaine.

Arlene thought of chalk lines on a schoolyard ready for Sports Day. The idea of trying to sniff something up her nose didn't appeal to her, and she shook her head. Sheila looked regretful, but also declined. "Very tired," they explained.

He nodded as he prepared two more lines of powder on the mirror. "I go out now." He nodded toward the cocaine and smiled. "*Hasta luego.*"

Using their packs as pillows, they were asleep almost before he was gone. Only a short time passed, however, and they were stunned awake by a firecracker exploding right on the doorstep.

"Jesus Christ!" They sat up abruptly. Arlene switched on a small lamp, disturbing a couple of cockroaches within her bleary line of vision. "Did you see those insects?" she asked.

"Yes." Sheila got up and examined the mirror on the table. She picked up one of the straws, leaned over, and gave a tentative sniff, finally snorting one of the lines. "Feels weird," she said, holding her nose, "but not bad."

Arlene shrugged. "What the hell," she said, and tried the other one herself. Her nose felt numb and she had to hold her nostrils together so she wouldn't sneeze. "I want feel active, no tired."

She stayed there, looking down at the mirror. "I read in a magazine somewhere that if you bend over a mirror like this, you can see how your face will look when you're middle-aged."

"You mean fat?"

"Sort of. Like your skin falls forward a bit."

"Let's see." They forgot, for a moment, where they were. They sat back down on the chairs, waiting for something to happen, until Sheila stood, suddenly manic, and zipped over to the stairway. She climbed up to the door and turned the knob, then rattled it. "Jeez. We can't get out of here," she said flatly. "You need a key to open it."

Arlene looked up at the staircase, then around the room. There was only one window, close to the ceiling at street level. It was barred and impossible to reach anyway. They were trapped. They both tried the door again, and then started to pace. "We have to get out," Sheila said. "I feel active for sure. I feel like joining the party." She nodded toward the outside world. "He must have locked us in by mistake."

The stifling little apartment seemed slowly to be taking on a chill. "The air in here," Arlene said, nodding her head wisely at Sheila, "is becoming sinister." She couldn't tell if the sensation creeping up her spine was drug or fear induced.

"It does have a sinister air," Sheila said. But neither of them laughed.

"We shouldn't have sniffed that stuff." A grain of hysteria scratched Arlene's throat. The two watched each other for what seemed a long time until the hilarity that hovered over them in a kind of mist eventually descended.

Giddy, euphoric in spite of, or perhaps because of, the possibility of danger, Arlene said, "We could have our own party, right in here."

"And do what? Play charades?"

"Let's look around. Maybe old Ramón has a crokinole board." At this they almost fell on the floor laughing. Arlene had another thought. "I bet he's a pimp," she said.

Sheila widened her eyes. "White slavery," she said. They sat in silence sorting out their thoughts. "If I had one more little sniff I bet I could knock the door in myself."

"It opens from the outside in," Arlene reminded her.

Sheila began to search systematically through the room for a key. She moved the mattress; she groped under clothes in open shelves. "Look at this," she said. A handgun lay gleaming, cold and threatening but unreal, Arlene thought, something from a mystery novel.

But this was no story. It was really happening. "Sheila. Maybe we should be afraid." Ramón had a gun. He'd locked them in. And the white powder, all laid out like that. All of this added up to something bad.

Sheila replaced a towel over the gun and moved on, her face pale, her pupils darkening her eyes. Arlene sat down at the table, her hand on her forehead, not knowing what she should focus on. Last of all, Sheila tried a small closet door. "Arlene," she said. She sounded supremely disgusted.

Arlene gaped at the open door. It opened, not into a closet but out into a hallway. A young couple dressed as mimes with white faces and black tears waved as they unlocked the door to their own place. A long, dimly lit corridor led to a hand-printed Exit sign with stairs leading up to the outside. Silent and sheepish, the girls shouldered their packs. "Maybe we should leave a note or something," Sheila said.

"Yes." Arlene found her pen and wrote "*Gracias*" on a piece of Chiclet package. They left it on the mirror. Making sure to lock the doorknob behind them, they walked quietly to the end of the hall, and ascended the stairs to the carnival.

The air outside, though laced with smoke from fireworks, smelled so fresh it felt supernaturally reviving. "I can smell the sea," Sheila noted happily.

"Maybe that's because Veracruz is a seaport," Arlene explained as they strode quickly through the streets toward the *zócalo.* Although it was almost dawn, the noise and music were still blaring. Their backpacks had become so light they hardly noticed them. They smiled at everybody, greeting people, stopping to listen and clap their hands to the beat of small groups playing the marimba or fiddles and guitars, Veracuz folk music or Latin American rock and roll. Open cafés taking up the sidewalks were crowded with men and women drinking *café con leche.* Roving bands of confetti-throwers called to them, or sprinkled them with light showers of the tiny paper discs as they passed by, but nobody threw any in their eyes. "Typical men," Arlene commented. "They only pick on you when you're down." She hoped they'd run into the guy from Mazatlán. It might be exciting to see him again, breathe the same atmosphere for a time even if he was with someone else and hadn't recognized her as anyone special. Sheila looked buoyant, ready to take off into the carnival sky unless Arlene could find a string to hold on to. This reminded her of an old dream.

"When I was a kid I used to have this recurrent dream that I could fly," she said.

"Really?" Sheila came back to earth for a moment, interested.

"Except," Arlene went on, "it was only ever inside the house. I'd bend over like this." She stopped to demonstrate. "And then I'd simply float up until my back bumped against the ceiling, like a balloon. I'd be able to float like that all over the house."

"You never dreamt you were flying up in the sky, way up over fields and cities and that?"

"No." Arlene considered. "Never. I was always in the house, floating up and down the stairs, bouncing gently off the ceiling. I guess for a flying dream it wasn't very exciting."

Sheila stopped abruptly, examining Arlene as if she were a familiar but still interesting phenomenon. "That's just like you Arlene. Not getting any higher than your own ceiling."

"Oh piss off." Arlene was annoyed until she said, "I'm higher than anybody's ceiling right now."

Sheila laughed. "If you think about it, it sounds to me more like an out-of-body experience."

They came to a huge open plaza, where a rock band was playing simulated Santana. They wanted to join the party. For a few centavos, a small boy volunteered to sit under a palm tree and guard their backpacks while they danced. Arlene danced with anyone who asked her: it was the rhythm, the music that was important and she felt part of it, fluid and graceful. The music changed to something that sounded Caribbean, exotic in a new way, and she flowed into it. Transported. The word came to her without her thinking about it, remained in her mind in wavery capital letters as something she'd become at that single moment.

But within a half-hour, she lost it all to an abrupt exhaustion. She excused herself from her partner, a young Mexican who, in spite of being too fat, had moved like silk through several dances. She plodded heavily over to the tree, where Sheila joined her, ready to pick up her pack and find some breakfast. The young backpack guard was talking to another kid who greeted them by name. It was Pedro.

"*Buenos dias.*" Pedro's shy smile and huge eyes seemed ethereal, as if he himself were in another dimension, and Arlene was greeting only his spirit.

After explaining their predicament, Arlene said, "I guess we'd better catch a bus out of here, go on down toward the Yucatán."

"*Momentito, momentito,*" Pedro held up his hand importantly. "I have cousin here," he said. "You stay, his wife her sister's house."

"A cousin? Really?"

"*Sí,*" he said, becoming officious. "Come. You have siesta there."

"Siesta," Sheila said. "What a great idea."

They followed him onto a bus that clamoured through neighbourhoods of tiny clapboard houses coloured salmon pink, sky blue, ochre, that through her exhaustion Arlene could see only as a wavy rainbow. Somehow, they managed to get off the bus at the right stop. Pedro led them to a pink cement square of a house with the sidewalk as the front yard, but with enough room for chickens and a goat in the back. He went in for a short time by himself, then opened the door and led them into a small room of polished red earthenware tile furnished with a table and chairs. A thin woman he introduced as *Señora* Perez greeted them. She nodded gravely, and with shy grace told them they were very welcome and indicated where they could sleep.

It was late afternoon when Pedro shook them awake. "Come," he said. "Eat." They saw that the table was set, and the family was waiting for them, the *Señora* coming and going from the kitchen. Two teenage girls were sitting beside two empty chairs. They looked cautiously friendly, smiling with curiosity. There were two boys about the same height as Pedro but younger. The father, they'd gathered from Pedro, was away, working on a fishing boat.

Señora Perez was a quiet, serious woman, but the girls, Juanita and Gabriella, warmed quickly and asked the two Canadians a friendly barrage of questions. Gabriella was seventeen and Juanita, sixteen. Like their mother, they were sure of themselves in a way that seemed exclusive to Mexican women, a way that had nothing to do with social confidence or attractiveness, though both girls were slender and very pretty.

Arlene was surprised at the amount of information they were able to communicate. Pedro hardly had to translate at all. The younger girl had a serious boyfriend. They liked rock music. Gabriella had had a boyfriend the year before but her mother disapproved of him. Now he was going out with someone else, someone whose parents weren't so strict. Gabriella and her mother still fought about him.

It was understood they would all go to *Carnaval* together. Arlene and Sheila had only their Mexican tourist blouses to wear with jeans, but they ironed the blouses and borrowed some of Gabriella's mascara and a hint of lipstick. Gabriella and Juanita wore colourful shifts, their legs left unshaven under nylon stockings. Arlene gave Sheila a surreptitious sideways glance. She'd caught Juanita glancing the same way at her sister when she realized neither of the Canadians wore a bra.

It felt peculiar walking arm in arm with women, Gabriella on one side and Sheila on the other. Arlene squeezed Sheila's arm tentatively, just above the elbow, as if she were testing a chicken thigh for freshness. "You're not exactly what I'd call muscular," she commented.

Sheila pinched Arlene's arm. "You should talk."

"Quit pinching." Arlene pinched her back. "God, it's bad enough having to put up with all these men." The confetti terrorists were out in full force so she had to wear her glasses. Men were heckling Mexican women here in the way she'd always thought was reserved for foreign tourists. "*Guapa, guapa, muy guapa,*" they would croon, bending sideways to look in the faces of all four of them. Two or three times in the press of the crowd, she'd felt an anonymous hand pinching her buttocks, though this didn't seem to happen to Juanita or Gabriella.

"I'd like to *guapa* all these guys on their little Mexican pinheads," Arlene said.

Juanita's boyfriend, Enrico, showed up, slightly drunk and gallantly ready to escort the four young women through the gauntlet. Pedro had run into a group of ragged acquaintances early on; he came and went, keeping track of his protegés while earning money guarding possessions or guiding people out of crowds. Arlene kept an eye on him when he was in her vicinity, worried that he might also be picking pockets. This wasn't a moral but a practical concern; she didn't want him in any danger from the *policía*, who were often in evidence though they didn't seem to be of much use.

They stopped at a square to dance, and at one point, over where the crowd was at its thickest, she noticed Pedro locking eyes for a long moment with a rather puzzling middle-aged man.

71

He had dark hair, was dressed in expensive jeans and T-shirt, and could have been either a tourist or a Mexican. She was shocked by the man's expression: in those unguarded seconds, he looked as if he were starving and had just happened upon a gourmet meal. He looked about to drool. Without thinking, Arlene shouted Pedro's name in a high, strained voice. "Come and dance with us." She beckoned to him, determinedly.

Pedro turned his winsome smile away from the man toward Arlene, and pushed his way over to her. He led her to a less crowded area, grinning cheekily as Sheila made room for them. Arlene felt awkward and heartsick.

"Pedro sure turned out to be a lucky break for us, eh?" Sheila called over the head of her dance partner.

Arlene smiled and nodded, glancing at their sensible young hostesses, and attempted to regain some carnival spirit. Maybe the man just needed a guide, she told herself, and he'd been struck by Pedro's angelic looks in a perfectly normal way. She recaptured the rhythm as Pedro danced; he was so involved in the music his partner didn't need to be more than adequate. "He's as good as Whatshisname, that youngest kid with the Jackson Five," Sheila said. Arlene nodded, beginning to enjoy this latest manifestation of Pedro's genius. But before long, he bowed gallantly and disappeared once again into the mob of merrymakers. She watched him for a moment, his clear outline merging into the crowd. She realized she was still wearing her glasses and took them off.

At breakfast, the family reminisced about *Carnaval* while Arlene sat quietly, half smiling, trying not to look as blank as she felt. Spanish seemed much harder to comprehend in the morning.

"Where's Pedro?" Sheila asked. "*Donde esta* Pedro?"

"*Con Jesus,*" said the *Señora.*

Arlene had a fleeting image of Pedro ascending on a cloud

until he reached a blue-robed Saviour, though she knew Jesus was Mrs. Perez's brother-in-law. Pedro referred to him as his cousin, but the *Señora* didn't think they were related. Jesus hired Pedro for odd jobs, though nobody was sure what kind of work he actually did.

They exchanged addresses with the Mexican girls, promising to become pen pals. Pedro showed up once again at the last minute to see them off at the bus stop. They shook hands all round, and kissed Pedro, slipping him a full pack of Fiestas. *"Muchas gracias por toto,"* Arlene said.

"I maybe see you sometime," he said, nodding his head calmly, sophisticated. "In America."

7. PALENQUE

Startled, Arlene jumped as a horn blasted directly behind her. She and Sheila had been pushed, along with dozens of others, into the path of one of the buses attempting to leave the Veracruz station. They looked up at the driver, who threw them a mockingly lascivious kiss. The destination sign said "Campeche, *Por* Palenque." "Palenque," Arlene quoted, remembering Tex and Dorothy's collection of tourist brochures, "is a paradise for the Mayan history buff and the ordinary sightseer alike." Sheila looked up at the bus driver, then shrugged at Arlene. "He's leering at us like a village idiot."

"So what? He'll let us get on, I bet, and what can he do then, he has to drive the whole way. Besides which, there's a hundred chaperones on the bus."

They rapped on the door. The driver laughed and swung it open; it was packed so full of people, they had to sit on the steps. "*Cuanto pesos* to Palenque?" Arlene asked. He quoted a ridiculously low price. As they counted coins, she said, "Maybe he'll expect real payment later on."

"Look at how crowded it is," Sheila said. "We'll probably have to get off when we're outside the city. We'll end up hitching again."

The bus made its way slowly past the carnival's centre, and Arlene was able to look, really for the first time, at the sixteenth-century plaza: the tall palm trees and tropical flowers, the cathedral, the colonial government buildings, the *palacio municipal* with its arched portals, which seemed as if it were acting as host to the cafés and hotels on the other side. Now that they were leaving, she realized they hadn't gone sightseeing. This was a major Mexican city, and they'd never even visited the cathedral. But she said, "Anything's better than staying in Veracruz. I've really had enough," and she meant it.

"Me too." They were sitting only inches away from the pavement and the celebration that still went on loud and vibrant as ever. For Arlene, *Carnaval* had assumed a supernatural quality. She would never be able to picture Veracruz as a normal city going about its business: she'd always see it as a perpetual *fiesta,* one of many carrying on all over the world without her. For a moment the bus stopped, and a man in a skeleton costume threw confetti at them, though only to get their attention as it scattered against the cracked glass of the doors. He took off his mask with a flourish and flashed the girls a smile. He was beautiful, virile and dark, intense but at the same time enjoying himself so much he radiated boyish pleasure. He was almost transcendently appealing. Arlene widened her eyes at him and ran her fingers through her hair as the bus moved forward.

"He looked something like Dr. Zhivago, only way handsomer," Sheila said, awestruck.

They craned their necks, and saw him at the side of the bus, walking fast enough to keep up. "He's got his mask on again." Arlene pointed him out. They waved at him. He stopped for a second and, holding his hand briefly to his mask's mouth, flung his arm wide in an exuberant gesture, a pantomime of a thrown kiss. Arlene nudged Sheila. "We're flirting with death," she said.

"Arlene. Look over there; there's another one." It was another guy in a skeleton outfit exactly like the first one.

"God. Are we even waving at the right guy?"

"I guess it doesn't matter. This one could look like Gomer Pyle and we'd never know the difference." The bus began to leave the crowd behind, now able to travel quickly toward the highway to Palenque.

The driver did not drop them off outside of town. They rode through long hours of humid heat, observing the countryside through cracked glass. Rainforest had been broken into farmland, small acreages with tiny huts beside crops of maize or yucca plants. Farmers wearing loose white pants and shirts and big straw *sombreros* worked the land.

It was late at night before they drove into Palenque. They stood silently among sleeping passengers and got off, feeling like ghosts. Three American women who'd been sitting anonymously in the back got off too. They had luggage strapped to the top of the bus, and a young man who'd been acting as the driver's assistant threw it down to them, Arlene watching with detached interest as suitcase after suitcase landed in the dust. The bus took off, leaving them at the small empty station, the women with a great pile of suitcases and no taxis in sight. The bus must have been unusually early or late, Arlene thought. Still, taxi drivers or boys eager to earn a few pesos must be around somewhere. Unless nobody bothered to show up for third-class buses.

The women's voices were all similar with mid-western accents. "This is the last time I'm listening to your ideas about economizing," one of them said dryly, not looking at anyone in particular.

Sheila and Arlene shrugged imperceptibly at each other, and started off toward a street with dimly lit buildings, where they assumed they'd find the way to a hotel. The town was unusually dark, with hardly any street lights.

"Uh, you two girls," one of the women called. "How would you like to make some money?"

"I don't know." Arlene stopped reluctantly.

"We'll gladly pay you young things to carry two of our bags each to a hotel." She hauled one of the suitcases toward Arlene. "And then we senior citizens can share the others between us."

Sheila and Arlene glanced at each other. The women were around forty, forty-five at the most. Any one of them could have out-wrestled both girls together. Sheila looked off into space, refusing to acknowledge the request.

"We don't know where the hotels are, and besides, we can barely manage our own backpacks," Arlene said, trying to sound delicate. "We can't lug those suitcases as well."

She and Sheila stood for a second, hesitating and impatient, then started rather stolidly on their way again. They noticed a group of kids hanging around a doorway. "*Hola!*" Sheila called. She waved toward the women and their suitcases. "Hotel," she called to the kids. "*Tres señoras.*"

"*Sí, sí, no problemo.*" Four of the young Mexicans detached themselves from the group and strolled over to the women. Once Arlene and Sheila saw them involved in negotiations, they continued on. When she looked back from a safe distance, Arlene saw the boys taking off with suitcases for parts unknown, the women hurrying after them.

After the Veracruz carnival, Palenque seemed dead. They saw only a few men, some young couples circling in slow promenades near the zócalo, the odd shopkeeper or café proprietor closing up for the night or standing reflectively in front of his establishment.

An old man in a Panama hat passed them, a tourist out for a stroll. Though his face was deeply lined, he moved in the relaxed, youthful way that seemed to be natural with a certain class of American senior citizen. "Excuse me." Arlene stopped him. "Is there a cheap hotel near here?"

"Considering Palenque is such a small place," he said, "there are several, but I think mine is one of the cheapest. I'm on my way there now, if you'd like to come with me. I drive here every year from New York," he said, "and I stay most of the winter." They reached the hotel, a two-storey motel-like building encircling a courtyard. "The very cheapest rooms don't have baths," he advised as he left them to the desk clerk.

"Thanks very much," the girls called out after him.

"Happy to be of assistance," he said, with a gallant wave.

They woke late the next morning, long after the steamy jungle heat had settled in for the day. At the café across the street, they met two young couples from Sweden who looked desperately hungover. All four of them had dark tans, their hair bleached almost to whiteness, yet they seemed unhealthy in a chronic way, as if they were undernourished. They reminded Arlene of documentary film footage of hillbillies or prairie farmers in the thirties. When Arlene asked them how to get to the Mayan ruins, they offered to give her and Sheila a ride. Their vehicle was an ancient jeep with a cow skull on the front that they'd bought in Texas. They weren't really enthusiastic about seeing the ruins again, they said, but that was all there was to do in Palenque.

The Swedes' lethargy was contagious. By the time they reached the ruins, the girls were half-dozing in the back of the jeep and weren't prepared for the sight of a lifetime, for the panoramic display of delicate stone architecture set amid lush sloping forest. "But this is amazing!" Arlene said reprovingly to the driver, who smiled bleakly at her. He said they'd decided to go to their campground and have a nap. As the Swedes drove off, Arlene and Sheila paid the entrance fee, awestruck at the magnificence of the ruined city. "Let's walk around first before we do any climbing," Arlene said. "Isn't this something?"

"What could have happened for the Mayans to just sort of leave everything?" Cleared areas around the monuments looked like cared-for lawns, with the buildings themselves set against hills of thickly foliaged and luxuriant jungle. Some of the architecture was ruined and crumbled, but much of it looked well-preserved, grand pyramids of stone with steps leading to single small temples with pillars and roofs that gave the impression, or the memory of an impression, of something oriental.

They headed toward a small group of tourists congregating by one of the pyramids. Three heavy-set women were waiting, ready to climb up to the entrance so they could go inside. "It's those ladies from the bus," Arlene said. "I wonder if they're mad at us for not carrying their luggage." They went up to one of them, who was standing aside smoking while her companions talked to a Mexican guide. The sun highlighted the fact that her hair was orange, which Arlene assumed was a hair-colouring mistake. "Hello," Arlene said, "your stuff made it safe and sound to a hotel?"

The woman turned to her. "Oh, hello," she said. "Yes," she answered tersely. The girls smiled politely and were about to walk on, when she nodded toward the other ladies still talking to the guide. "We're all going into the crypt to see the stone sarcophagus. You can join our group if you want. It's only a couple of pesos per person."

"Oh," Sheila said, surprised. "Sure, why not?"

"Whose tomb is it?" Arlene asked.

"A Mayan ruler named Pacal. I don't know much about what the archaeologists think, but I've done some reading about the tomb. The sarcophagus lid is supposed to be one of the finest works of art from ancient Mexico. The building is called the Temple of the Inscriptions."

The third woman beckoned to Arlene and Sheila and introduced them to the guide as part of their group. As they reached the entrance, he handed each person a flashlight although there were dim lights illuminating the entrance. Switching on his own light, he escorted them down a long damp flight of narrow and treacherous stone stairs. *"Tengan cuidado, por favor,"* the guide cautioned at intervals, as if intoning a chant to ward off evil spirits. "Be careful please."

The carved figure was typically stylized with the flat forehead and hawklike nose of all the Mayan carvings. The lid was decorated with symbols, intricate designs of setting suns and creatures with feathers radiating like flower petals, serpents extending their bodies toward the sky, various geometric discs and knobs that could have been anything. The figure of Pacal seemed to be in an enclosure. Maybe it showed his afterlife inside the tomb, Arlene thought. Maybe that was as good as it got; the Mayans didn't believe in any kind of heaven.

They took grateful breaths of fresh air when they got to the top and out again. Arlene's crypt partner tried to convince her companions that the carvings on the tomb depicted an astronaut inside a spaceship. "It's exactly like what that Von Danekin described. The Mayans were familiar with space travellers; they might even have been aliens themselves."

Arlene and Sheila decided the orange-haired woman had been experimenting with henna on grey hair, and discussed the advisability of Sheila trying it out, walking aimlessly until they came to one of the highest pyramids. They started up the mountain of stone steps, finally making it to the cool doorway of the temple, where they sat, recuperating. "I wish we had something to drink," Arlene said. She put on her glasses to appreciate the view. From this height, the surrounding structures, built in among startling green growth and rounded treetops, looked like stone and ivory figurines set in moss and broccoli.

They examined the vestiges of stucco that still clung to the temple. The colours and designs were faded almost to extinction but they could still make out stylized figures harvesting crops or doing something mysterious with snakes.

"These guys look like they're playing some kind of ball game."

"This is that game Murdoch was talking about. Remember? Where the losing team was sacrificed to the gods?"

"You'd think if they really wanted to please the gods, they'd have sacrificed the winners."

"Maybe they tried that and found the teams started to sort of lose their competitive spirit."

"They didn't want to play their hearts out."

"I think it was the Aztecs who cut out people's hearts. Or was it the Incas?"

"I thought all of them did. On big stone sacrificial slabs. Murdoch would know."

"He might be here now, too, him and his girlfriend. What was her name?"

"That redhead." Arlene looked scornful. "She was sort of a loony-tunes, I thought." She recalled Jeanette and Murdoch recounting various adventures over their last supper in San Blas.

"No kidding," Jeanette had said, her feigned wisp of a voice gaining animation, "the bus actually left the road on a curve, just like in a cartoon, out and over the cliff, then scrabbled back like a live thing. The wheels managed to grab the side of the road again and we continued on, careening toward Mazatlán. I swear, I was sure we were all as good as dead."

Murdoch, on the other hand, had a talent for understatement. "So there I was, going for a little walk in the jungle," he said casually, his face expressionless, "and instead of stepping over this vine, I stumbled on it, and it bit my boot."

"The vine bit your boot?" Arlene asked without thinking.

"Yes. The famous Fanged Vine of Palenque." He had a peculiar dry grin just behind his expression that Arlene found familiar. It was Canadian. A certain species of Canadian male. He smiled innocently.

"I bet it was a garter snake." She was annoyed at herself for feeling foolish.

"It was a nawiaka snake," he said, unperturbed, "five feet long. Its venom can kill within an hour." He held up his right boot. Two holes that could well have been fang marks indented the leather.

Arlene and Sheila walked around the temple back to the stairs now, appearing in time to startle three young men just finishing the climb. "*Ai carumba!*" one of them said, and then they all laughed.

"I can never believe people actually say that," Arlene said.

Sheila was looking at the guy who'd uttered the exclamation.

She smiled. He wore faded jeans, and had long hair, black eyes, a lovely chin, nice shoulders, and skin the colour of caramel. Arlene noticed Sheila lick her lips and thought, oh shit, here she goes again. Beside him the other two looked like boys. Even so, Arlene regretted having her glasses on, but felt it would look self-consciously vain to take them off now. They were students from Mérida, in Palenque for a holiday. The attractive one was named Manrike.

The young men took a quick tour of the temple, returning immediately to make sure the girls weren't leaving without them. They descended the stairs slowly, Manrike providing competent English conversation and information about the ruins. "In Mayan," he said, "Palenque was called Lakam ha, which means Big Water." He pointed out high stone walls forming tunnels that used to be aqueducts. "Many, many *arroyos*. Dried streams," he clarified. "And many springs. Waterfalls."

"*Mucho agua*," Sheila said.

"*Sí. Sí!*" He nodded, evidently delighted with her and her impressive command of his language.

Arlene asked if the Mayans made human sacrifices. "Oh yes," he said. "And also only blood."

"Only blood?"

"Yes, no dying, only cutting. Lords and their wives. How do you say? Aristocrats. Cut themselves to give blood for, uh, good luck with the gods." His "uh" was pronounced more as a short e, and sounded charming.

"Cut themselves?"

"*Sí*. Piercing the tongue. Or men, ehh –" He motioned toward his genitals. Arlene made a face, but in his enthusiasm Manrike was oblivious. "Also," he said, "so much lost blood made people see – how do you say – pictures from the mind that are not real. Very, very important."

"Like vision quests," Sheila said. "Only North American Indians just didn't eat for many days, and then one day, poof, a hallucination of a flying moose."

Manrike nodded seriously. "Vizh-on quests." He was impressed with the words, and repeated them with different emphases, "Vision *quests*."

The day was becoming hotter, and once on the ground, Manrike became pensive, strolling quietly past several sites that he couldn't or didn't bother to identify. After more pleasantries and, to Arlene, rather obvious and unnecessarily extended sultry looks, he and Sheila formed the twosome she'd expected from the beginning. They were kind enough to give an appearance of including their friends for the rest of the afternoon, but Arlene could see they were simply existing until later. They gazed into each other's eyes. They kept touching each other on the arm, the shoulder. Manrike tenderly pushed a lock of Sheila's hair behind her ear, ostensibly describing Mayan jewellery. They held hands.

Arlene lagged behind, ignoring Manrike's friends who, besides their adolescent lack of appeal, were far less proficient in English than he was. She examined details of stone carvings and hieroglyphics that so far, Manrike informed them, had remained mostly indecipherable even to the most expert of linguists. The flat foreheads of the figures, he said, were not the result of stylized imagination, but came from fact: in ancient times, Mayan babies' heads were squeezed that way between two boards. Arlene began to wonder if he knew what he was talking about.

The sun shone heavily, seeming to press the top of her own head. She could feel sunlight compelling the damp forest to flourish, could sense the jungle as a living creature eager to repossess the ruins. What was that called in lit class? Pathetic fallacy.

She pictured the first modern excavators, digging through centuries of topsoil and old growth, cutting the stone city out of the jungle as if carving it all a second time. She felt dizzy, and sat down in the shade of a temple that had half crumbled to the ground. This is what she got for running around without a hat, she thought, mimicking her mother. She waved the others on. She relaxed in the hot shade and closed her eyes, but even then, emerald green continued to glow somewhere under her eyelids.

Back at the hotel, she sat and smoked a couple of cigarettes under a tree in the quiet courtyard. She knew enough not to expect Sheila that night. She looked up at the full moon visible through fig leaves and clouds and thought, with some surprise, it wasn't so bad being by herself for a change. The old man who'd guided them there stopped to talk to her on his way home from dinner. "I leave New York every year in late October," he said, "so I arrive in Mexico for the Day of the Dead."

"Day of the Dead?" she asked.

"Yes. An old friend of mine is buried in Tampico. It's on the way here." He didn't elaborate, but continued on to his room in the more prosperous side of the hotel. She assumed the Day of the Dead to be the Mexican name for Halloween. She supposed when a person was as old as he was, death might become a preoccupation. She had an urge to look over her shoulder, but went inside instead.

In bed she read a Spanish romance comic book she'd found in the bathroom. The front cover featured a glossy young woman with bright yellow hair, a crystal pearl trickling from her tear-sparkled blue eyes. "*Por qué yo?*" she asked in the dialogue balloon growing from her luscious lips. A darkly handsome young man stood glowering in the background. Inside the cover, the pages were filled with small black and white photos, still shots taken of a soap opera. The character in the photographs looked nothing like the cover artist's version, although her hair was bleached blonde and she also seemed to feel inordinately sorry for herself.

When Arlene started to doze off, she had to get out of bed to pull the string on the single light bulb in the centre of the ceiling. This woke her up again, and she lay on her side, scrutinizing a slim shaft of moonlight cutting across the dark wall, until she fell asleep.

8.

"I've decided," Arlene announced, "that whatever you guys want to do today, I'm staying here on my own."

"We haven't even told you what our plans are," Sheila said. "We want to go on a trek in the jungle." She was breaking the last of her tortillas into crumbs.

Arlene stared at her. "A trek in the jungle?" she repeated. "Are you out of your mind? You don't have the right shoes or anything. Remember those heavy boots Murdoch wore?" She didn't bother to mention the snakebite marks; Sheila would remember them.

"Manrike says my *huaraches* will do fine. He and his friends have gone on this kind of trip from here before, and there are some beautiful sights. They know how to live in the jungle, and Manrike has a tent."

Arlene looked skeptically at Sheila and the three young men. Her perspective shifted. The guys all looked older, relaxed and manfully sprawled at the table, and Sheila looked like someone else. With her dark eyes, tan, brown hair, and Mexican earrings, she could have been Mexican. Or Spanish, Italian, Arabian, gypsy. Something exotic. "Actually," Sheila went on, looking hesitant, "only Manrike and I want to go. These two," she nodded at the others, "have to be back in Mérida tomorrow."

This wasn't a mere camping trip; it was as if they were going off on a honeymoon. What if Sheila decided this was the romance of the century? What would Arlene do if she wanted to stay with him? She put her fork down. "When do you have to be back?" she asked Manrike.

"In ten days," he said. "We start later today, go camping eight, nine days." He started to count the days of the week. "Sunday, Monday, Tuesday night after next we be back."

Nine days! Arlene counted silently on her own fingers, then prolonged the silence on purpose. She looked grimly across the table at Sheila until her anger became swamped by self-pity. Sex and romance would always pass her by, all her friends would eventually leave her in the dust to go off with men, and she'd ultimately be left alone to dedicate her life to her work, whatever that might turn out to be. Teaching underprivileged children. Nursing in a leper colony. She would never have sex with anybody. She would remain an outsider, an observer of other people's relationships. She would be Jane Austen. "It's fine with me I guess," she finally said. "I can always visit the ruins." She pushed her plate away and lit a cigarette. None of it was up to her anyway.

Sheila was eyeing her, watching her thinking. "We were expecting you to come too," she said. "We really wouldn't mind. It's an adventure, Arlene."

Manrike nodded. "Sí. Most certain you are welcome."

Arlene raised her eyebrows, then examined the torpid fan on the restaurant ceiling. "Charmed, I'm sure," she said with a fake British accent, "but I think not."

Sheila gave her a look. "Let's go back to the hotel, then," she said. "I want to pack the stuff I'm taking."

On the way, Sheila scuffed her sandals against the hard-packed earth of the street, slowing herself and Arlene down. The heat hovered ahead of them in steamy waves. "I know you're pissed off, Arlene," she said, "but it's only for nine days."

Only? What was she supposed to do for a week and a half?

Study the ruins? But she said, "Why should I be pissed off?" She didn't look at Sheila. "We're travelling companions, not each other's chaperones."

"Arlene," Sheila said. She remained silent for a moment. "I'm in love. You wouldn't believe what sex is like with him. It's like –" She stopped, considering.

"It's like what?"

"It's as if I've been only part of a person without knowing it and now I'm whole."

"Really?" Arlene asked stiffly. She didn't know how to react in the face of this earnest pronouncement. She felt green, with envy and inexperience. She felt like a new piece of wood. She changed the subject. "You'd better leave your birth certificate and stuff with me," she said. "You don't want to lose them in quicksand or something."

That night, after Sheila and Manrike were gone, Arlene had trouble getting to sleep. She'd moved into a cheaper room, little more than a cubicle, for one person. She tried to put herself to sleep with the Spanish comic book but it didn't work, although this room was so small she could reach the light bulb string from her bed. It was stifling hot, and this mattress was even lumpier than the other one. When she finally dropped off toward morning, she dreamed she was in the jungle, looking for Sheila. She pushed leaves and vines out of the way, calling her name until she sat down to rest on a hollow log. She heard Sheila's voice coming from inside. "I'm whole," she said. "I'm whole."

"You're a hole?" Arlene asked, peering into the log.

"You know that's not what I said." Sheila's voice echoed, annoyed. "You're not even funny."

Arlene decided she might as well give up on sleep and have another shower. She would go out to the ruins whenever the first bus went, or catch a ride with some early-bird tourists. She could do some sightseeing in the cool of the morning and come back for breakfast later. Maybe it was so early she could get in without having to pay.

But the streets of Palenque were already busy. The small sidewalk cafés were bustling with people, men and women walking energetically past her on their way to work. Of course. This was why Mexicans took siestas in the afternoon. She made her way past the little marketplace toward the bus stop, feeling enlightened. She would get up this early every day from now on. A fruit vendor called from his stall, holding up a ripe papaya, a pineapple, a bunch of bananas, sending her an odour of fermenting sweetness. Farther on she held her breath past the meat market, where carcasses of beef and poultry hung exposed, raisined with flies.

She stood in the dense morning sunshine waiting for the bus, feeling her damp hair bleach blonder by the minute as passing men cheerfully hissed at her. It struck her again how unfair it all was. Why should *Sheila* be the one having the time of her life in the jungle?

From high ground she could see scarves of mist obscuring part of the greenery, transforming the ruins into mirages. Down on the paving stones where the grass gleamed almost neon between the rough structures, she tried to imagine herself as a young Mayan going about her business. But she knew too little about the ancient society. Who was it who said we're in a cage made up of our own language and culture? Somebody they'd studied in philosophy. She noticed a figure standing alone at the top of the highest pyramid, and felt desolate. She missed Sheila. She had no one to compare notes with.

She was beginning to feel hungry, but she walked farther on toward an area of the ancient city she hadn't seen before. Maybe she'd find the sacrificial altar. She pictured a bunk-sized slab of stone worn smooth by the slaughter of thousands of virgins. She was reminded of the steps in the Saskatoon Army and Navy Store, now worn concave by years of shoppers. Of course, the comparison wasn't really apt. Lying down on a stone wouldn't be as abrasive as walking on it. The sacrificial slab likely wasn't smooth at all. It would be rough, it would cut into your shoulder blades. She stopped at the highest structure. These stone steps weren't worn smooth. Maybe they'd originally been covered in marble, or some other more valuable stone that had since been ripped off, like the Egyptian pyramids.

As the mist cleared, she noticed the antlike figure on the top begin to climb slowly down. She peered up, shading her eyes from the sun, thinking even at that distance there was something familiar about the way he moved: methodically, with a stubborn, deliberate patience. In fact sort of like an ant, she thought as he came further into focus. She stood at the foot of the giant stairway and waited until she could see him clearly. It was Murdoch! She waved and called his name.

Startled, Murdoch looked down. "Arlene, isn't it?" He seemed pleased to see her. He made his way with surprised alacrity to the bottom, where they stood grinning at each other awkwardly. "So where's your sidekick?" he asked.

"Sheila? She's gone for a while. Went on a ten-day hike in the jungle. I decided to stay here by myself."

"Not your bag, eh?" They ambled companionably toward one of the smaller buildings the guide to Pacal's tomb had called the Temple of the Sun.

Murdoch looked unhealthy. He'd become thinner and because his face was very pale under his tan, it had a yellowish tinge. "Have you been sick or something?" she asked.

"No," he said, shortly. They walked in silence until they came to the pyramid. "Why don't we climb up here and have a toke or two?" He displayed the contents of his shirt pocket, which, along with some toothpicks, contained a couple of joints.

"I was sort of hoping to find a sacrificial altar," she said. "You know, where they used to tear people's hearts out and offer them to the sun god or whatever."

"The Mayans did make some human sacrifices, but I don't think there's an actual altar here in Palenque. There's a site, though, that they might have used for that kind of thing. I'll show you later."

She gauged the distance they'd have to climb to reach the temple. The redheaded girlfriend was either doing something in town or she was already out of the picture. "Where's your friend, What's-her-name?" she asked. They started to climb.

"Jeanette." He blushed and looked away, but not before Arlene noticed tears in his eyes. "She left me for a guy from Toledo," he said. "She dumped me before we got to Palenque."

"Oh." Arlene didn't know what to say. Poor Murdoch.

"It was at a huge party in the mountains," he recalled, his voice froggy and damp. "She just, well, went off with him." He shook his head. "Toledo," he said bitterly.

Swift Current, Arlene thought uncharitably, but said, "I've been sort of abandoned too. Sheila's having a mad love affair with this guy in the jungle. Who knows, she might want to stay with him."

Murdoch had recovered. "It's not exactly the same thing," he said scornfully. "Unless you two had a lesbian relationship."

"God no. What would make you think that?"

"I don't think that. It just logically followed from what you said about being abandoned too, comparing your situation to mine. Jeanette and I were lovers, you know."

"Of course you were. Don't be ridiculous, I was just sympathizing. Quit trying to be annoying on purpose." They continued up the stairs, panting, until they reached the temple.

He lit a joint and handed it to her as they sat in silence enjoying the view. Arlene gradually began to glow with knowledge, with a sense of order, of the existence of a grand scheme within the universe, though even as she became aware of the feeling, she knew it to be false. That was the thing about smoking grass; some part of her was always aware of the difference between the real and the artificial. When she felt happier after a couple of drinks, it felt like genuine joy. Dope encouraged either a silly sort of giddiness, or a mildly unpleasant paranoia. She did, however, appreciate the way marijuana clarified sight, the way it encouraged focus on detail. This reminded her she had glasses. When she put them on, sharp outlines of stone and jungle cut almost violently into her line of vision.

She'd almost forgotten about Murdoch, who was exploring the outside of the temple, climbing dangerously along a small ledge on the side. "Be careful," she called apathetically. He began to teeter on the edge. "For god's sake Murdoch, what are you doing?" Her voice became genuinely anxious and Murdoch, satisfied, sat down beside her again.

"I contemplated suicide after Jeanette left," he said. "I was devastated. It's worse than somebody dying on you. I mean not only is the person gone but there's all that rejection to deal with."

Arlene nodded. She lit an ordinary cigarette and watched the match flame burn down almost to her fingers. It seemed to take forever.

"I spent a whole week drunk on tequila, I hardly even came out of my tent."

"Tent? Are you still camping?"

"Yes. In the campground right here, near the ruins." He took a drag from her cigarette, and she offered him one from her pack of Fiestas. Everything now seemed so slow and off-centre, she wondered if this dope was different from ordinary marijuana. She thought she heard music from somewhere, and the colour yellow. She clicked her tongue at herself and giggled. How can you hear a colour? She caught a glimpse of dancers out of the corner of her eye. They were playing touch football with something yellow, and singing "Lemon Tree Very Pretty." That was it, that was the music. When she turned her head to look at them, they disappeared, along with their lemon. She could still hear the song, but she knew it was coming from inside her head. She gave Murdoch a sour look. "This," she said heavily. She couldn't quite articulate a full thought. "This," she tried again, "is disconcerting." The word seemed immense; her tongue had to stretch in order to wind its way around it.

Murdoch turned his face towards her in slow motion. "It's mixed with mushroom," he said, which seemed to Arlene at that moment to be the most mysterious thing anyone had ever said to her.

"Mixed with mushroom," she repeated with reverence. They sat like that for an unfathomable time in the pleasant shade of the temple, Arlene bothered by small glimpses of hallucinations like ghosts of mosquitoes. She was relieved when she felt herself coming down, coming to herself, although Murdoch had come full circle too and returned tenaciously to their initial conversation.

"After Jeanette," he said, "I came here anyway and set up my tent on my own. That first day I wandered around the ruins, going over in my head all the stuff about the Mayans I'd been going to tell her about. And I found myself at the top of the Temple of the Inscriptions. I just about jumped. But," he added, somewhat unnecessarily, "I didn't."

"There are probably more appropriate places to kill yourself anyway," she said. "Like the sacrificial site." If all he was going to do was whine about Jeanette, she'd go back to town and have breakfast by herself. "I'm really starving," she said, attempting to get to her feet. "I haven't even had breakfast yet and it must be lunchtime by now."

"I've got cheese and tortillas and some pineapple," Murdoch offered. "We can walk to the campground from here if you'd like." He took her hand to help her stand up, and they began the descent.

"Sounds delicious," she said. Salty Mexican cheese and the soft mealiness of tortillas took over her entire imagination. It wasn't until they'd been walking for some time and were leaving the ruins that she realized she and Murdoch were still holding hands.

9.

Small brightly coloured tents bloomed under the giant trees of the campground, set off by low and luxuriant vegetation. There was a variety of camping places: cement pads for vehicles, rough grass *palapas* set up as extra shelter for tents or hammocks. Murdoch led her to his well-used orange tent, which seemed smaller than it had on the beach at San Blas. It looked like a kid's toy in a backyard fern garden: Barbie and Ken go camping. Murdoch crawled in and brought out the food wrapped in layers of wax paper. Arlene caught a whiff of old socks and tequila breath. "Don't look inside," he said. "It's disgusting." He placed the cheese and tortillas carefully on a piece of plastic in front of Arlene.

"At least you're aware it's disgusting," she said. She wolfed down a hastily constructed tortilla sandwich. "These are very good."

"I hope the cheese is still okay," Murdoch said with his mouth full. "It should be; I just bought it yesterday."

"Where's the pineapple?" she asked. The cheese and tortillas had disappeared in a matter of seconds. They sliced the fruit in half moons like a watermelon and ate the pulp voraciously, juice running down their chins. Voices drifted over from other campsites. A group of Americans passed by, noisy and dripping wet. Water would be nice, Arlene thought. "Is there a swimming hole nearby?"

"The falls. There's a river with a waterfall."

"Really?"

"Where are you staying?" he asked.

"La Paloma, one of the hotels."

"Do you have a shower?"

"Yes, there's a bathroom at one end of the courtyard. Isn't there one here?" She was sucking the woody, spike-ridden rinds, relishing the last of the juice.

"There's a trickle from a few taps and otherwise everybody uses the river. I could use a regular shower for a change."

"We'll go into town then. We can take showers and I'll have a nap." Now that the pineapple was gone, she felt drowsy. She felt like sleeping right there in the shade. "It must be siesta time by now," she yawned. While Murdoch carried the remains of their feast to a garbage can, a vehicle came backfiring and grinding its way through the campground toward the exit. It was the Swedes. One of them nodded to Arlene as they drove by, and she waved them down. "Are you going to town?" she called.

"Where else?" the driver said, sadly.

"Can we get a ride?"

"Hop in."

Arlene beckoned to Murdoch, who was hastily throwing his towel and a couple of other items into a small pack.

"Oh," one the women said, evidently amused at seeing Murdoch instead of Sheila, "what happened to your other friend?"

"She's gone for a few days. On a hike in the jungle."

"Good lord." The woman looked dismayed. "A hike."

"In the jungle." The other young woman seemed almost offended.

Arlene felt obliged to explain. "With a man," she said. She regarded the other two coolly, trying to seem as sophisticated as they were.

"Ah." Both of them looked satisfied though still disdainful. The one in front made room for Murdoch and the driver revved the engine, making it backfire once more as they left the campground.

The Swedes were hungover again. Even with the top of the jeep down, they seemed saturated in an atmosphere of smoke and tequila. Though the vehicle was too noisy for conversation, Arlene tried to recall a couple of the Swedish phrases her father had taught her. All she could come up with, however, were the numbers from one to ten.

Once they picked up speed, the motor settled down to a steady ordinary hum. "It's a magic engine," the driver said to Murdoch. "It fixes itself."

As the woman beside her lit a cigarette, Arlene noticed her hands shaking quite dramatically. "We have all been ill," she explained when she saw Arlene staring. "Montezuma's revenge."

"We never drink the water any more," her companion said, "only beer and tequila."

Arlene shook her head, lighting her own cigarette with difficulty in the breeze. She suspected the shakes were caused by the cure, not the disease. It occurred to her it wasn't only in documentary films about hillbillies she'd seen this sun-bleached lethargic hopelessness, this white-trashy look, it was in old photos of some of her own relatives. She gave everybody a quick once-over. What with Murdoch looking skinny and peaked too, she felt absolutely robust. Speeding over a jungle road in an open jeep with the hot wind blowing through her hair, she felt like a hearty buxom heroine from an old Bob Hope comedy. She pictured Sheila raising her eyebrows at her: "buxom," she would say, was going a bit too far.

Americans might have invited her and Murdoch to go for coffee or a drink with them, but the Swedes simply dropped them off at the hotel. *"Tack så mycket,"* Arlene said, and they all nodded. Nobody acknowledged her attempt at Swedish. The driver seemed ready to throw up.

Drowsiness caught up with her again as she unlocked the door to her room. "I'm having a siesta now," she said to Murdoch. "You can shower over there across the courtyard." She noticed her fingers sticking together with dried pineapple juice. "Or just follow me. I have to wash my hands anyway." Murdoch trailed her to the washroom, unfolding his stuff out of his pack. She gave him and his towel an appraising glance. "I have some laundry detergent," she hinted.

"I just wash everything with me in the shower, with soap. Shirt, cut-offs, everything." He grinned at her. "I'll wash my towel later, Mom."

She was sleeping by the time he'd showered and returned to her room. She woke up once to find him lying beside her, wearing only his towel but breathing so easily she knew he'd fallen asleep. She turned over on her stomach and drifted off. The second time she woke, Murdoch was rubbing her back with a slow expertise so sensual she wanted to arch like a pet cat under his hands. She kept her eyes closed, pretending she wasn't awake but knowing he knew she was. He scratched gently between her shoulder blades and she felt ready to purr. He reached under her panties. "Mmmm," he breathed. "Smooth." She moaned softly. He continued his massage. "Take off your clothes," he suggested. "I may not be very swave or deboner, but I'm good."

She started to laugh into her pillow. "Jesus, Murdoch." She turned on her side and they kissed; he peeled her pants and T-shirt off as if she were a Christmas orange: something juicy. "I've never done this before," she said.

"Really?" Murdoch's fingers were diligent, exploring.

"I mean I've done *this*, but I don't think I can go any further. I tried a couple of times," she lied, "and couldn't go through with it." She'd said the same thing to an old boyfriend, she recalled, and he'd given up.

"Don't worry," he said, "you're so horny you'll hardly feel a thing." He guided her hand to his penis.

"It's way too big," she said, matter-of-factly.

"Gratifying as that sounds," he said, breathing so heavily she could hardly understand him, "it's not true. Let me try only the tip." He maneuvered carefully on top of her. "Just the very tip." He pretended to wheedle, joking but urgent, indicating a fraction of an inch with his other thumb and forefinger.

Arlene knew he was right. She bet it would feel good. He certainly seemed to know what he was doing. He flicked her nipples expertly with his tongue and she gasped. Her body felt like creamed velvet. "Well okay, let's try it," she said. She still didn't believe actual intercourse to be possible, but what the hell, it was only Murdoch.

"Creamed velvet?" Murdoch was sitting up in bed, grinning, smoking a cigarette.

"That's what I felt like. It's what I thought of." She felt dazed, euphoric. She'd done it. She reached for a cigarette and looked down at the sheet, now decorated with one bright red drop. They were silent for several minutes, until she said, "I'd make a pretty pitiful Sicilian bride."

"What?"

"I read somewhere they hang out the sheets after a Sicilian wedding night. You know, to show bloodstains proving the bride was a virgin."

Murdoch had heard of this too. "Some of them used to fake it with bladders of sheep's blood and that," he said.

Count on Murdoch to know more about it than anybody. She leaned over and kissed him, but felt too hot and sticky to cuddle. They lay back against the lumpy pillow, smoking Fiestas. "I guess," Murdoch said hesitantly, "You're not on anything, eh?"

"On anything?"

"Like the pill, I mean."

"Oh. Well, no. Not yet."

"I'd better pick up some safes."

"Yes. I guess so." She wasn't worried though. Her period was due soon, and anyway, she wasn't an unlucky person. Not that she was the type to win door prizes or raffles, either, but she knew she'd never be so unfortunate as to get pregnant after one time.

"I like you a lot," he said, stroking her face and looking mildly concerned. "I'm not usually the irresponsible type."

She gazed at him with what she thought was a contemplative expression and he tickled her. "Don't laugh at me," he said, "or I'll give you a hickey."

"Don't even think about it." They started to wrestle like sibling puppies, soon lying back on the pillow again. It was too hot. Murdoch lit another cigarette, but it wavered dangerously over the sheets as he fell in and out of sleep, until Arlene reached over and stubbed it out. He began to snore lightly with his mouth closed; his newly gaunt face featured interesting cheekbones and an aquiline nose. In spite of his round forehead, with his tan and no glasses he looked slightly Mayan. She smiled to herself, picturing him standing over an altar wearing feathered headgear and gold amulets.

The experience itself hadn't been anything wonderful, she realized, except for the incredible fact that she'd been able to go through with it, that she was normal. She was as capable as anybody. She lay on her side of the small bed examining the cracks in the ceiling, feeling she'd accomplished something all by herself, as if Murdoch hadn't had much to do with it. She thought of him as the first of a long line.

A rlene moved out of her room into the campground. She stood by, impatiently holding a flashlight for Murdoch as he cleaned out the tent. His supply of socks and gotch, long used up, were piled in a steamy mass beside the tent, and a fair number of tequila bottles had to be stashed in the garbage before she was allowed inside to spread out her sleeping bag. They'd decided to leave Murdoch's outside to air out.

Arlene was drifting off to sleep when she was startled awake by a monstrous roar. "Jesus!" She sat up. "What was that?"

"Oh." Murdoch had been asleep. "I forgot to warn you."

"Warn me?" It was as loud as a lion. "It's not a jaguar, is it?" She pictured a huge cat clawing at their tiny tent.

"It's howler monkeys. They howl like that every night. Sometimes you can catch a glimpse of them in the evening or early morning."

The sound came again, and it was true, it wasn't like a big cat. It started with a spine-tingling moan that rose into something hollow and ghostly, only to change into the lionlike roar before ending in an echoing parody of a gigantic monkey: Ooh, ooh, ooh.

"That was a lot more like a roar than a howl."

"Whatever you want to call it, it's made by howler monkeys."

Reassured, she nuzzled against him in the dark. "Now that you're awake," she said, "you might as well make yourself useful." His penis stiffened instantly at her touch: she could imagine it making a sound, something boing-like from a cartoon. She wondered if all men were like that.

The campground was shady and inexpensive, and the waterfall was ice cold and spectacular. They drank beer. They made love in the stifling tent, crawling out gasping to go swimming under the falls. They lay steaming in the jungle sunshine on the riverbank eating pineapples and mangoes. They forgot about the ruins. Arlene forgot about Sheila.

Murdoch had seventeen dollars to get him across the continent and back to Swift Current. It had long been time for him to start the trip home, so when the Swedes said they were leaving right away for Mexico City, he decided he'd better catch a ride with them. He could hitch north from there, or take the train.

Someone had told him a third-class ticket from Mexico City to the States border was only a few dollars.

He rolled his tent into a little orange bundle, tied it onto his pack under his sleeping bag, and was ready to go. The Swedes were waiting for him. "I'd give you some money to stay longer if I could afford it," Arlene said. "You could be my gigolo."

Murdoch grinned, adjusting his glasses over the bridge of his nose. Lighting one of her cigarettes, he said, "I mean it, Arlene. You have to call me when you get home." She had his parents' number and he had hers.

She was sorry he was leaving, but now that she'd finally crossed the sex bridge, she wanted to get on with her life. She could hardly wait to tell Sheila, although on the other hand she knew Sheila wouldn't envy her choice of lovers. She tried to remember if she'd ever said anything derogatory about Murdoch. Not that Sheila would bring it up to her. But then, that was the thing, they never had to say anything to each other. Everything was understood. The reason she'd gone to bed with Murdoch was because he was there and he'd tried. "You're really something, Murdoch," she said before they kissed goodbye.

"So are you," he said. They stood together for a moment, their foreheads touching.

"Take care, now," she called, waving as the morose Swedes drove away with him. She felt like somebody's aunt, waving him off at a bus depot. She felt slightly let down at the lack of romance. She couldn't convince herself even if she wanted to that she was in love with Murdoch, or that he was in love with her. They had certainly, however, cheered each other up. She packed her stuff and took the bus from the campground, returning to her old room at the hotel.

The hotel manager's wife smiled rather stiffly as she gave Arlene the key. Her name was Louisa but she was known simply as "the *Señora*," at least to most of the young tourists. She was a stern-faced, solid woman who oversaw the running of the hotel, all its guests and employees, with an energetic zeal. She seemed to be everywhere at once, efficient and imposing. Arlene felt she was slinking back to her room in a dormitory under the eyes of a disapproving den mother.

She would wait until Sheila came back before exploring the ruins one last time, and then they'd head for the Yucatán. She looked forward to lying on a beach by the Caribbean, enjoying the breeze off the sea. The jungle air of Palenque seemed to hang in damp nets that almost brushed against her face as she moved. Now that Murdoch was gone, her arms and legs seemed weighted down until she hardly had the energy to leave her room. None of this really bothered her, though. Her normal laziness was simply being taken to extremes. She didn't even mind having no one to talk to, now. Conversation of any kind would have involved some form of effort.

The day after Murdoch left, uninvited sex fantasies began to plague her. Over early afternoon coffee she pictured herself with the guy from Mazatlán or the man from Veracruz without his skeleton mask. She pictured herself with both of them. She felt damp and miserably excited. She squirmed in her chair and crossed her legs. She hadn't realized how strong a habit sex would become once she started. She needed it; she suffered, having to quit cold turkey. It had become a necessity like flavour in food, like keeping warm in a cold spell.

She didn't know until much later what a find Murdoch had been. It wasn't just that he was good in bed. Good, as far as she was eventually able to figure out, was simple: a bit of experience, the ability to hold an erection for a reasonable amount of time, and a certain willingness to please. No, with Murdoch, it was that they were good together. She'd found him so comfortable she'd been able to experiment, to find the exact positions and ways that suited her. She found that sometimes better-looking men weren't as easy to be with.

The only other customer in the café, an old Mayan Indian sitting alone at a corner table, looked up from his drink and stared at her, his rheumy eyes regaining a black intensity for several seconds. Arlene decided she'd better go and take a cold shower and have a *siesta*.

"Señorita Nelson!" Someone shouted outside her window and she jumped out of bed, making herself dizzy. "Just a minute!" she called, pulling on her jeans. She stumbled over her backpack, steadying herself on the warm grey cement of the wall, and opened the door.

"*Señorita.*" Two Mexican policemen stood outlined in the doorway, as immobile as if they'd been planted in front of her room. Their attitude of grim authority was tempered by that air of satisfaction peculiar to messengers of disaster.

PART TWO

10.

Arlene woke up bleeding. She felt nothing but blind misery as she stumbled to the washroom: Sheila was dead. Sheila had died in the jungle. She wasn't coming back. Nobody seemed to be around; the *Señora* had tapped on her door in the evening, just as she was falling asleep, and she remembered answering. She wasn't sure what time of day it was now. Back in her room, she pulled the sheet off her bed then made another trip to the shower to wash it out. Everything was always slightly damp in Palenque's climate but the heat would dry it as much as possible in an hour or so.

She lay on her sleeping bag, paging through the romance comic, feeling the blood seep out of her more and more insistently, sometimes with clots that felt massive, giving her a sick, sinking feeling, as if she were in a rowboat that kept springing leaks. The thought crossed her mind that at least she couldn't be pregnant. Every cloud had a silver lining.

An image of herself walking into her parents' house after her first trip out of the country, carrying Sheila's ashes and Murdoch's baby, cheered her, somehow. What could have been worse? She knew her mother would be relieved she was home no matter what, as long as she was alive. But how far could she go before her dad would refuse to have anything to do with her? She knew there was, with him, a breaking point somewhere. She didn't think pregnancy would do it, but she wasn't sure. Drugs. That would be the final straw, her getting stoned at home: he'd go off his rocker, slamming out of the house in a sort of panic at not knowing what do with his rage, until he'd calm down into morose acceptance, complaining to the neighbours, and not exactly throwing her out, but sending her away. Alcoholism ran in the family, so he might feel it his duty to put up with that, but drugs involved hippie decadence, a willful pursuit of evil.

It occurred to her that she was an adult and didn't have to think about her family. She didn't even have to go home unless she felt like visiting. She was free. Certainly her dad couldn't control her life anymore. His approval no longer mattered. She lay on the bed with the towel between her legs, looking up at the ceiling. She was free to lie here and bleed to death if she wanted.

She would be feeling better about Sheila, she noticed, even if she weren't preoccupied with herself, with having to run to the bathroom every twenty minutes. She realized with relief that intense grief couldn't be sustained indefinitely. Even though she was always thinking of Sheila's death on some level, she didn't have to be overwhelmed with sorrow every minute of the day. But she would never be finished with it altogether.

Having to change pads so often became even more worrisome when she saw that she'd soon run out of supplies. Her tampons were long gone. She felt weak, and although this could have been caused by her shock at Sheila's death, she knew she was losing blood at such a rate she might have to find a doctor. Maybe she should see this as an unanticipated vision quest. Maybe she'd have a life-transforming hallucination, like the ancient Mayans. Maybe she'd find her totem. She changed once more, put a sheet on top of her sleeping bag, and replaced the towel between her legs. If she went to sleep, perhaps it would stop. She might wake up and find everything had been a nightmare. A bluebottle fly buzzed drunkenly around the bed. With her luck, it would turn out to be her totem: she'd have a vision of a giant insect. She drifted off with the rather disgusting thought that she'd be able to sleep because it was ignoring her face.

She regained sudden consciousness to find someone standing over her, having hysterics. "Good lord. My God. Get a doctor quick. Quick!" It was the orange-haired American woman.

Arlene was so bewildered she sat up politely. This was not the vision she'd been hoping for. "Hello," she said. "It's nice of you to come by." Then she noticed the woman's companions running past her window, and looked down to discover her sheet and towel drenched with blood. Christ. This was like something from a horror movie. Even part of her sleeping bag was soaked. She felt the mattress, relieved to find it dry. "Oh. I'm really, uh, sorry. I've been having this problem since morning." She swung her legs over the side of the bed, wrapping her sleeping bag around her waist. "I have to get to the bathroom."

"I don't know if you should attempt it. But if you feel strong enough, I'll try to help you," the woman said, brisk now that she could see the situation wasn't as bad as it had looked at first sight.

Arlene made it there and back, but just barely. She felt faint. And no wonder, the woman said. "Is this a miscarriage?" she asked. "You didn't do anything to yourself did you?"

Arlene was confused for a moment, then said, "Oh god, no. I'm not that stupid." She hesitated. Could a miscarriage happen after such a short time? Could a fertilized egg only a few days old cause this much trouble? "It's the right time of month, I mean it just started out as my regular period. I can't understand it."

"Shock."

"What?"

"Shock over your friend's death. I had a cousin once who bled for three months straight after she caught her husband in bed with his podiatrist. But," she added, looking at the sheet, "it was nothing like this."

Arlene lay back on the pillow, shaken. She had actually forgotten about Sheila. She looked across the bed at the blue tin box and nodded at it. "My friend's ashes," she said.

The woman shook her head. "Awful," she said. "Just awful."

They were quiet for some time, waiting. "I got too much sun yesterday too," Arlene remembered. "I felt sick after I went for a walk."

The other two arrived with a harried-looking doctor. When they realized Arlene wasn't on the brink of death, they shrugged at him apologetically. He looked from her to the woman. "No baby?"

"No. No, nothing like that. Really," Arlene added impatiently. Her impromtu nurse mentioned possible sunstroke. He nodded and quickly gave Arlene a shot, handing two more syringes to the orange-haired woman. *"Una esta noche,"* he said slowly.

"One more tonight," she repeated.

"Y la otra mañana."

"And one more tomorrow."

"Do you know how to give needles?" Arlene asked after he was gone.

"She was a student nurse once," one of the others said. "We told the doctor that."

The would-be nurse almost said something, then thought better of it, blandly eyeing her companions.

"They expect people to know how to give needles here," the third woman said. "Drugstores will often give syringes out with a prescription." They finally all introduced themselves. As Arlene had suspected, they were all related: sisters, in fact. Their names were Lily, Blanche, and Iris. Iris was the one with the bad dye job. She brought the cane chair in and sat down, while her sisters, relieved, went off to do some shopping. Time dragged. After long silences broken by the odd exchange of travel anecdotes, Iris asked hopefully, "Do you feel any better?"

"I think so." The clots had quit, at least.

"The doctor left you a package of sanitary napkins."

"Thank goodness," said Arlene. "You know, I'm sure it's better," she continued. "I think I'll try the washroom." Iris accompanied her again. "It's much better," Arlene called from the cubicle. It felt to her like a miracle.

After seeing her settled back in her room, Iris cheerfully left to join the shopping expedition.

Arlene dozed all afternoon, waking up that evening for her second shot. Iris came alone, kind, efficient and silent, and told her to get some more sleep. When she left, Arlene heard Fred Muckle call to her from across the courtyard. He and Iris must be getting to know each other. Nothing like coming across a walking disaster to break the ice. Of course Fred was too old even for Iris and her sisters. Arlene strained to hear some of the conversation. The word "suspicious" came up more than once, and something about that Manrike character and not trusting the Mexican police.

This time what he was implying registered, but she rejected the thought altogether. Manrike wasn't a weirdo. She knew it, just as surely as she knew Iris and Fred were solid citizens, kindly concerned with helping her out.

A horrible thought caused her to sit up in bed. They were so responsible and conscientious, they might feel called upon to contact her parents. The hotel had her visa information with her home address, and the *Señora* would be sure to help. But no. Surely they'd at least ask her first.

She lay back on her pillow, weak tears coming effortlessly: not the hard sobs of grief, but the easy weeping of self-pity. Once she'd started crying at the thought of having to go home, she lay staring at the tin box and wept for her best friend, for how bleak and sad her own life would be from now on without her. Ashes, all that was left of Sheila. Without warning, she envisioned herself back in Saskatchewan presenting the little box to Sheila's parents. She snorted into her pillow, hysterical with rage, until her stomach hurt. "Sheila, you fucking idiot," she said aloud. "I'll never, never forgive you for this." Death was nothing, she felt at that moment, compared with having to face Sheila's mother.

She needed time to recover and to think. She certainly wasn't going to make any phone calls until she could face the idea of it, the prospect of hearing her own parents reaction, let alone Sheila's. Maybe she wouldn't phone at all; she'd just take the ashes and board any mode of transportation she could afford and go straight home. She'd get her mom to tell them. She pictured her mom and dad's faces showing a mixed medley of emotions: grief and horror for Sheila and her family mingled with relief that Arlene was safe, then finally, a certain grim satisfaction. Their fears, after all, had been justified. Her rage against Sheila was replaced with such extreme exasperation with her parents that she wanted to beat her head against the wall. Oh Christ she wished she and Sheila were both orphans.

The next morning, she found she'd quit bleeding entirely, and within a couple of days she felt quite well again. But she wasn't yet ready to deal with collecting Sheila's stuff from the police station. Maybe she'd never be ready. She had Sheila's ID, and her ashes, of course. That was all she really needed to go home with. But she should at least pick up her visa, and her travel diary and sketches. She wondered if the notebook had been damaged in the jungle.

Fred Muckle asked her out for supper. "First things first," he said when he'd knocked on her door with the invitation. "I must apologize for providing the disturbing news about the ashes not uh, being all there, while you were still so, uh. I have worried about it, thinking how insensitive that was."

She was touched. "Really, what I said then was true. Nothing could have made it any worse."

"It's just," he went on, "that when my wife died her ashes required an urn three times that size. It struck me at the time."

"Please don't worry about it. I really appreciated you being there."

Once they were in the restaurant, she felt like eating everything on the menu. She'd developed a voracious craving for tortillas and beans, and meat.

While she stuffed herself with roast pork, he seasoned his beefsteak and talked. She asked him what he did in New York, expecting him to be maybe a retired teacher. He was, he said, fairly wellknown as a painter. "I can make a claim," he said, "to being a contemporary, in my own modest way, of Edward Hopper."

"Really?" she asked. For all she knew, Edward Hopper was a tap dancer. The waiter, noting her empty side plate, brought more tortillas. Fred Muckle was folding his own tortillas with natural authority into triangles, without eating them. He began to talk about writers and artists who had work set in Latin America, or who lived there. She could tell he was used to respectful attentiveness. She tried to take smaller bites, to chew silently and look intrigued.

What did it mean, she wondered, being a contemporary of Edward Hopper? She liked the sound of all those homely American names. Hopper. Wyeth. Whistler. Muckle. Who was that playwright her English prof had talked about, whose name reminded her of a Dr. Suess book? Horton Foote. She smiled, and Fred Muckle thought she was reacting to something he said. "No, I'm perfectly serious. Only a Latin American could write *One Hundred Years of Solitude*." He cut substantial portions off his *bistek*, and chewed heartily. He had very good teeth for someone his age, she noticed. "Society here," he continued, "has the capacity to contain magic within its cultural context."

Arlene raised her eyebrows in an attempt to convey intelligent attention. She took a tortilla and wrapped it into a tube. She wanted, suddenly, to stuff the whole thing into her mouth. She couldn't remember ever feeling this ravenous. "Religion," she said, nodding sagely.

"Catholicism," he agreed, "but intermingled and crossbred with the pure magic of ancient times." He chewed another forkful. "Have you ever read D.H. Lawrence?" he asked.

"Oh yes." Her dinner was disappearing far too quickly. She tried to slow her progress by rolling yet another tortilla. *"Lady Chatterly. Women in Love."*

"You should read *The Plumed Serpent*. It's about the power of the old ways, and about –" he hesitated, couldn't seem to find the words. His shoulders sagged for an instant. "It's set in Mexico."

The word "serpent" touched her with a brief chill. She finished off her beer, not able to think of anything to say. Reading was something she'd always done in solitude. She wasn't used to discussing literature.

After a period of companionable chewing, Fred tried again, expounding on the paintings of Diego Rivera and Frieda Kahlo, the literature of Juan Rulfo, Carlos Fuentes, Graham Greene and Malcolm Lowry, while Arlene had second helpings.

Trying to think of a topic she could bring up herself, she recalled him mentioning the Day of the Dead, and asked, "Who was your friend, the one who died in Tampico?"

"What?" He looked so disoriented by the change in subject she was sorry she'd asked.

"Remember, you told me once you had a friend buried in Tampico? You always stop there to celebrate the Day of the Dead? Or, well, not celebrate but. You know what I mean." Now that she'd mentioned it, she wondered why they hadn't noted the connection between their two experiences before. He knew what it was like to have lost a friend in Mexico.

"Celebrate is the word," he said. "That's what the Day of the Dead is, a celebration. Everyone gathers by the graves of loved ones and they eat, drink and make merry."

Arlene looked at him, shocked. Make merry? She tried to

imagine her and Sheila's family gathering for a party on her grave. It was inconceivable.

But Fred's gaze went straight through her to another time. "She *was* an old friend," he continued. "She was my wife."

"Oh! Oh yes, of course, you said. About the container for her..." she hesitated.

"The ashes. Yes. Tampico is where we used to have a house. Our winter home."

"How did she...?" Arlene stopped. Really, since he hadn't volunteered to talk about it, she should mind her own business. "Never mind." She swallowed the dregs of her *cerveza*.

In the space of a few seconds, his face had taken on a bitter, malignantly aged look. "I try never to mind." He examined his coffee cup. "I've tried for years to allow the hate to leave me but it won't go away."

"Hate?" Arlene was now too interested to stop herself. "Was she *murdered?*"

"She may have committed suicide," he said bluntly. "I'll never know. She drowned, so theoretically it was an accident. However. She went swimming alone on a beach notorious for its undertow. No one ever swam there except the odd ignorant tourist, and she was neither ignorant nor a tourist. Even if it wasn't deliberate, it was such an extremely *stupid* thing to do..." He stopped abruptly, his face assuming its former expression, as if he himself had been briefly under water and had surfaced again.

Arlene recalled herself wishing Sheila were alive so she could strangle her. "It isn't hate."

"How would you know?" he said, obviously offended by her having an opinion.

"I do know. It's anger, it's not the same thing at all."

"No." He bit his lip, as if preventing himself from saying anything else. "You don't know."

Arlene knew enough not to insist. Instead she asked, carefully, "Was she an artist too?"

"A poet. You wouldn't have heard of her." He smiled cheerlessly. "One couldn't have called her successful. But then what poet in North America can call himself successful? We don't value them; we let them starve, for attention if nothing else." He was off on another tangent, and Arlene returned to her own thoughts, and to dessert.

Toward the end of the evening, he told her he'd like to paint her. For an uncomprehending second, she pictured herself standing straight and still while he plastered her body with green paint from a hardware store. Then, "I'm leaving soon," she said. "There wouldn't be enough time." She thought he'd had too much *cerveza,* and thanked him very much for the meal, saying she felt tired. She thought of his wife and all the women he might have painted over the years.

Back in her room, she examined herself in her tiny hand mirror, wondering if a seventy-year-old would have the gall to flatter her thinking he had any hope in hell, or if he'd been serious. Maybe he was a famous American artist. Maybe after he died, a Fred Muckle would be worth millions.

Her hair was now a definite yellow blonde with lighter highlights, and it had picked up a natural curl in the jungle climate. Her face was tanned but pale. She wasn't any thinner, really, although perhaps her cheeks were less rounded, maybe her cheekbones showed to better advantage. Maybe her brush with death had given her an interesting, ethereal look, she thought hopefully. She pictured the guy from the Mazatlán bus depot watching her stroll sadly through the ruins, looking fascinating and melancholy: a young woman with a tragic past, alone and palely loitering like the Lady of Shalott. Or whoever it was who'd loitered palely. Ophelia, maybe.

She was sick of being grief-stricken. She wanted to relish feeling like a tragic heroine. She wanted to skate on the surface of her sorrow, to contemplate the impressive depth her character must be gaining and to enjoy it.

The evening Sheila and Manrike had been intending to return to Palenque, Arlene made her last trip to the ruins. She was still feeling a strange sabbatical from mourning, finding in herself the ability to shove grief away and think about superficial concerns: her looks, practical travel plans. She could go for several minutes without thinking about Sheila at all, without even being aware of an undertow, but then the inevitable shock of remembering induced that sense of vertigo. Because she was new to sorrow, she thought this would never go away, that it was something she simply had to get used to.

She strolled through the grounds of the ruins, not attempting to climb any of the structures. She wore her glasses, wanting to have a clear picture to take home with her. It seemed to her that even without glasses, she'd developed a heightened clarity of vision. Vegetation seemed greener, Mayan stonework more sharply delineated. She had lost the desire to inhale anything chemical: inhaling reality was proving to be too much. In spite of her ability to dull thought, her surroundings were too sharp now. Everything seemed designed to give her, on the one hand, pain, and on the other – well, what? She was suspicious and ashamed of the hints she'd had of joy, of radiant relief that death had chosen Sheila and not her.

Maybe after all she would like to go home: to sit and drink coffee with her parents at the kitchen table; to watch *Bonanza* on the couch while her mom scratched her back; to go for long walks down the grid road with her brother Vic; to play with the dog; to bring lunch out to her dad cultivating barley in the south quarter. To recognize everything as so familiar she didn't have to look at any of it.

She decided to borrow Murdoch's plan and take a bus to Mexico City and a train to the border. Then she'd see how much money she had left, whether she could manage a standby flight. She wondered if she'd be able to forge Sheila's signature on her traveller's cheques without looking guilty.

The prospect of going home allowed her to see it, to picture her parent's kitchen clearly, as if she'd stepped out of it a minute ago: the cream and red battleship linoleum that never wore out; the grey arborite table; the painted wooden chairs; the off-white fridge that didn't match the stove. The smell of floor wax and Co-op dishwashing detergent wafted through her memory, making her almost as homesick as she'd been when she was eight, her first week at Camp Tapawingo.

On her way back to the hotel, she considered making a detour to the police station. Sheila's notebook would be there, all her stuff, maybe there'd be a letter she'd been intending to mail, although she doubted it would be more than a postcard.

She noticed a commotion in the distance, by her hotel. She plodded down the street, kicking up dust and wondering what the problem was. People were standing outside the front door, gesturing. Towards her? Others were coming around from the courtyard. One of them started to move quickly in her direction, waving. It was Angel Delgado, the policeman.

Was it possible another disaster had occurred? At least it couldn't be news from home; nobody there knew where she was. She rubbed her upper arms to stimulate circulation, assuring herself that she, at least, was alive and healthy. And really, who else was left?

Angel had almost reached her. *"Señorita!* Happy news! Happy news! We make much great mistake."

"What?"

He came up to her and patted her shoulder, grabbing her arm gently but insistently. "Come. Come, I show you big, big happiness."

What was he going on about?

They walked into the noisy chaos of a mob, although she realized later there were only about a dozen people. Luckily, Iris and the *Señora* were there, and they took over from Angel. Appropriating Arlene's arm, Iris led her into the courtyard and sat her down on the chair outside her room. Her orange hair seemed particularly frizzy and spectacular that evening, as if she were a cartoon character who'd put her finger in a light socket.

"What's going on here?" Arlene demanded.

"Prepare for a shock," Iris said. Louisa stood behind her, silently encouraging.

"Well, what?" A possibility struck her numb. Those Swedes. They were terrible drivers. "*Murdoch's* dead?" she asked.

"No, no," Iris said. "Happy news, like Angel said! It's Sheila. Your friend Sheila. She's alive."

11.

Arlene felt dizzy, but she took deep breaths, trying to keep some sanity in what must be a bizarre dream. They must be mistaken. Sheila was dead. Arlene had just been so sick, had practically died herself with the grief of it.

"Sheila's here!" Iris said. "Her and that Mexican boy are in your room."

"Here?" She couldn't take it in.

"Have you told her yet?" It was Sheila, calling from inside.

"*Sheila?*"

Sheila appeared. Arlene recoiled, bewildered. This was some sort of delayed hallucination, a mushroom flashback or from all that blood loss. Or maybe she'd fallen asleep, passed out. She desperately tried to remember what she'd just been doing, to grab onto an explanation that made sense. Her breath came in short gasps; she felt she was drowning.

"It's me," Sheila insisted, standing uncertainly in front of her. She looked the same as always, though her brown eyes were wide with concern and her hair was straggly after ten days in the jungle. Her jeans were torn above the left knee, Arlene noticed, and she wondered stupidly if the thread and needles had been in the stolen duffel bag.

Sheila finally bent over and gave her an awkward hug, which she returned automatically. She blacked out, slumping forward, and sat with her head down, Sheila holding her steady. When she recovered enough to sit up, she stared at Sheila for several minutes, shaking her head. She couldn't think of anything to say. "You're not dead. Holy shit, you're not dead, holy shit," came out in a sporadic unconscious litany. Sheila's quiet presence finally convinced her to calm down.

Sheila handed her a cigarette, and pulled up another chair. "That wasn't my body they found in the jungle," she said unnecessarily, "it was somebody else's. It was all some horrible mistake."

The policeman kept a low profile, finally disappearing altogether. The other people who'd happened in on the reunion, the hotel employees, a few hotel guests, some vendors and shopkeepers from down the street, were eventually herded away by the *Señora*. Iris remained standing there, shaking her head. When Arlene stood up, Sheila took her hand, and Manrike came over. "What a horror-ful time for you," he said gently, and she began to sob in great gasps of relief first on his shoulder, then on Sheila's. Manrike handed her Kleenexes until she was through, then helped her into the room. She leaned against him a moment longer than necessary, feeling, in spite of her joy and relief, a needle of envy when he sat her down on the bed and took himself and his warmth back to Sheila. "I have tequila," he said. "We go to campground? Or stay here?"

"I'm not moving," Arlene said. "Let's just sit in my room."

They invited Iris to stay for a drink and she had several, using lime and salt like an old pro. Half the town had noticed Sheila and Manrike return, she told them. The hotel manager had phoned the police, and the *Señora* had sent one of the maids to fetch Iris to help supervise the reunion. "What the hell they figured I could do I have no idea." She took a good slug of tequila and glanced from Arlene to Sheila and back again, her expression taking on a jaundiced humour. "I leave my troubles at home and come for a holiday to see the Mayan ruins and jungles of Mexico and what do I run into? Other peoples' kids and their disasters." She got up, ready to leave. "Those idiot cops," she went on. "Those fools should all lose their jobs. They really did cremate some poor girl; her visa and stuff are still at the police station. What I can't figure out is why they just assumed she was Sheila. Can't they *read?*" She glared at Manrike as if he were somehow to blame.

Manrike shrugged his shoulders at Arlene. "It all big, big mistake. Angel say you became sick, did not come in to see papers and so on."

Iris told them she and her sisters were leaving the next day. "You make sure and write, now," she said to Arlene. "You've already given me nightmares about my own kids."

Arlene, still dazed if not in acute shock, nodded her head. "Thank you again," she remembered to say as Iris left.

The three of them had another drink. "My mother," Manrike said, *"ai carumba.* She scream at police over telephone, I talk to her, she cried only. I must go home early tomorrow." He looked tenderly at Sheila. "We have very good time, no?"

"Sí." Sheila smiled. "Beautiful time." Arlene looked at the two grinning complacently at each other and felt anger radiate through her along with the tequila. She wanted to knock their heads together. She remembered wishing she could wring Sheila's neck for dying on her. She wanted to wring her neck now. There she'd been, in misery, in real agony, thinking Sheila was dead, when all along she was having the time of her selfish little life. And there she was now, smiling away as if it had been a picnic. Well it had been no picnic for Arlene. She wanted to tell them both to piss off out of her room, go back to the campground and fuck themselves. "You know," she said. She hesitated, watching them coldly for a moment. "I think I need some time alone here. Why don't you guys go back to your tent?"

"We'll come back here tomorrow morning," Sheila said, nodding earnestly. "I know this must be, uh, you must be pretty crazy with all this and you need some time to adjust."

Manrike looked surprised, but readily agreed to go. He pointed to the remains of the tequila. "You like it? Or?"

"Take it with you." She tried to regulate her breathing. She tried not to look at them. She felt as if doing so would injure them, that such profound anger was dangerous. After they left, she sat on her bed, panting. She walked around the room, for some reason needing to feel the rough texture of the cement walls under her palms. What the hell was wrong with her? She was furious, but about what? None of it had been Sheila's fault. They hadn't even been late getting back. Of course there was the fact that Sheila had deserted her in the first place, but after all it was for a lover. Arlene knew what was important. She knew what friendship was, and what priorities came before it.

She shouldn't have asked them to leave. She thought about catching the bus to the campground, but it was already dark. She turned on the electric light bulb and sat on her bed, staring at the blank grey wall until she felt tired enough to crawl in. Against all odds, she slept.

By the time Sheila and Manrike came by in the morning, Arlene felt able to assure them she was back to her old self, though this wasn't true. She would never again feel invulnerable, never again know for a fact that tragedy happened only to others. She had become aware of reality, the possible consequences of risk, and couldn't undo the knowledge. On the other hand, this tragedy had turned out to be a mistake, so she made up her mind it wasn't going to ruin her trip. She would carry on as if nothing had happened. She would follow Sheila's lead, try to rely on the beneficence of fate. And she could, after all, rejoice in the fact that Sheila was alive.

"Oh Arlene." Sheila didn't speak for a moment. "You must be just – I mean you got sick and everything. I feel terrible. I shouldn't have gone off in the first place."

Arlene wasn't feeling generous enough to disagree, but she said, "Well, it's done. And now it's all over with and we can continue travelling." Part of her was still astounded to find Sheila standing in front of her. She wished she could shrug her shoulders and say she'd known all along nothing could happen, there they were, Sheila and Arlene, inseparable as always.

Sheila looked relieved. "I thought maybe you'd want to pack it in and go home."

"God, no. I just want to get out of Palenque. Today if possible. And never come back. Let's go to the Yucatán, to the Caribbean coast, like we planned."

"We can get a ride to Villahermosa and then take a bus," Sheila suggested, then hesitated, "unless you're not well enough yet."

"I'm fine. I don't know why I bled like a stuck pig in the first place, but it's stopped now completely. Those shots Iris gave me did the trick. Now I'm just eating like a pig."

"Well," Sheila said, grinning. "That's nothing new."

Instead of reacting, Arlene again felt disoriented seeing Sheila right there, teasing the same as ever. "You know the funny thing is, I'm glad you're back, but I don't feel like jumping with joy and slobbering all over you."

"God. Who'd want you to?"

Arlene picked up the blue tin of ashes from the fruit crate by her bed. "Do you know anything about these?" she asked.

"Not as much as you do."

"Everybody thought they were your ashes. Not only that, but they lost half of them in the jungle."

"Lost half of them? How?"

"They were in a leaky container. Fred Muckle said his wife took up an urn three times this size."

"Who's Fred Muckle?

"That old man, the American who showed us the way to the hotel."

"Him? That distinguished old gentleman? His name is Fred Muckle?" Sheila watched her with a puzzled smile ready to break into something wider.

But Arlene didn't answer her. Some strand between them had been untied or snapped, and right now she wanted to make it worse. Giggling over a funny name didn't seem appropriate any more. She was too old for that now. Manrike watched them, silently. "Sheila, my true love," he said, "I must go."Arlene said goodbye to Manrike and went to the washroom, where she stayed brushing her hair, somberly examining her face until they'd had time for a proper goodbye. My true love I must go. God. Did everything have to be trite? Even death had turned into a farce, all that sorrow wasted on a stupid mistake.

When she returned to the room, Manrike was gone.

Sheila was sitting on the bed contemplating the ashes, weighing the tin box in her hands. "Have you taken a look at them?" she asked.

"Are you kidding? I didn't want to see them even when I thought they were yours. Anyway the lid is closed and tied together with that wire. I'm not even sure how you're supposed to open it."

"There's no lock on it or anything. It's like a cookie tin, you just pry it open." Sheila unwound the wire and grasped the lip of the lid with her fingernails.

"It's somebody's ashes, Sheila," Arlene warned. The thought of opening the tin had never crossed her mind. She was surprised at Sheila's lack of squeamishness.

"Jesus look at this." Sheila put the lid on the bed beside her. The contents were a greyish colour, looking more like powder than ashes, containing pale fragments that must have been pieces of bone.

They replaced the lid, clamping it shut tightly. They looked at each other, grimacing in distaste. "Like I said," Arlene continued, "they belong to some person, whoever she was. They did find a

123

girl's body." Now that she was getting used to Sheila's miraculous resurrection, the significance of this struck her. "When her family finds out she's dead, they're going to go through the kind of grief I did when I thought it was you. We should try to make sure the police find her next of kin. Maybe we can help them write a letter or something."

"Yes." Sheila looked a bit pale. "I hope she forgives us for opening the box."

"Jeez Sheila." She knew Sheila had a vague, Ouija Boardy idea of an afterlife that up until now she'd found interesting and quirky. She stood up. "Let's go to the police station; we have to get rid of these ashes anyway, and maybe they've contacted her relatives, now that they know I won't be doing it."

"Or maybe they want to contact them and their English isn't good enough," Sheila said. "Maybe one of us can make the call."

"Huh. You can do it then." The prospect of actual conversation was far less palatable than writing. They got ready to go out. "You know," she recalled, half-joking, "the worst thing about your being dead?"

"What?"

"The whole idea of having to tell your parents."

"You didn't phone them did you? Or write?" Sheila's tanned face took on a blanched shade.

"No. I kept putting it off and then I got sick. And then I put it off again. I thought I'd just go home. Maybe phone my mom so she could break the news first."

"What a coward," Sheila said, understanding perfectly.

"You're right," Arlene agreed. They left the hotel with Arlene carrying the blue box in the crook of her arm like a library book, and headed downtown to find Angel the policeman.

The police station was located in a less savoury section of town, where some of the buildings were missing small, curiously round patches of stucco, as if they'd been shot up by *banditos*. The girls walked into a fly-blown square of cement with a reception counter, and asked for Angel Delgado. Arlene recognized the man behind the counter, though he didn't look quite as fat here as he had when he'd blocked her doorway. He smiled broadly and shook her hand. *"Señorita* Arlena," he said, batting his long eyelashes at both girls and going on to shower them with Spanish. *Señor* Delgado was out, he said, but would be back *momentito.* In the meantime, Arlene and Sheila were ushered into another room with a desk and green plaster walls, and left alone to examine the grainy images on out-of-date Wanted posters.

Señor Delgado arrived, looking uncharacteristically officious. He glanced balefully at the tin box, which Arlene was still holding. He took it from her and set it on a pile of manila folders on his desk. God, she thought. A paperweight.

"I want show you, how become this big, big mistake," he said rummaging in an adjoining storeroom. "Here, this, dead *señorita,* her backpack." He produced an expensive state-of-the-art camping pack. "Now, here, her papers. See name. Same your friend." He handed them to Arlene.

Arlene looked at a crumpled visa. Shelley Stewart from Phoenix, Arizona. "Shelley Stewart?" So that's what had happened. She gestured toward Sheila. "My friend's name is Sheila Stuart." She spelled it out.

"Sí. Shelley, Shella. Stu-art. We see name in hotel book. Same, same." He picked up the tin of ashes, as if he were going to use it to demonstrate. But he only nodded his head and closed his eyes, as if he were supremely tired of the whole thing. As no doubt, Arlene thought, mentally shrugging her shoulders, he was.

She raised her eyebrows and looked at the ceiling fan, then at Sheila, whose face had taken on a pinched expression. Nothing more could be said or done. The mistake had been made and that was all there was to it. She looked up again. The fan was moving impossibly, uselessly slow, making the whole situation seem lazily demented. "I would like," she said succinctly, "to at least make sure the ashes get to the girl's family."

"*Sí.*" Angel sat behind his desk, facing them silently for some time. Then his back straightened as if he'd been hit with something. It turned out to be inspiration. "You keep!" he said abruptly. "You take papers, take backpack. You can use, no? Very good pack, no cheap." He nodded enthusiastically, as if he were trying to sell it to them.

He pointed at the tin box. "You take to Phoenix?" he asked. "I beg of you," he said formally, before either of the girls could react. He took an atlas from a drawer. "You go home north to Canada, see first Phoenix." He pointed out a prospective route. "We have *muchos problemas*. We telephone Phoenix. *Nada*. We try *la embajada*, the embassy *americano*, they say, we try send maybe to Phoenix but –" the complications were far too profound and numerous, he indicated, for his English vocabulary. "You take!" he reiterated. "Take backpack, nice, nice things." He dove into the pack, coming up with treasures: an expensive-looking dress, jewellery, a jean jacket.

Arlene and Sheila looked at each other. Although Arizona would be on their way to Saskatchewan overland, it was still an outrageous favour to ask.

"Here, you look." He put the pack down between them. "I must go, *uno momento*." He left the room, taking the ashes with him.

"Well," Arlene said, "I don't want any of her stuff."

Sheila was examining the floor. "Jeez. Shelley Stewart. Sheila Stuart. Was I ever close to kicking the bucket! Doesn't it give you the creeps?"

"I can see how it would give you the creeps. But *you* didn't come close. I mean," Arlene tried to organize her thoughts. It was pretty creepy. "You aren't close to being the same person."

"And both of us being here at the same time. Going into the jungle. What was she doing there all by herself, though, anyway?"

"I don't think she was more than a couple of miles from the ruins. Maybe she just took the wrong path. Or she was exploring."

"Why did they *cremate* her right away? Aren't they supposed to investigate or something?"

"They could tell right away it was a snakebite. So that was the official cause of death. And then it's so hot here, well. The body had been out there for a couple of days already."

Sheila made a face. "God."

Out of curiosity, they started to sort through the pack. They found a carved light wooden jewellery box with several sets of earrings. When Arlene held a lovely jade pair up to her ears, Sheila said they brought out green lights in her eyes.

Sheila dug down to the bottom and came up with a plastic bag. When she opened it, her eyes widened as if she'd discovered gold doubloons. "Arlene, look," she said. "American birth control pills." Along with Shelley Stewart's toothbrush and soap, there was a six month's supply of Ortho Novum 150. Three months each.

Before they'd left Saskatoon, they'd gone to a clinic where they were given enterovioform tablets to protect against the intestinal bugs tourists picked up in Mexico. Only Sheila had been brave enough to ask the doctor for a prescription for birth control pills, and he'd refused point blank.

They stuffed everything back in the pack. Arlene tried carrying it. It was far less awkward, far more comfortable than her old one. Sheila tried it, too. "Gee," she said appreciatively. "We could take turns. And look." She pointed to a neatly rolled sleeping bag attached to the bottom. "You had to throw yours out, didn't you?"

Arlene nodded. "We could just drop everything off someplace in Phoenix, like with a church organization or leave it with a note at, well maybe in some office at city hall," she said. "We wouldn't have to deal with the police or look for her family." They put the pack down between them and stared at it. "You know what?" she asked.

"What?"

"I bet Shelley Stewart's family will never find out anything unless we take this pack to Phoenix. And I bet her ashes will just sit here caught up in red tape. Or whatever the hell the big *problemo* is with the police here."

"Yes."

"I sort of feel we owe her something. For me thinking she was you. For being like us and dying. You see what I mean?"

Sheila nodded. "And like you said, you know what her family will feel like. It would be a good thing to get her stuff to them. Not to mention her, uh, remains."

This gave Arlene pause. "Remains? Jeez Sheila. Maybe we should..."

But Sheila was becoming enthusiastic. "Not to mention the fringe benefits for us."

When Angel returned, Arlene watched him as he settled himself at his desk. Didn't he realize the amount of trouble and inconvenience he and his police department had already caused her? And wasn't she taking on a new responsibility when what she wanted was to forget all that had happened here and go off, free to start over again? She was on the verge of giving up the whole venture. But what about Shelley Stewart's family? And what about the sleeping bag and birth control pills? She glanced at Sheila, giving her an imperceptible signal, and Sheila nodded back at her, smiling at Angel. "I guess we'll take them with us," she said.

His face brightened. "I must go *mañana* to Villahermosa. I drive you to bus depot for México." He placed the tin of ashes inside the pack, taking particular and ceremonious care, and solemnly handing it to Sheila. "I typewrite papers. I come to you *mañana*, ten o'clock *pronto*."

"*Sí, sí, bueno. Hasta mañana,*" Sheila said, so naturally that Arlene was surprised. Her Spanish had certainly improved. They both shook hands with Angel, sealing the deal.

On the way back to the hotel, Sheila carried the pack. "It's already adjusted to fit me," she said.

This sounded ominous to Arlene. It occurred to her she might not want to sleep in Shelley Stewart's sleeping bag. "How can we be doing this without even considering how –" she searched for the word, "how *ghoulish* this all is? Are we crazy or what?"

"Practical and hard-headed and kind I would say. Besides, we're doing her spirit a big favour. Maybe Shelley will watch over us."

Arlene ignored this and decided, for now, to change the subject. Something else nagged at her conscience. "He said Villahermosa for bus to México," she reminded Sheila.

"So?"

"So he thinks we're on our way to Mexico City; that we're going straight home."

"Yes. I guess so." They walked on, thoughtfully. "But it doesn't matter, really. Once we're in Villahermosa we'll take the bus to Mérida."

"Anyway, it's none of his business how long it takes us to get home. It's not as if we owe him anything."

At the hotel, they unpacked the backpack and washed it and most of the contents after it occurred to them Shelley Stewart would have been carrying it when the snake bit her. "I guess we'd better not risk doing the sleeping bag," Arlene said squeamishly. They didn't expend much effort, but swished everything around in soapy water and threw it all under the shower for a good rinse. One of the handy items in the pack was a real clothesline, easy to hook up anywhere. "Old Shelley thought of everything," Arlene said after they finished hanging up the last of her shirts.

"I can hardly wait to lie on a beach again," Sheila said.

"I can't wait to get the hell out of Palenque for good." Arlene was reading the directions on the back of a light green birth control package. She turned the little dial and popped a pill into her mouth. The small yellow disc lodged for a moment at the back of her throat and she thought of Shelley Stewart intending to take this very pill. She took a drink from her water bottle, quelling a mild queasy sensation. "You're supposed to wait until just after your next period," she informed Sheila.

Sheila looked off into space, calculating. "That should be next week sometime. As long as Manrike's condoms worked." Arlene shook her head. Pregnancy would be such an inconvenience, such a disaster, neither of them had considered it possible. Now she knew anything was possible. But at least she didn't have to worry about being pregnant herself. "Here," Sheila said, "give me a couple to put in my bag."

Arlene doled out three packages, feeling as though she were dividing the take from a bank heist. "I was going to start practising your signature," she remembered. "So I could forge it on your traveller's cheques."

"Arlene. I know you. You'd never have gotten away with it."

She remembered something else she hadn't yet told Sheila. "Guess who I ran into at the ruins just after you left, before all this trouble started?"

"Who?"

"Murdoch."

The next morning they sorted through Shelley Stewart's things. A pair of expensive jeans fit Sheila perfectly and two elegantly casual dresses of a lovely soft linen and a cotton blend fit both of them, although they were shorter on Arlene. Neither of them wanted the jean jacket or shorts, but they were pleased to add one or two shirts and sweaters to their sparse wardrobes. Arlene could see that besides having more money, Shelley'd had better taste than either of them. They left everything else, except the earrings, on the bed for the maids, and carefully packed the tin box at the very bottom of the new backpack. Over the box, they folded Sheila's old canvas pack, with all her belongings over that. Though they both found Shelley Stewart's pack easier to carry, Arlene realized that because it had a frame, it would be unwieldy to manage on buses, not to mention small cars or train carriages. Besides, they never walked far with their packs anyway, if they could help it. Since she was taking the sleeping bag, she graciously insisted Sheila have the pack.

"I wonder what Angel did with Shelley's money and traveller's cheques?" Sheila asked.

"I wonder what he did with all her underclothes," Arlene said.

Sheila made a face. "Jeez. You had to point that out just before he's coming to pick us up, didn't you."

"Oh well. I mean really. Maybe she didn't wear any. Anyway, Angel isn't the only person who works there."

Sheila's expression didn't change. "Remember that guy on the bus? El Kafkasito. He got those scars from the police, didn't he?"

"Angel is a nice man. He was good to me during this whole thing; he might be a bit sleazy, I don't know if he ever takes bribes or anything, but he's not...he's a decent person."

He appeared at their door only a half-hour late, beaming. He handed Sheila a closely typewritten official paper, along with Shelley Stewart's visa. "For border crossing," he said. This caused the girls to pause and look at each other, but he minimized any concerns with his hands pressing down the air in front of him. *"No problemo."* His gold teeth glinted in a wide smile, and he insisted on carrying their packs to the car.

"Aren't we all little rays of sunshine this morning," Arlene said, feeling elated herself.

"Qué?"

"I mean we are all very happy."

"Oh, *sí*. Is happy ending, like in cinema."

"Not so happy for poor old Shelley." Sheila nudged Arlene.

"No indeed." Arlene put on a false primness. "Shelley might beg to diffa." For a moment, a black glee took hold of both of them.

They went around to the hotel desk to check out and say goodbye to *Señora* Louisa. She was her brisk, efficient self, hugging both of them with a certain gracious disapproval. "You will come here when grown women," she told them in English, "and visit me."

131

"We are grown women," Sheila said cheerfully.

The *Señora's* laughter was the last thing they heard before getting into Angel's car. Since Sheila headed straight for the back seat, Arlene resigned herself to the front.

As they were about to drive off, Fred Muckle came to say goodbye. Arlene had knocked on his door earlier but he was out, so she'd left him a note. "The police here," he said, ignoring Angel, "well, I don't have words. It's like something from a farce." Angel gunned the motor. Fred handed each of the girls a postcard of a painting. "This is the artist I was talking about the other evening. Diego Rivera's wife."

"Oh, yes," Arlene said. They examined the cards, politely at first, then with real interest. "Thank you. They're beautiful," she said to him as warmly as she could out the car window. Though she hardly knew him, she felt she'd failed him somehow, and wished she could make it up to him.

Arlene's postcard was called *The Dream*. It showed the artist as a young woman sleeping in a huge stylized bed. Vines were growing over the blankets, covering the top part of her body, the leaves almost reaching her face. Above her, on a top bunk or canopy of the bed, lay a skeleton holding a bouquet of flowers. For some reason, the picture seemed familiar.

"You young ladies take care now," Fred Muckle said, waving them off. Instead of taking one last look at the town, Arlene examined Sheila's postcard, *Self Portrait with Unbound Hair*. She was impressed by the subject's proud intensity. She noted the eyebrows forming one strong line, the shadow above her lips. The woman looked as if she could take on anything and emerge strong and disdainful. Arlene felt an obscure resentment. "She could have toned down the moustache," she commented.

"My mother would recommend tweezers and peroxide paste," Sheila agreed. They put the cards carefully away in Arlene's denim bag, and sat back to watch yucca crops and jungle flash by from the comfort of the beat-up police cruiser. Arlene caught a faint whiff of vomit from somewhere in the back and wondered if Sheila noticed. Served her right for always maneuvering her way to the back seat.

By the time they hit the highway to Villahermosa, she knew Angel had no intention other than to drive happily along. He began to whistle, producing a haunting lilt as lovely as flute music. Sheila leaned forward, either to avoid the atmosphere or so she could hear better. *"Esta bonita,"* she said. They demanded an encore. He entertained them the entire way to the city, producing everything from classical to Mexican folk music to "Stairway to Heaven" and "Nights in White Satin." He imitated birds. Arlene was enchanted, dumbfounded.

She shook her head. Sheila had come back from the dead. Murdoch had saved her from old maidhood, set her on her way to further adventures. They had all survived the jungle. She felt as if she were starting out again, as if everything that happened now were part of a brand new journey. She could put Palenque behind her for good.

12. MÉRIDA

They arrived in Mérida that evening, looking forward to a night out. They had Manrike's phone number but Sheila didn't want to try it. If Manrike's mother answered, it would be curtains for him, she said. "Anyway, it was a beautiful love affair for a short time. We knew we wouldn't be able to stay together even if we wanted to, and now we've ended it. I don't know if I'd phone him, mother or no mother."

"That's a sensible attitude."

"See? Sensible is my middle name." But Arlene could see from her bright-eyed attention to the people they passed that Sheila was hoping to run into Manrike by accident.

The hotel room they found had a ceiling fan and a bathroom with a full-length mirror. "God, what luxury," Arlene said. "I would have killed for my own bathroom in Palenque."

"I bet."

They showered and dressed up in Shelley Stewart's elegant dresses and expensive earrings. The outfit that suited Arlene was a soft green that complemented her hair and brought out the green tints in her eyes. The dress draped elegantly from her shoulders, emphasizing her breasts, clinging to her hips, making her feel like a model. The jade earrings were perfect. She supposed Shelley had picked them to wear with the dress. "What do you think?" She turned to Sheila after brushing her hair.

"Wow." Sheila said. "Really."

"You too." Arlene looked Sheila up and down in amazement. She looked as elegant as Joan Baez in a delicately faded rust-coloured number that suited her eyes and brought out the sun-tinted coppery highlights in her dark hair. Her earrings were opal teardrops set in silver; they made her look exotic and mysterious.

They watched themselves and each other in the mirror, speechless with admiration at the transformation brought on by something as simple as an expensive dress. Arlene thought she looked like someone else entirely, as if she'd become someone only vaguely familiar. With a start, she studied her reflection more closely. That couple in the restaurant in Veracruz. The girlfriend had been wearing a green dress. She'd been about to go off on her own. It couldn't possibly be. "I wonder what Shelley Stewart looked like?"

"God Arlene. You really know how to add the final touch."

"Remember that cool guy I liked and his friend? The Bacardi girl? In Veracruz." She hesitated. "Does this look the same colour as her dress to you?"

Sheila's face took on the pinched look that Arlene was beginning to associate with references to the ashes. She examined the dress seriously and then said, "No. It's definitely different. God. I was just getting used to carrying her ashes around with us. You can't start trying to relate Shelley Stewart to anybody we've actually seen."

If the girlfriend really had been Shelley, Arlene thought, he'd certainly be single again. There in San Cristóbal all by himself.

Guiltily, she brushed this thought away. Imagine if the ashes were his girlfriend's. They couldn't very well show up on his doorstep wearing her dresses and jewellery. Carrying her remains in a box. Like something from a myth. Or a Monty Python sketch. How attractive would he find *that*? She let out an inadvertent snort.

"Oh don't be such a sissy," she told Sheila. "These are all Shelley's things, in case you've forgotten. They suit us so well, I bet she'd be glad they're not going to waste rotting somewhere in the jungle."

Sheila gave her a baleful glance. "Let's go eat. I'm starving."

They went out to join the parade of people strolling in the *zócalo*, where they were greatly appreciated. Sheila seemed to have developed a tolerance for being called to or hissed at. It had become, according to her, if not a fundamental attribute of Mexican society, at least an innocuous eccentricity.

"That's only because tonight we feel beautiful," Arlene said. "Usually we feel plain and dowdy and they still hiss at us, and then it seems like they're jeering."

"No. Well, that might be part of it, but not all. It used to make me so mad, I used to think of it as an attack of some kind. Now I hardly notice it; it's such a small thing really." They sat down for a cigarette on one of the peculiar S-shaped benches that were designed so courting couples could face each other without their bodies touching. They were near the main bank, an ancient building fronted by carvings of Spanish soldiers standing on the heads of conquered Mayans.

"Do we need to change any money, or should we wait till we're in Puerto Juarez?"

"I changed some in Palenque, remember?" Sheila said, grinning at her. "After you let me have my cheques back?"

They found a sidewalk café with the desirable mix of young tourists and Mexicans. They knew people were staring at them. Arlene felt powerful; she felt as if other people didn't matter. Before they were ready to order, two young Americans crossed the patio to their table. They were handsome, tall with long hair and moustaches. Definitely cool. "Mind if we join you?" they asked, lazily confident.

Arlene and Sheila sent each other slight negative signals. "Uh, my friend and I haven't seen each other for awhile and we want to talk."

"Maybe some other time," Sheila added politely.

After they'd gone back to their own table, Arlene said, "Imagine us turning those guys down a month ago?"

"A month ago they wouldn't have noticed us."

The menu featured a tempting array of seafood and Yucatecan beef and pork specialties. They ordered a substantial feast. "I could eat a horse," Arlene said.

"Me too."

The food began to arrive, and they discovered turtle soup to have an appetizing, delicate flavour. "You haven't told me much about the sights you *saw* on your jungle trek," Arlene said between spoonfuls.

Sheila was downing her soup like a labourer who'd just spent a day ploughing the back forty. Arlene realized she was doing the same, and self-consciously slowed down. What, actually, was the back forty anyway?

"Pay attention," Sheila said, kicking her lightly under the table, "and I might tell you some of them."

"I was wondering what the back forty was," Arlene said.

"What?"

"Never mind. I was just thinking we were both eating like farmhands."

"Oh." Sheila stopped. "I guess our etiquette hasn't caught up to our wardrobe."

"Maybe Shelley's ghost could drop by and give us a few pointers."

"Very funny." They started to imitate someone with impeccable manners, as Sheila talked about her trip. "The first day," she said between tiny mouthfuls, "we walked about five miles up a sort of mountain path. Well at least it seemed like a mountain. It wasn't all through jungle, some of it was farmland." She took a drink, holding her little finger delicately away from the glass. "I thought I'd die of the heat, but then we got to this cave, with a waterfall and pool right inside it. It was heaven." She forgot about acting cultured, and her eyes widened. "Really. We were on a cliff, and the view from the mouth of the cave was amazing. We could watch sunsets. It was like a pirates' hideout. We stayed there two days, just us in this cave and crystal cold waterfall." She fell silent.

"Then what did you do?"

"We walked along the top of a cliff sort of overhanging the jungle, until we came to another waterfall, an outside one that was really spectacular. Then," she examined her spoon, considering something. "Then we went down, into the dense jungle where sometimes Manrike had to use his machete to cut a path. His grandmother was Mayan, did I tell you that?"

"No."

"She taught him a lot of stuff about the ancient ways, some of it magical."

Arlene tore a tortilla in half. "Manrike the Magician."

"I'm not telling you anything else, you wouldn't believe it anyway. But," she stopped for a moment, looking daring and mysterious, "it was a very strange and exhilarating time."

"I believe you ate some magic mushrooms or something." A month ago, Arlene realized, she would have been eager to hear all details, magical or not. "Murdoch had some in Palenque, mixed with grass. We smoked it at the ruins. I hallucinated a bunch of people singing 'Lemon Tree Very Pretty,' and playing Frisbee."

Sheila laughed. "You might as well stick to tequila and beer." She ate quietly for a while. "I have to tell you though, we didn't eat or smoke anything weird. And," she hesitated, taking another drink, "we were able to become things."

"What do you mean? *Become* things?"

"Like jaguars. We became jaguars and were able to get through the jungle in only a few days, where ordinary people would have taken weeks."

"Jaguars." Arlene shook her head and mopped up the remainder of some hot sauce with a piece of tortilla. She absently licked her fingers. "You know one thing I learned through this?" she said. "I mean, thinking you were dead and getting sick and all that?"

Sheila's eyes did seem to have become rather catlike. "What?" she asked.

"To survive you have to rely on yourself, not on any outside spiritual hocus-pocus."

"You always believed that," Sheila pointed out. "And anyway, you had some help surviving. What if Iris and her sisters hadn't come to visit?"

"That was physical, practical help. You can always use that. Besides," she paused to order another *cerveza*. "Besides, I would eventually have called the *Señora* or someone to get a doctor. I wasn't unconscious." She pointed her spoon at Sheila. "You know very well what happened on your trip. Manrike slipped you something like peyote. Or you simply took some and you choose not to remember, because you want so badly to believe in magic, like a little kid."

"That's not even close to being true. You have no idea." Sheila wasn't angry, she was just stating a fact.

Arlene knew Sheila wasn't lying, either, just misguided. There was no use becoming hot under the collar against simple faith. Still, she needed to have the last word. Jaguars. Jesus Christ. "You're as gullible as some idiot Baptist who thinks he's going to change into an angel after he dies."

"I just know what happened to me." Sheila shrugged, and concentrated on her meal again.

For some reason, Arlene was reminded of their philosophy class. After a long pause, she said, "Remember that Heidegger quote, *The being that exists is man. Man alone exists?*"

"Yes," Sheila said, "You memorized that whole paragraph didn't you? Although I can't remember why."

Arlene wasn't sure why, either. "It talks about self-consciousness as being the key to really existing. I mean, the consciousness of self." She wanted to elaborate, to pin down a vague idea, but hesitated, not sure how to put it exactly. It was something about not being real unless you knew you were real.

"I'd like to know what's with all this 'man' business," Sheila said, interrupting her thought.

"What do you mean 'man business'?"

"*Man alone exists.* I mean, what about woman? Women are, but they don't exist, right?"

"Jesus, Sheila, you know he means man in the sense of human beings or people."

"Hah. None of those old farts thought of women as people."

"That's not the point. What you do with these guys is take all their ideas and apply them to women, just the same as you do men. Even if they were male chauvinist pigs, that doesn't mean everything they ever thought was totally wrong."

"Yes it does." Sheila nodded emphatically. "I've thought about it, and I think in the end, it does mean they're totally wrong."

Arlene was so irritated she could feel it in the pit of her stomach. "How can you of all people say that? You're the one who had a big love affair with a Mexican." She said this more scornfully than she'd intended. "Don't you know what Mexican men think of women?"

"God, Arlene, what has that got to do with philosophy?"

"You know sometimes you're such a pain I can't believe it."

"Ad hominem," Sheila said. She had taken Logic 100.

Arlene watched her tucking her hair behind her ears as she finished her meal and thought that if Sheila dropped dead tomorrow, it wouldn't be half as terrible as when she died the first time.

She glanced over at the two guys who'd tried to pick them up. So far, she'd had no opportunity to act on her plan to take a long line of lovers after Murdoch. She appraised both of them more openly. Either would do. In fact, maybe if Sheila wasn't interested, she could live out one of her fantasies and spend a night with both of them. She should take control, take advantage of her freedom, of being far from home where no one but Sheila would ever know. It would be a shame to waste Shelley Stewart's birth control pills. She turned back to Sheila.

"Seafood?" Sheila asked politely, holding up the last of the shrimp.

"Yes please."

Sheila opened her mouth, displaying the remains of a chewed tortilla with hot sauce. This was a stupid joke they'd shared in junior high. "See?" she said. "Food."

"Sheila." Arlene shook her head. Words escaped her.

A religious procession moved slowly past the café. It was made up mainly of women and children carrying sparklers and singing "Ave Maria," or at least that's what the refrain seemed to be. It didn't sound like the hymn Arlene had heard. Who'd recorded it? Marion somebody. This tune wasn't as beautiful, and it was sung in a quick singsong way, the voices high and nasal. The women wore head coverings, shawls and scarves hanging down past the shoulders of their dresses. The children wore black and white, likely school uniforms. They looked scrawny and wan in the streetlight, with a patina of poverty that for a moment Arlene couldn't ignore. It reminded her of Pedro, who couldn't even afford to go to school. She looked at her empty plate and felt hungry again.

On the way out, they were invited by a mixed group of young Mexicans to a nightclub. The two guys with the moustaches were still there, watching to see what they'd do.

"Should we go?" Sheila obviously wanted to go dancing.

Arlene sensed everyone watching her: the Mexicans, the Americans, Sheila, other restaurant patrons. Her skin crawled with an unexpected attack of shyness. Now she wanted nothing more than to be away from all of it. "I'm going back to the hotel. I'm not in the mood." As soon as she said this she felt a needle of panic. Sheila would go. She'd go off to the dance and leave her.

But Sheila acquiesced. She turned to the Mexicans, said, *"No gracias,"* and they walked out. When they reached their hotel room, Arlene pulled off her dress, dazed with relief and self-disgust. So much for living out fantasies.

It turned out that in order to reach the Caribbean coast, they had to take a bus to the Mayan ruins at Chichen Itza and transfer there for Puerto Juarez. Arlene said she'd seen enough ruins to last her a lifetime, so she sat in the shade close to the bus stop where she drank cola and ate snacks from a vendor while Sheila explored a small section of the ancient city. Arlene had a perfect view of the grand pyramid, which was huge, bigger than any at Palenque, featuring a temple at the top that might, Arlene thought, if you were very athletic, be worth the climb. The grounds, though, were bare and quite desolate, not lovely and lush as they were in Palenque.

Sheila didn't want to climb up to any of the temples in case the bus showed up, so she returned to join Arlene in the shade. "You can see the main one best from here anyway," she said. According to a sign, the bus was due now, which meant another hour or so. Meanwhile several young tourists joined them: three couples, one waiting for a bus in the opposite direction, back to Mérida, the other two also going to Puerto Juarez. The people going west said they'd just come from Playa del Carmen.

"That's where we're headed," said a man with a New York accent named Ian. He was tall and weedy-looking but substantial, with a modified Jimmy Durante nose. Molly, the young woman with him, was thin and dark with long black braids. "We thought we'd find some place on the beach to camp out," she said.

The guy from the third couple, Joel, was from Oregon. He was about twenty and built like a dancer: slim, delicately muscular and graceful. Red hair tumbled down his back in a mass of tangles. His girlfriend, Philippa, had an English accent, long light brown hair, and looked voluptuous but had a devout, artless air about her that seemed to nullify her curves. Playa del Carmen turned out to be where they were planning to go too. So, without thinking much about it, were Sheila and Arlene.

The westbound couple looked at each other; they had important information. "We stayed in a cabin," the man said, "or, well it's more of a shack, I guess, but it's by a freshwater well, in a cove about a mile down the beach from Playa del Carmen. Great beach. Free, nobody hassles you, a fisherman now and then, no tourists. It's far out. We even left some canned supplies and a few books. And there's still pots and pans there from someone before us."

"You only need the shack if it rains, really," his girlfriend added. "It's lovely sleeping out under the stars."

"It sounds too good to be true," Arlene said. "A well and everything!"

As it happened, their bus was to continue on to Playa del Carmen, after a stop at Puerto Juarez, the driver said, of maybe an hour. "It seems too easy," Arlene commented quietly to Sheila once they were on their way.

"Arlene," she said. "You're still in disaster mode. This is the way it always goes, remember?"

"We can shop for supplies in Puerto Juarez," Ian suggested. Everybody agreed, naturally assuming without any discussion that they'd all live together. They talked, relaxed and optimistic, about possible activities for the next few weeks, and the bus trip went quickly.

Puerto Juarez was larger than a fishing village, but couldn't be classified as a city, either. Small fishing boats crowded the dock area. Farther down, a ridge of grassy beach dipped abruptly into a small strip of sand washed by the Caribbean. It was pretty, but as beaches go, disappointing. The town itself had stores and cafés, and they discovered a vendor near the beach who made delicious *licuado de plátanos*, a kind of banana milkshake. At the market, they bought two weeks' supply of dried beans, rice, oatmeal, coffee, canned milk, tins of meat and vegetables, and some fresh fruit. "Cookies," Joel said. "Don't forget the munchies. And peanut butter. Let's see if anybody has peanut butter."

Arlene grinned at him. Both he and Ian seemed laid-back enough to be friends with so she didn't have to be bothered by tension or attraction. Anyway, they both had partners. Comfort and security: that's all she really wanted right now, and it looked possible. The bus honked its horn and they piled on for Playa del Carmen. "I hope the beach is better there than it is here," Arlene said.

"It will be just fine no matter what," Sheila said, somewhat tartly.

"Now, now, girls," Ian said.

"Does anybody know how to cook all these beans?" Arlene asked.

"I do," Molly said. "Ian and I are quite good cooks, aren't we?" She arched her eyebrows at him.

"I'm not bad myself," Philippa said.

"We're totally useless as far as cooking goes," Sheila said cheerfully. "But we can do the grocery shopping if no one else wants to."

Speak for yourself, Arlene was going to say, but stifled it. They had to volunteer to do something.

Joel was silent. "Joel can be the chief dishwasher," Arlene suggested.

"As chief," Joel said, "I can delegate employment."

"Everybody," Ian said, "takes turns doing dishes."

"And Ian's word," Molly said, "is the law."

Molly was teasing him, but still, Arlene hoped Ian wouldn't unwittingly appoint himself the family patriarch. She knew his type: a little bit older, an unquenchable sense of responsibility. She wanted none of it. Oh, cut it out, she told herself. She was becoming morose and pessimistic, a regular Eeyore. She looked out the window past Sheila's cheerful face at flashing glimpses of the Caribbean. It occurred to her she hadn't read a book in ages. She'd better find something decent to read soon if the only literary reference she could come up with was from *Winnie the Pooh*.

13. PLAYA DEL CARMEN

The living arrangements worked out very well. Molly and Ian slept in the hut. It was known locally as Chunzibul, which, a fisherman told them, means "bark of a tree" in Mayan. The others all slept in a row out on the beach except for the time or two it rained. Every evening they sat on the beach watching the stars come out. Later, comfortable in their sleeping bags, they drifted off to the sound of waves, sheltered by the full brilliance of the night sky. From the beginning, they formed an easy group, although it remained clearly comprised of individual couples, each minding their own business, spending most of the days on their own but drifting happily together for meals and to sit around the fire in the evenings.

Ian was always the first one up in the mornings. He started a fire in a rusty barrel under the lean-to attached to the hut, and made coffee, cooking porridge in a huge aluminum pot left behind by other campers. Each couple threw together what they could for lunch by themselves, fruit and buns or tortillas, and dinner was rather an occasion, with soup, fish or beans managed over a careful fire by Molly and Philippa. Joel, Arlene, and Sheila contributed what driftwood they managed to glean from lethargic sun-beaten walks down the beach, and helped sort beans for soaking.

Evenings were often spent planning outings and group activities: a baseball game with the local kids; a walk to find a freshwater lake that was reported to exist a couple of miles inland; an excursion on one of the fishing boats; a walk to the village to meet the ferryboat and gawk at the tourists. Nothing came of any of it, except eventually Joel and Ian were invited to go fishing.

When the time came to buy supplies, Arlene and Sheila walked the mile and a half of beach to the village and missed the grocery truck. Since the truck only came to Playa del Carmen once a week, Arlene knew the others would not be pleased. The local store charged three times as much for everything except buns.

The two of them sat glumly in the shade of the restaurant's *cerveza* sign, sipping beer and smoking Fiestas. On the other side of the fence, one of the fishermen's wives knelt outside her hut making tortillas on a charcoal-heated griddle. She slapped each tortilla rhythmically from one hand to the other until it was the proper thinness, threw it on the hot griddle for exactly the right amount of time, and piled it on top of the others. They were sitting so close to her Arlene could see the sweat in the creases of her forehead, but after an initial friendly nod, she'd politely ignored them. She stood up, moved into the light and looked out to sea. The neck and sleeves of her shift were embroidered with flowers blooming in almost fluorescent colours. The white cotton of her dress shimmered in the sun and her braided hair was as black as the bluebottle flies buzzing behind the curtains inside the restaurant. A mild breeze from the Caribbean ruffled her dress as she stood outlined against the turquoise sea. Arlene wondered if Fred Muckle would want to paint her.

Thinking of Fred Muckle brought Shelley Stewart's ashes to mind. They were never, in fact, very far from her thoughts, and she was getting sick of them. Just as she'd feared, they weighed on her and she knew Sheila felt the same. She wished they were rid of them. The idea that the longer they stayed in Playa del

Carmen, the longer they were prolonging the ignorance of the dead girl's family nagged at her conscience. She felt she should write to the address on the visa informing them of Shelley's death and that within a month or two, her ashes and backpack would turn up in Phoenix. But not specifying a time, just indicating some vague point in the future, might seem too much like a sadistic hoax.

"We'd better get back to Chunzibul." She picked up her denim purse. "What time is it?"

Sheila examined her bare wrist. "Two hairs past a freckle," she said.

Arlene studied the sky. "It must be at least eleven-thirty."

Two fishermen passed the restaurant patio, leered at them and hissed. "*Mamacita,*" they crooned, puckering their lips in exaggerated Latin kisses, swaggering, enacting a parody. For a moment, the desire to run after them and knock their heads together left Arlene breathless; she could almost hear the sound they'd make, like two coconuts. But she made her way slowly off the patio onto the beach.

"Sheila."

"What?"

"Why do Mexican men wear pointed shoes?"

"Pointed shoes?" Sheila looked mystified, then realized it was a joke. "Why?"

"So they can step on cockroaches in corners."

"Very funny." Sheila gave her a look. Arlene had heard the joke on a bus in San Diego and hadn't let herself tell it until now. She knew racism when she heard it. But she didn't care any more; she was sick of Mexican men and their macho strutting, their hissing at her as if she were a prime specimen of livestock. Sick to death and didn't care if Sheila was still sensitive about Manrike or not.

What really irked her was that these past several days, with nothing in her life but sun and heat and swims in warm salty water, all she could think about was sex. The thought that she could take advantage of some of that macho swagger if she felt so inclined was sometimes excruciating. If it weren't for obscure hopes about Joel, she might have done something about it.

The village houses were either cement boxes painted in tired pastels or thatched huts with sand floors. There was one hotel, a block of four cement rooms with a restaurant. The rooms were never used except by stranded tourists who had missed the ferryboat to the islands of Cozumel or Isla Mujeres. Few people stopped at Playa del Carmen by choice, although the beaches were long and white and lined with coconut palms and the Caribbean was as clear and blue there as by the islands. It was, as yet, undiscovered by regular tourists and Arlene considered herself a privileged pioneer. There was not much to do, though, but lie on the beach, swim, eat, and sleep, which had sounded fine until they'd tried it for three weeks straight.

By now she and Sheila were so bored that, although Joel had initially seemed more brotherly than anything, he'd developed the magnetism of a minor cult figure. Molly and Ian were in love, they were a couple, but Joel and Philippa never slept together, never made love at all as far as anyone could see. They talked about levels of spiritual existence. They never wore shoes, they said, even when it was cold; they were teaching their feet to feel. Joel assumed an aura of mystery, the fascination of an unreachable priest, a celibate mystic. Whenever Arlene considered making a play for him, she was stopped not only by the existence of Philippa, but by the knowledge that she herself had seen better days as far as sex appeal was concerned. A diet of beans, tortillas, buns, fish, coconuts, oatmeal and beer was not conducive to creating a svelte body. Since their arrival at Chunzibul, her and Sheila's main passion, in spite of Joel, was food, although they told each other that Shelley Stewart's birth control pills were causing them to swell with excess fluid.

As they entered the tiny store, the sudden gloom snapped her mind back to present reality. *"Buenos días."*

"*Buenos.*" The storekeeper eyed them balefully. They bought enough supplies to last a couple of days, and Arlene counted their change carefully.

By the time they started back, the village was entirely deserted; even the dogs sat in the shade. It was almost high noon. They wrapped scarves on their heads to protect themselves from the sun and began to walk, kicking the fine white-sugar sand that sifted between their toes. They splashed aimlessly in the shallow waves where the sand was hard, the bottoms of their rolled-up jeans becoming soaked. They could see the heat shimmering in waves almost as substantial as the water.

"The guys got to go fishing again didn't they?" Arlene stopped and scraped some beach tar off her feet. "What a piss-off we can't go. At least it would be something to do." Women on board a fishing vessel were considered bad luck.

Palm trees lined the white beach, feathery fronds waving in the Caribbean breeze. The water was a vivid turquoise even when the weather was cloudy, and today it sparkled in aquamarine splendour.

"I guess we can always go swimming," Sheila said.

"Yes. Joel might be skinny-dipping at this time of day." Even though they knew Philippa would be with him, they both started to walk with more purpose toward Chunzibul.

J oel and Philippa had met on the road. Joel had calm grey-green eyes that changed colour with the sea. He carried nothing with him but a sleeping bag and a toothbrush. Apparently, he had sat down at Philippa's fire one evening when she was camped near the Mayan ruins at Tulum. After drinking a cup of tea, he got up to do his Tai Chi exercises. Philippa had watched him perform his slow-motion ballet and decided he could stay with her. She told Sheila and Arlene this was what she'd been looking for in America. It was all right with her if he was seeking purification to prepare himself for a higher existence. She decided that's what she'd been seeking too.

Arlene and Sheila started speculating more often about the apparent chastity of Joel's and Philippa's relationship. They hunted for clues to his soul, listening to his rather vapid opinions about the meaning of life, questioning him about his past and insinuating themselves into his and Philippa's conversations, even though he hadn't done anything unusual or particularly interesting except refrain from having sex. Arlene didn't think he liked men; at least he didn't give that impression, and the way he sometimes looked at Philippa seemed to rule that out. She knew Philippa must just be biding her time.

Ian and Molly were mature: they'd had real jobs once. Molly told stories around the campfire on the beach, about herself and her family. Her father had been a Catholic priest who'd lived five years with her mother before finally giving up the priesthood, becoming a social worker and marrying her. Now Molly's mother wouldn't speak to her because she was living in sin with Ian. "I'll never get over it," she said, her eyes darkening with hurt and anger in the flickering light. "If she lives to be a hundred, I'll never forgive her, it's so blatantly hypocritical and unfair."

Joel and Sheila were playing with the fire. Sheila added small dry combustibles that produced sparks. Joel rested the end of a stick in the coals until it glowed, then waved it in the dark, creating phosphorescent red designs in the night sky.

"Your mom," Sheila said to Molly. "If she's so religious, she probably thinks she's made this awful choice, a real sacrifice, given up her soul for the love of her life. Maybe she even thinks she's going to hell. And then, there you are, living with Ian and, compared to her, taking it all so casually." They watched Joel create a continuous radiant spiral.

"Yes." Arlene nodded. "None of our parents know what it's like to be young now. Everything's changed so much."

"My word," Philippa said, "we all have such sympathetic

insights into other people's parents." Arlene laughed. "How come," Philippa asked her, changing the subject, "you two have such different backpacks? Is Sheila richer than you?"

"No," Arlene said. "It's a long story."

"We've got nothing but time," Ian said lazily. So Arlene recounted her adventures in Palenque, from the time she was told Sheila had been killed by a snake to when the *policía* convinced them to take Shelley Stewart's ashes. She didn't go into details of her illness; she just said she'd been sick for a few days.

"God." Philippa looked at Arlene with new respect. "What an awful experience." Joel added a piece of driftwood to the fire and they watched sparks float upward, blending with the stars. Their evening campfire was away from the cabin, along the beach close to the water. The soothing wash of the surf provided such a constant accompaniment to their days and nights that Arlene sometimes wondered if she'd manage to exist in the same way without it.

"Can we see them?" Philippa asked.

"See what?" Arlene asked.

"The ashes."

"You've got to be kidding. Why on earth would you want to see them?"

"It's all so interesting. I'm curious."

Then Arlene thought maybe Philippa didn't believe her. For a moment she felt like telling her to fuck off. She looked at Sheila.

"You could look at the tin box," Sheila said hesitantly. "But it's sort of hard to open. Besides, we looked at them once and that was enough."

Ian and Molly looked gravely at each other as Sheila went into the hut and returned with the tin. "It's not as big as most urns because the container they had at first leaked on the trail back to Palenque. This is only part of Shelley Stewart." She set the box on the sand, where it flickered, reflecting the fire.

Molly shook her head. "You can't take something like that over the border. God. I mean, think about it. Even if all it is is ashes, customs will detain you forever to examine it."

Ian nodded. "There could be cocaine or heroin in there."

Joel sat up, interested. "Holy shit," he said.

"How can you trust this Angel character?" Ian asked. "The police here are all corrupt to some extent."

"And really," Molly said. "Over the years there must be thousands of tourists who've died in Mexico. There's got to be some kind of ordinary arrangement that can be made to send them home."

Arlene felt foolish for not considering any of this. She glanced at Sheila. Neither of them mentioned the extra benefits they'd received.

"On the other hand," Joel said, "Mexican officials rely on bribes, and even then things don't get done. I bet with no one to claim the ashes, they could sit in Palenque for years until the police or whoever finally threw them out."

"No." Ian looked hard at Joel. "This is serious. You girls don't *ever* want to risk having anything to do with the police here. I mean maybe that Angel was all right, but..." He looked at Arlene. "Just get rid of them."

"I guess you're right." Arlene looked at the fire. "One time we met a Mexican student who'd been in jail. He had scars all over his back."

The others were shocked silent. Finally Ian said, "You see? You don't even want to think about trying to get this past border police. You may be arrested."

"But we can't just throw them out," Arlene said.

"No," Sheila said. "We're sure they're a real girl's ashes."

"But they may be mixed with something," Joel said, sounding hopeful in spite of the others' gravity.

"Why don't you bury them here somewhere," Philippa suggested, "and then you don't have to worry about them until you leave? Then you can decide to take them or leave them; meanwhile you'll have your good backpack to carry groceries with."

Since they hadn't bought any groceries yet, Arlene felt this to be a mild dig as well as a sensible suggestion.

Sheila looked depressed. "That's not a bad idea," she said. "I've been meaning to put all my stuff in my other pack anyway so we can use the good one."

"Maybe the best thing would be to send the girl's papers to her address in Phoenix, with a letter telling what you know of her death and that her family should contact the Palenque police," Molly suggested.

"Yes, I've been thinking of doing that," Arlene said. "I don't like the idea that we know she's dead but none of her family does yet."

"But make sure you sign only your first names," Ian said. "You don't want anybody to be able to trace you."

"Who actually saw her body?" Joel asked. "Are you sure it was a snakebite that killed her? Who had her cremated?"

"The Palenque police, I guess," Arlene said uncertainly. "But really, they seemed okay. At least Angel did. He was kind to me."

"We could spread the ashes here," Ian suggested. "Have a bit of a service, sort of a funeral."

"But if there's drugs?" Joel sounded alarmed.

"If there are any drugs in there, good riddance," Ian said. "It's likely all nothing anyway; that Angel guy just saw an opportunity to get rid of a minor problem. But it's not worth taking any chances."

"We'll think about it tomorrow," Arlene said gloomily. Telling the story hadn't been a good idea. It seemed to her the others were taking it over, putting in their two cents' worth like dirty shirts. Slightly cheered by her silent mixed metaphors, she said, "I'm going to bed." She stepped into the cabin for her toothbrush, taking the ashes with her, and held the coolness of the tin against her forehead before placing it once more in Sheila's pack.

Now that Molly and Ian had pointed out the foolhardiness of taking the ashes over the border, she felt caught. How could they just scatter them? She felt they'd been entrusted to her. Not just by Angel but by, well, fate. Or the universe or something. She knew the importance Shelley Stewart's family would place on the ashes, how they'd feel when they heard the news. She knew the chasm of grief that would open up in front of Shelley's mother. Or her sister. The memory of her own grief returned for a moment with such force she put her hands over her face and stood breathing carefully. She heard Sheila laugh, and thought, after all that, there she was alive and kicking and flirting with Joel over the fucking campfire.

Later, she brushed her teeth standing alone in the night sea breeze, and crawled out of her jeans into her sleeping bag. Shelley Stewart's sleeping bag. But since it had turned out to be so comfortable, she'd become used to the idea. There were no gnats or sand fleas on the Caribbean coast, and she always slept well. Looking at the dark sky and sea, hearing the comforting buzz of voices as the others put out the fire and set about their own preparations for sleep, she noticed Orion had dipped farther toward the horizon. Joel shook his sleeping bag a few feet down from her. He undressed completely, folding his jeans and T-shirt, carefully placing them at the mouth of his sleeping bag to use as a pillow. Arlene wondered if he could sense her watching him, watching his naked, graceful outline. But no. In a matter of a couple of minutes, he was lightly snoring. Hopeless. Completely hopeless. Philippa joined them, giving Joel a light prod with her toe before crawling into her own sleeping bag beside him. He rolled over and quit snoring. Sheila was taking a walk in the moonlight.

Arlene lay awake listening to the sift of the sea, frustrated, quietly masturbating. It occurred to her this was all that damn Murdoch's fault. Because of him, nothing would do any more but the real thing. She'd give anything for him to show up out of the blue to spend one more night with her. She brought herself off embroiled in a confused image of herself sandwiched between Joel and Murdoch. She fell asleep before Sheila returned.

The next day, mealtime conversation focused on the perfect location to bury Shelley Stewart's ashes, until finally that evening Ian dug a hole in the corner of the shack with a plastic shovel he'd found on the beach. "No one can see us burying anything in here. Who knows who hangs around during the day? Who knows who sneaks past here at night?"

"The shadow knows," Joel said. "Bwa ha ha ha."

"We need to find something to do," Sheila said. "Let's go to Puerto Juarez tomorrow. I have a craving for one of those *licuado de plátanos*." Her and Arlene's obsession with food seemed to be getting out of hand. On their failed shopping trip, they'd bought dozens of sweet Mexican buns at the store and had eaten thirty by themselves.

"We need peanut butter," Joel said. "We didn't really have time to look for it the last time we were there."

"The bus only goes in the evening though, and not every day either," Molly said.

"We can hitchhike," Sheila said.

"Not all of us," said Philippa.

"Why don't Arlene and I go?" Sheila said. "Make up for missing the supply truck."

Arlene was bored enough now to consent to almost anything, though since leaving Palenque, she was happy to have avoided hitchhiking. Her sense of security was permanently eroded, though she'd barely admit it to herself, let alone to Sheila. But she suggested, carefully trying to avoid focusing on either Joel or her nervousness, "One of you guys could come along as protection if you want."

"Protection." Joel smiled.

"Well, I don't mean you have to be a bodyguard, but it's sometimes more comfortable having someone of the male species along."

"I don't want to go anywhere anyway," said Molly.

"Me neither," Philippa said. "It's too bloody hot."

"Why don't you go, Joel, you're the one who's the peanut butter addict," Ian said.

Next morning, late, the three of them started off. Joel, as the token male, carried the empty backpack. Traffic was sparse on the road from Playa del Carmen and the few vehicles they did see passed them by. They sat at the side of the road sweating, the atmosphere hot and damp as a greenhouse.

"We would have been there by now if it had been just the two of us," Arlene complained. It hadn't occurred to her that with a guy along, no one would pick them up. They each picked a palm leaf to protect their heads from the sun, and sat there.

"You look like elves," Sheila said. Arlene knew she was refraining from pointing out whose idea it had been to bring a man along in the first place.

"If I could be sure you'd look seriously for peanut butter," Joel said morosely, "I'd go back to Chunzibul and leave you to it."

A half-ton finally stopped, and they rode in the back all the way to Puerto Juarez. The hot wind in her hair provided little relief, Arlene found, but it was better than being steamed alive, or for that matter, better than having to sit beside the driver.

When they got there, they raced to the *plátano* stand on the beach. They had two banana milkshakes each and then went shopping. Peanut butter was nowhere to be found. "No kidding," Joel said, "I'm getting desperate."

"I thought you were seeking a higher level of existence," Arlene said. "Peanut butter doesn't seem very lofty to me."

"A level of existence without peanut butter isn't worth reaching," he said. He asked everyone they met: storekeepers, vendors, people on the street. *"Tiene la mantequilla de cacahuete?"*

By late afternoon they were hot and thirsty. "Hey" Sheila said, inspired. "We have a male escort!"

"So?"

"So, maybe we can have a beer in a real *cantina*."

Without further discussion they went into the bar they happened to be passing, one of the few *cantinas* they'd seen with an open entrance giving the impression of something more than a crowded cave or a sinister hole in the wall. They sat at a tin table, contentedly drinking their *cervezas*, not saying much. Arlene watched the people around them until she realized that since they were far from inconspicuous, she'd better mind her own business. Unshaven fishermen dressed in baggy pants and threadbare open-necked shirts glowered at them, muttering to each other. There were no other women in the bar. Now and then one of the men hissed, a pressure cooker not able to contain itself. One or two spat on the floor. Joel took out his little book of Zen kōans and read to himself.

Tense now, Arlene looked down at the table but didn't say anything. She didn't want to be a wet blanket. They had a second beer before realizing how late it was. Joel stood up and stretched, then lifted the backpack to his shoulders, flexing his muscles a bit, looking around him nonchalantly as he strolled out of the cantina herding Arlene and Sheila before him. More relaxed after a second beer, Arlene caught herself watching him with a jaundiced expression, and for a moment he looked sheepish.

They left the village, hiking down the road. "At least it's a bit cooler now," Sheila said. The girls stopped to use some of the dense greenery at the roadside as a bathroom.

"Sheila," Arlene hissed as they crouched in the underbrush. "Watch out for snakes."

Sheila laughed.

Back on the road, the three of them fooled around like bored school kids, elbowing each other, searching for the pressure points on the backs of each other's knees. "Read us something from your book," Arlene suggested. This was something they'd asked Joel to do before, but he wouldn't. He kept the book to himself, refusing to share the wisdom of the Zen Masters with anyone but Philippa.

"You'd just make fun of it," he'd said when they'd first asked him about it.

"I wouldn't," Sheila had said, looking accusingly at Arlene. But so far he hadn't budged. His kōans were sacred.

Now Arlene wheedled, "Come on. Just one poem. I wouldn't laugh; I mean, what kind of person do you think I am anyway?"

"Do you think," he said disdainfully, "that I'd care whether you laughed or not?"

"No. I don't. So read one, or we'll bug you the whole way back to Playa del Carmen."

"They're not poems, they're kōans."

"Pomes, cones, whatever. Enlighten us."

He ignored her. He was still carrying the full backpack, although Sheila offered to take a turn. "Why don't we just quit walking?" he said. "If nobody picks us up we'll have to go back to town anyway."

They sat on the side of the road, standing up whenever a car or truck passed. No one stopped for them. "All right," he said after a long silence with no vehicles. "I'll read one, but you have to promise not to ask me again."

"We promise," Sheila said.

"Yes," said Arlene. He looked so cute and earnest with his straight sunburned nose buried in his book.

"This one is by Hakuin Ekaku. He wrote the one about one hand clapping."

"I've heard of that one," Arlene said.

"So has everybody." He cleared his throat. They were far enough from town for Arlene to sense wilderness. The jungle was in full chorus. "Here it is, it's called 'Monkey': A monkey searches for the moon in water, / not stopping until death / If he lets go he'll drop into a deep pool. / The light is bright and pure in ten directions."

Arlene was quietly impressed. After a respectful moment, she asked, "It's beautiful, but what does it mean?" It seemed to her like the flashes of insights she had when she was stoned, the sense of something deep and significant just out of reach.

Joel shrugged. "You're supposed to meditate and find the truth in it for yourself. In fact I think the meaning has something to do with searching for truth."

It was dusk. Soon the sudden Mexican night would darken the countryside. "It's getting too late," Sheila said after another silence. "What a bummer, we'll have to go back."

A noisy contraption that looked like a giant VW beetle appeared on the horizon, and they stood up hopefully. It turned out to be an ancient Chevrolet; unexpectedly, it screeched to a stop. The three men inside seemed rowdy but since they all sat in the front, any hitchhikers could sit together in the back. They decided to take the ride. It was better than nothing. The men each had the slicked-back hair and pencil-thin moustaches of film stars the same vintage as their car. Arlene thought she'd seen them in the *cantina.*

They sang *mariachi* songs through several miles with the car swaying from side to side along with the rhythm. A few weeks ago Arlene would have found this to be fun. Now she held onto the front seat, white knuckled, and hoped they'd make the Playa del Carmen turnoff without going off the road. Joel and Sheila sat on either side of her on the springless back seat, smiling over the success of their day. "Maw and Paw will be so pleased," Sheila drawled.

"And Sister Phil too," Arlene added, giving Joel a sideways look, regaining some of her equanimity.

The car came to a stop, in the middle of nowhere, or so it seemed, until Joel pointed out the lights from a shack with a Coca-Cola sign. The driver, after a quick consultation, started toward the building, and Joel scrambled out of the car after him. "Checking for peanut butter," he called back. It was almost too dark to see anything.

The other two men got out as well and stood leaning against the hood, passing a bottle back and forth between them. They moved to the back and disappeared as they bent over, busy with something behind the open trunk. When they moved away from the car, Arlene pointed wordlessly at the taller man, now outlined with a shotgun against the darkening sky.

"They're hunters. The other guy has one too." Sheila said, not seeming too concerned. The men were both swinging their guns around carelessly, aiming into the jungle, which seemed abruptly to become stiller. Only frogs and insects continued to saw and chirp away, too low on the food chain to know better. Arlene was reminded, quite stupidly she knew under the circumstances, of a Walter de la Mare poem she'd had to memorize in grade three. "Do you remember, 'Someone Came Knocking'?" she asked.

"No," Sheila said shortly, now watching warily as the two men swaggered back toward the car, shouting, *"Señoritas!"* One of them pressed his face against the window on Sheila's side. "They're drunk as skunks." She moved away from the door. "Those guns make me nervous."

"No kidding," Arlene said. Now that something was actually happening she felt – not calm, certainly, but cold, alert, ready for panic. "Should we get out, or stay in here?"

"Where the hell's Joel?" Sheila's voice was strained. The man still had his face against the glass, leering.

"Our hero, searching for peanut butter."

"We could lock the car."

"That might just piss them off. They can open it anyway, they have keys. Look, that guy's fly is open."

"Is he flashing?" Sheila didn't look.

"No, he's just been pissing in the ditch. But give him time." He zipped up and approached the car in a stupid, exaggerated way like a comedian acting drunk. He shoved his leering companion aside and opened the car door just as Joel and the other guy got back. "They've got shotguns," Arlene said to Joel, trying to sound calm.

"Oh." Joel stood stock-still, then moved tentatively toward the car. "You hunting?" he asked conversationally. He mimed shooting a gun. "Pow, pow? *Los animals?*"

"No," one of them shouted. *"Señoritas."* Expected to laugh, Joel managed a watery grin. The night seemed suspended for a long moment, as if time had slowed. None of them knew what to do next. Even the drunks didn't seem sure what would happen. A narrow beam of light emerged from the darkness, along with a click that sounded like a gun being cocked. This was followed by a torrent of incomprehensible Spanish. Arlene and Sheila decided it was time to get out of the car. This could be help of some kind, or it could be worse trouble, from which they might want to at least attempt escape. They stepped awkwardly into a beam from a high-powered flashlight. Arlene shaded her eyes, too confused to be frightened. The light was immediately lowered.

"Buenas noches, señoritas." It was a *policía.* Sheila grabbed the backpack from the back-seat floor. The policeman flashed his badge and pointed his gun at the drunk who'd opened the car door. The other two were moving toward him in a wavery semblance of belligerence, but they thought better of it after he blasted them with another volley of Spanish. Arlene understood only one word, *vámonos,* and was greatly relieved to see the men follow the suggestion. Mumbling darkly, they tossed their guns in the trunk and slunk sensibly into the car, not half as drunk as they'd been a minute before. They drove off carefully until they reached a safe distance, then gunned the motor and sped into oblivion.

"Tsk tsk tsk." Their rescuer clicked his tongue and slowly shook his head. *"Señoritas.* Hitchhike is not safe, *comprenden?"*

They shook hands with him in shocked silence, hardly believing their luck. *"Muchas gracias, Señor,"* Joel said formally.

"De nada. De nada," he repeated. "Come, I drive you to Puerto Juarez. I going back there." His car was only a few yards down the road. He must have crept up to them with the lights off, Arlene thought, mystified.

"God. What luck." Sheila looked dazed. Arlene climbed into the police car, feeling euphoric. As they drove off, they began to chatter like school kids on a field trip, telling him about Playa del Carmen, about their grocery shopping, about their favourite *licuado de plátanos* stand in Puerto Juarez. In town, he stopped the car in front of a small police station. "I am here," he said. "And you?"

"We'll just camp a ways down the beach," Arlene said.

"I walk with you, show good camping place. I need walk," he said, patting his flat stomach as if it were flabby. He insisted on carrying the pack of groceries, walking with them along the grassy shore away from town. The water of the Caribbean was a mirror that night; the moon's reflection shone brighter than the real thing. "The light is bright and pure in ten directions," Arlene remembered. She quoted aloud, pleased with herself. Joel stopped and waited, then continued on beside her, his hand resting lightly on the back of her neck. Bliss enveloped her for one shining moment.

Sheila was walking with the policeman. "You're our hero," she said, smiling up at him. Arlene could see she was only half teasing.

"*Sí,*" he said, grinning. He was young, Arlene realized, not much older than they were. It occurred to her he had a gun, too, and it might not be such a good idea to flirt with him. It also occurred to her that nothing had ever happened to them, nothing dangerous at all, until she'd started to worry. She'd invited danger in by expecting it.

Ahead of them, she could see a strange-looking rock that looked like a giant bowl upside down. "Is sea turtle," the *policía* pointed out in the manner of a tour guide. "From today, morning." The huge amphibian had been captured by fishermen and left on its back. Its legs waved pitiably in the moonlight as the four humans formed a circle around it.

"He's been here the whole day?" Sheila said. "We can't just leave him like that."

"I'll turn it over," Joel said.

"Come," the policeman said, beckoning. He gestured toward the turtle. "He is eatings for much peoples." He rubbed his fingers against his thumb to indicate money.

They plodded on, Sheila and Joel conferring suspiciously. The *policía* waited for Arlene. They walked silently for a while, Arlene glancing over at him. She found his tough wiriness, his cocky but respectful authority, attractive. She walked on his right, where the beach slanted down toward the water, so he'd seem taller than she was. It must be a sort of damsel-in-distress syndrome, she thought, mildly disgusted with herself.

"You were in *cantina*," he said, reprovingly.

"Yes," she said. She expected a lecture, but he continued to walk silently for several minutes.

"I may visit you at Playa del Carmen." It sounded almost like a question.

"Yes, of course," she said. She wasn't sure exactly to what she was agreeing. Did he mean visit her, as in, for want of a more modern word, courting? Or did he mean drop in for a friendly cup of coffee with all of them? Or was he warning her he might show up so if they had any dope, they should get rid of it? She'd never been any good at reading men, even familiar Canadians; foreigners were entirely incomprehensible.

"Here. *Muy bueno* camping." He dropped the pack and called to Joel and Sheila, pointing out a flat sheltered area behind coconut palms. "Be careful," he said. "No more hitchhike, no more *cantinas*. *Adiós*." He walked away abruptly. Outlined in the moonlight, he was visible for a long time as he made his way down the narrow beach toward Puerto Juarez.

It was warm and, using palm fronds, they were able to make a tolerable camp even without their sleeping bags, but they spent a restless night. When she finally managed to doze off, Arlene was haunted by a nightmare: a jaguar was following her. She would feel relieved for a time, thinking it had disappeared, when all at once she knew she was being stalked again and she'd catch a glimpse of yellow eyes and a sleek black outline creeping gracefully through the jungle. She was awakened in the middle of the night by Joel and Sheila rustling around in the dark. For a jealous moment, she thought Sheila had seen her chance and was seducing him, but after she caught a few whispered words she understood they were on a turtle-saving mission.

She lay awake, waiting for their return. She got up to sit on the beach but couldn't remain still. Wading into the water, she found herself in the midst of a sea of luminescence. Light sparkled in the waves, from a phosphorescent water plant or creature with a built-in radiance, like fireflies. Maybe it was algae or something that reflected the moon's brightness. When she put out her hands to touch the lights, she could feel nothing but sea water.

She fell asleep as soon as Sheila and Joel came back trying to be quiet in the ridiculously noisy way of kids at a sleepover, through suppressed snorts of laughter. She was eventually chilled awake by the early morning mist. Joel and Sheila were already up, building a fire. They sat, warming themselves in the opal dawn. They all watched the sun rise seashell pink over the waves, speechless with fatigue, early morning bad temper and awe. Since they were camping near coconut palms, Joel decided to try and get a couple of the nuts for breakfast. "It will be easier than rope climbing in gym class," he said.

"In case you've forgotten," Arlene said, "we have a whole pack of groceries here."

"I just want fresh coconut," he said. "And they're right there, so why not have some?"

"It's your funeral." Arlene said. Maybe he just wanted to prolong the sense of proximity to danger. Coconut palms flourished near Chunzibul too, but they'd always bought the fruit from local kids who sold them for next to nothing, holes for the juice already cut. She tried not to picture him falling, lying awkwardly in the sand, his neck broken.

He managed surprisingly well, shinnying efficiently up the

palm, his bare feet as tough as the tree trunk. Arlene watched his sinewy back and shoulders, remembering her imagined night with him and Murdoch. He cut down three nuts with a pocket knife Ian had lent him. "Bombs away," he called as each one thumped into the sand below. He descended as quickly as a monkey.

They cut the ends off the green husks, sawing at them with the knife. "This is a lot easier if you have a machete," Sheila informed them. They drank the sweet juice, then cracked the whole nuts with a stone to relish the crisp white meat. The day seemed to be starting out quite well, all things considered.

On the way into town, Arlene noticed the turtle had disappeared. She considered pretending she'd forgotten about it, but said, "That was eatings for much peoples." Joel and Sheila looked at the sky. Arlene fell behind.

She spotted an interesting-shaped piece of driftwood sticking out of the sand, and stopped to dig it out. "Look what I found," she called, holding up a wooden toilet seat, worn smooth as satin by the waves.

They waited for her, laughing. "We certainly don't need that," Sheila noted. They'd all become used to the freedom of the great outdoors.

"Better leave it for posterior," Joel said. They all found this so unaccountably hilarious it was several minutes before they found the strength to continue on to town.

Since there happened to be a bus that day going to Playa del Carmen, Arlene insisted on taking it. Her hitchhiking days, she said, were over. The three of them shared the *camione* with one other person, a very old woman in black, who sat just behind them with a watermelon on the seat beside her. After an initial friendly nod, she stared at Arlene's hair for the rest of the trip.

"This turned out to be sort of an expensive shopping excursion," Sheila said tentatively. Arlene knew she still wanted to hitchhike in spite of last night, and didn't reply.

"Aw shit," Joel complained, reminded of something. "I still

haven't found any peanut butter." He turned hopelessly to the old lady. *"Tienes la mantequilla de cacahuete?"*

She shook her head, pointing to her watermelon. *"Melone,"* she said, looking melancholy, *"Sólo melone."*

Arlene noticed a distinctive shimmer in the distance, as if the sun were reflecting off another body of water more silver than the blue of the Caribbean. She didn't realize what it was until they were almost at the turnoff to the village. "Sheila, look." It was an Airstream caravan. Silver trailers were parked in a long row by the sea like suckling pigs lined up against their mother. "Stop. *Halto."* She stood up and the bus driver pulled over. "I'm getting out to see if I can find Tex and Dorothy," she said to Sheila. Do you want to come?"

"You have friends in a caravan of *Airstreams?"* Joel asked.

"We got a ride once with these people who were really nice, and I want to see how they are." The driver hissed the brakes impatiently.

"Can you manage the groceries alone?" Sheila asked Joel.

"Huh. As if I've been doing anything else."

"Okay." Sheila and Arlene both jumped off the bus. "See you later then," they called, and started toward the encampment. Another incentive to visit besides her sudden longing to be around Tex and Dorothy's particular brand of comfortable American decency occurred to her. "Gee, I wonder if they still have any peanut butter."

They reached the encampment and walked along the trail at the rear, looking for Tex and Dorothy's window sign. Arlene was puzzled at her own pleasure at the thought of seeing them, at the idea of them still on the road arguing and joshing with each other, making pancakes and coffee every morning.

They couldn't find the sign. "I hope Tex is all right, that they didn't have to go home or something."

At the front, the beach was a hive of activity with Airstreamers setting up barbecues and lighting systems. "Excuse me." They finally approached a friendly-looking elderly couple. "We're looking for some people named Tex and Dorothy Wurlitzer."

"Wurlitzer?" The woman glanced up from putting a plastic cloth on a folding table. She looked all right from the waist up, but her shorts emphasized thighs that, riddled with cellulite and varicose veins, looked like gigantic parsnips. "Don't know anybody here by that name; do you Paul?" she called to her husband, a stringy-looking man hanging an elaborate system of kerosene lamps.

"Nope," he said laconically, "but if it's a big organ you're looking for you've come to the right place."

His wife ignored him. "You must have the wrong caravan honey," she said to Arlene.

"Oh. Of course." How could she have thought these caravans were uncommon?

"Well, so much for peanut butter," Sheila said, only half joking. "We'd better start walking back if we want to get home for lunch."

"You looking for some peanut butter?" The man stepped down from a stool set precariously in the sand.

"Yes." Arlene grinned. "We're going through withdrawal; we're craving it. That wasn't the reason we wanted to visit the Wurlitzers, though," she felt compelled to add.

"Here." He ducked inside and came out with two jars. "Take them. We got way too much stuff like this here."

Arlene looked at the woman, who nodded. "Go ahead, honey, take them. And put your wallet away."

The girls thanked the couple profusely and made their way, dazed, down the road to Playa del Carmen. They bought a bag of buns at Aguillar's and hid the jars at the bottom. "Joel will be just ecstatic," Sheila said.

"Yes," Arlene agreed. She was silent on the walk back, looking forward to the prospect of watching him eat it all up.

14.

Chunzibul now looked like home. They trudged down the beach toward the cove where the rough little shack leaned comfortably against the background of palm trees and jungle. It was almost lunchtime, and Arlene could see both couples outside in the shade, throwing together their snacks. Ian was the first to spot her and Sheila. Arlene could see him pointing them out, waving. They quickened their pace, ploughing through the fine sand. "Well, well," he said dryly as they walked up. "I hear you had quite the adventure."

"I bet you're glad to be back!" Molly was rolling up a tortilla with leftover refried beans. Philippa smiled calmly.

"So did you find your buddies in the travelling old folk's home?" Joel asked, grinning.

"It was the wrong caravan," Sheila said. Joel snorted.

"I'd be careful if I were you," Arlene said to him, nodding mysteriously at their bag. They flopped down cross-legged on the sand in the shade of the hut. Molly handed them warm soft drinks.

"Oh yes," Sheila said. "We got some extra supplies from a couple of Airstreamers that you in particular might not want to miss out on."

"What kind of supplies?" Joel asked.

Arlene could see a suspicious hope beginning to bloom somewhere behind his grin. The heat beside the hut seemed so intense she could almost hear it, but the thought of teasing him settled over her with refreshing glee.

"Oh, this and that," she answered, reaching across to touch Sheila's ankle with her toe.

"Yes." Sheila agreed. "This and that." She put on her goofy country girl voice. "And the other," she added.

"The other." Arlene nodded, imitating her. "Two jars of something or other."

"Cheap like borscht too. Free in fact."

"But not borscht. Smoother and creamier."

"Yet, somehow, nutty."

"Sort of like you two," Ian said. "Somehow nutty."

Joel grabbed the bag of buns. "You'd better not be joking," he warned.

"Hey!" Sheila tried to grab it back. "Get out of that."

"Aha." He held up a jar of peanut butter like a victory trophy. He hugged it to his chest and fell over, mimicking ecstasy. "It's Kraft too! Oh thank you thank you." He grabbed Arlene's hand and kissed it several times, "Mwa, mwa." He grabbed Sheila in a neck hold and pretended to try and give her a hickey. They wrestled just a slight bit too long. Arlene could see Philippa sizing them up. She got between them and showed Joel the other jar as if she were distracting a couple of two-year-olds.

Once he settled down, she said, "What makes you think you're going to get any?" He smiled brilliantly. "This one is for all of us to share," Arlene directed primly, "and that one is just for you." She handed one of the jars to Molly, who tried unsuccessfully to open it, then gave it to Ian.

"Lucky to have me around aren't you?" he said, his big hands easily unscrewing the top.

"Lucky for me you're good for something."

"It's a good thing you bought some more buns," Philippa said.

"With these two around," Ian said, indicating Arlene and Sheila, "they won't last long." Arlene made a face at him.

Joel was holding his jar of peanut butter like an alcoholic with a mickey of gin.

"Help yourself," Molly said, handing him a bun, a knife, and the open jar. He savoured a finger full first, a true connoisseur, then spread some on the bread. "I would do anything for you two," he said. He gave Sheila and Arlene a brown-tinged smile. "I could kiss your feet."

"How about taking our turns at doing dishes this week?" Arlene suggested. This brought no response whatsoever. He sat chewing, his expression beatific, his eyes faraway and blissful. They all helped themselves to peanut butter sandwiches.

Though they didn't dwell on what had happened at Puerto Juarez, the six of them hung out together that afternoon, staying quietly in the hut. They lounged around drinking coffee, reading parts of *In Watermelon Sugar* aloud, fantasizing about American food. After gorging on peanut butter, Joel sat cross-legged in the middle of the room, playing his still-concave stomach like a pair of bongo drums. Ian belched and stacked firewood. Molly told a story about having to shave her legs when she was in a swimming club, Philippa sat placidly staring off into space, and Sheila and Arlene quietly stuffed themselves with the last of Aguillar's sweet pastry.

Time passed, each day flowing lethargically into another, like the waves washing the beach. At dusk the six *compañeros* would sit out on the sand, waiting for the sun's last rays to shine through the palm trees and catch the ripples on the surface of the water, turning the sea to liquid gold. Sometimes, the four women waited alone for Ian and Joel to get back from a fishing trip.

"Here they come," Sheila said one evening, shading her eyes. "It looks like the big ones got away."

"How come you're so late?" Molly asked when the guys finally reached them.

"We had to stay out until we caught something, and then there weren't even enough fish to take any home with us." Ian pushed his hair back from his forehead. "They're not going to invite us again I bet. I heard them saying something about us looking like women. Because of our long hair, the Virgin Mary thinks there's women on the boat and that's why they aren't catching enough fish."

"That doesn't even make sense." Arlene looked up from sifting sand through her fingers.

"Why not?"

"Well, Jesus had long hair. I mean, Mary sure as hell wouldn't mistake you guys for women when her own kid had long hair. Why don't you just point that out?"

Ian hesitated. "The real problem is, I think a couple of them find us, uh, attractive, especially Joel. Tell them about Manuel." He nudged Joel.

Joel kicked at the sand, not commenting. "Aw, just forget it," he said. "We just won't go fishing any more." He looked over at Molly. "So what's to eat?

Later, he came out to the beach and sat cross-legged, the setting sun framing him in radiance, his hair forming an aureole around his head as he chanted quietly to himself. Arlene was reminded of the paintings she'd seen in a book called *Old Masters*. "Madonna with Beard," she thought. "What's he saying?" she asked Philippa.

"His mantra."

"I know but what's the word? Om?"

"I have no idea. It's a personal thing." Philippa stepped gracefully through the sand to the cabin. Her hair had turned taffy-coloured in the Mexican sun. It was long and thick, and she wore it loose. She was the only one of the four women who couldn't run along the beach comfortably without a bra. Arlene still found her and Joel's chastity mystifying. If he was really searching for a higher level of existence, he hadn't shown much evidence of it otherwise.

She sat down on the sand beside Joel, who had ceased chanting and was now staring out to sea. "So how are your feet coming along?" she asked.

The sun had almost set and his eyes were becoming midnight blue. "What?" He looked suspicious.

"Have they learned how to feel yet?"

He smiled, and his face was radiant. "Piss off," he said.

They sat watching the waves, Arlene staring off and on at the growing flab bulging over the waist of her jeans and feeling peaceful and slobbish. Maybe she could simply ask him about his relationship with Philippa. She picked at one of her toenails, thinking of ways to introduce the subject, but he stood up to do his Tai Chi. Sheila sat down beside her to watch.

Joel was performing with grace and precision, his slim dancer's body silhouetted against the fading light. Arlene smelled something that reminded her of high school gym class, then realized it was Sheila. She bent her face slightly, taking a surreptitious whiff of her own armpits. "I stink therefore I am," she said. They sat in silence, still watching Joel. Next shopping trip they'd have to look for more Halo Shampoo. "We'd better go home. We can't live here forever, we'll be total vegetables in another week."

"Who said I think therefore I am, anyway?"

"Some French guy; I forget his name," Arlene said.

"It wasn't the same guy whose quote you memorized from Philosophy 100?"

"Philosophy 102, you mean. No. That was Heidegger."

"Say it again."

"Heidegger."

"You nit, I mean the quote."

"'The being that exists is man. Man alone exists.' It goes on to say that rocks, trees, horses, even angels and God *are*, but they don't *exist.*" They contemplated this silently, still watching Joel. "So in other words," Arlene continued, "consciousness of self is the key to really existing. The problem is, what's God doing on that list then, or angels for that matter? If they existed wouldn't they be conscious of their own existence? I guess I don't understand what he meant at all."

"Maybe," Sheila said, "you should have read the whole essay."

"Hah, you should talk. You can't even remember the name of the class."

"One thing's for sure, whatever Heidegger thought," said Sheila. "We exist right now and he doesn't. And neither does poor Shelley Stewart," she added quietly.

Arlene was on the point of asking Sheila about her theories of a so-called afterlife, but decided to change the subject. She was sick of thinking about Shelley Stewart. Certainly, as far as Shelley was concerned, it was just as well there wasn't an afterlife. Imagine if she could look down from some heaven or hover around as a ghost, watching them wearing her clothes, carting her ashes around Mexico, even procrastinating about getting word to her parents in Phoenix. She continued to pick thoughtfully at her toenail. "When we first got to Mexico, were you sort of disappointed?" she asked.

"No. Not that I recall. Why? Were you?"

"Yes," Arlene said. She hesitated, trying to gather her thoughts into some sort of coherence. She examined the hairs on her legs, noticing that they were yellow now, bleached as blonde as those on her head. "Because I realized that there I was, on the beach in Mazatlán, and I hadn't changed a bit from when I was in Saskatoon. It was still me, Arlene, with the same old consciousness, viewpoint, everything, walking along in the heat eating corn on the cob with hot sauce instead of ploughing through the cold to get to the Ritz. I couldn't understand why people always talked about finding themselves, when I couldn't seem to get rid of myself."

"I have changed since I've travelled," Sheila said. "I feel as if I've become almost a different person."

"Really?" Arlene peered at her, sifting sand through her fingers. "You know in Palenque? When you finally showed up? I was mad as hell at you. I felt like strangling you but couldn't think of a good reason for being so angry, so I stifled it." She could feel her voice becoming strained. "It sounds awful, but part of me was even disappointed you weren't dead, since I'd already gone to all the trouble of coming to terms with it."

Sheila thought about this for a time, eyeing Arlene with an ambiguous expression.

"Now I have all this knowledge about what grief is like," Arlene went on, "but it turned out to be for nothing. It's as if I did change, as if I learned something, but it was all bogus, so now I feel like it's excess baggage." Like Shelley Stewart, she thought. She tried to smile. "Like our old duffel bag."

Sheila nodded seriously, pondering. "I wonder whatever happened to El Kafkasito? We didn't even ask him what his name was."

For a time, they watched Joel perform against the backdrop of darkening water. Arlene didn't want to wonder about El Kafkasito's scars or about Tex's heart attack or about Pedro's ways of making a living. She didn't want to think at all about Shelley Stewart. She wanted to imagine herself getting it on with the guy from Mazatlán in San Cristóbal. She wanted to kiss the salt off Joel's chest and shoulders and down his wiry body, licking him as if he were a popsicle.

"You know in the jungle? When I was with Manrike and we turned into jaguars?" Sheila stopped.

"Well what?" Arlene asked, though she didn't really want to hear about it. She recalled sitting in a campground watching silver trailers and wishing for magic. Maybe she'd changed in more ways than she was conscious of. And what was more, maybe she disdained her earlier self. Sheila had eluded the serpent, but

174

through chance, not because of any particular strength of her own. Arlene felt she had come through Palenque all right because of something in her own self which wasn't changed, but tempered. Something that had nothing to do with her new carefulness.

"I felt I was part of the jungle," Sheila went on, "of all of nature, as if that was the place I was meant to be."

"Shit. You belong everywhere you are, Sheila. You always have."

Sheila stretched voluptuously, looking suddenly slender, with long cat muscles. "But being a powerful cat, hmmm, it was so, as if I really was a part of something magnificent." She gazed at Joel, reminiscently.

"Did you hunt? You must have eaten raw meat, eh?"

"What?" Sheila looked shocked.

"That's what jaguars do, after all."

"No. We were human when we ate. We just travelled as jaguars. Once."

Arlene snorted. "Maybe Heidegger included God and angels and stuff because he meant that they're things, like horses and rocks and ideas. Like something seen in a vision quest. They're ideas, figments of someone's imagination, so they're *things*. Not beings."

Joel had been holding a position on one foot for five minutes. Arlene quit staring at him and stood up. She walked to the water's edge, but instead of wading in, went deliberately up to him. She took his face in her hands, putting him off-balance, and gave him a long kiss. She led him toward the jungle growth that lurked down the beach behind the palm trees, and he went along with her as if he were a small boy being led into an ice cream parlour, his eyes dark and expectant. She could feel Sheila watching them. "Arlene," she called. "Watch out for snakes."

Ian, the first one up in the morning as usual, was cooking porridge and coffee on the old barrel under the thatched lean-to they called the veranda. The iguana that lived on the roof of the hut scuttled over the corrugated tin. "The patter of little feet," Ian said, when the girls trooped in for breakfast.

"Where are Joel and Philippa?" Molly asked.

Joel and Arlene had meandered back separately in the evening, and eventually crawled into their sleeping bags as usual. Arlene was awake half the night smelling his sweat and semen, his salty oysterish smell on her own body, until she washed it off, swimming in the calm sea at dawn. She'd noticed Philippa sit up and watch her for a moment, but she and Joel had both still been lying there next to Sheila when Arlene settled back in for another couple of hours' sleep.

"I don't know," Arlene said. "I thought they'd be in here." She looked down to adjust her sandals.

"They must have gone," Sheila said flatly.

"Is Philippa's pack here?" Molly asked. Joel had nothing but his sleeping bag anyway.

"No." Ian looked bewildered. "It's gone."

Molly was eyeing the girls. "Did something happen?"

"I guess so," Arlene said, feeling like a badly behaved child.

"It's time we started to think of leaving too," Sheila said.

Molly shrugged and gave Ian a look. He snorted to himself and continued to stir the porridge, and the atmosphere eventually returned almost to normal.

Arlene was relieved they were gone; she didn't want to worry about having to face Philippa. She opened a tin of canned milk and mixed it with well water. Sheila set out the brown sugar and Molly set the coffee pot in the sand. The four of them ate, companionably leaning against the wall, and Arlene helped herself to seconds now that there were two extra helpings. "Waste not want not," she said to Ian. Ian shook his head and added milk to his coffee.

Molly and Ian went off to town, and the girls sat in the shack, reading. "Listen to this." Arlene read a passage from *The Prophet* about the earth delighting to feel your bare feet. She wanted to court Sheila, to entice her away from sulking. Joel wasn't the love of either of their lives, after all. But this time Sheila had lost, she'd lost her advantage, hadn't grabbed her chance when she could have.

"Listen to this." Sheila was reciprocating. She read a passage from *The Electric Kool Aid Acid Test,* and Arlene laughed a bit louder than she normally would. They were meeting each other halfway.

They prepared to leave. They washed their underwear in well water. They bathed, floating nude in the Caribbean past the anchored fishing boats, Arlene conscious of nothing but sun and sky, the colour aquamarine, the salty lukewarm seawater, all of which by then had permeated her existence as profoundly as a Saskatchewan wheat field, so that twenty, thirty years later she would catch the warmth of sunlight on her face or see an ad for rum or a tacky Club Med beach resort and be overwhelmed for a fraction of a second with – how would she describe the feeling? Not nostalgia, not longing, not a desire to go back there, but simple physical lust. Lust for the recipe of the offering, the combination of sun, sand, sky, water, all that clear heat and brightness laced with too much time, with deadly luxuriant boredom.

The next morning, they announced they were going to pack up and take the evening bus from the village as far as Chichen Itza and then see if they could get a ride with some tourists into Mérida. They were ready, they said, to start the trek home.

Ian nodded slowly. "We'll miss you," he said.

"I guess," Arlene said hesitantly, "we'll dig up the ashes." She looked at Sheila. They'd already composed the letter they planned to send to Phoenix. "We'll sprinkle them in the Caribbean. Shelley Stewart would have liked it here."

"Yes." Sheila nodded. She started paging through *The Prophet*, presumably to find a quote suitable for a funeral service.

Ian gave Arlene the toy shovel he'd used to bury the tin box. "It's only a foot or so down."

She dug in the sand at the place they remembered and found nothing. She dug further: still nothing. "Let me try," Sheila said. She shovelled two feet down, a little farther away from the corner, with no luck.

Arlene felt strangely resigned to the fact that the ashes were gone. Ian and Molly each took a turn, digging in the general area until the floor looked like a kid's sand pile.

"Joel and Philippa," Ian said.

"But we were sleeping in here the night they left," Molly objected.

"They could have planned beforehand," Arlene said, "and dug them up any time."

Sheila had another thought. "Maybe Angel the *policia* or his drug dealer friends decided to keep an eye on us and dug up the ashes when we were all out somewhere."

Ian nodded. "Maybe your police friend from Puerto Juarez did show up for a visit."

"Oh, who knows what the hell happened," Arlene said. Fate, or whatever it was, had put the ashes in her keeping, and now the same force had taken them off her hands. "Let's just get moving."

That evening, Ian and Molly looked lonely as they stood in front of the hut, forming a portrait as solemn as the farm couple in *American Gothic*. "Keep smiling," Ian called, waving as Arlene and Sheila started down the beach.

"Don't worry, Paw," Sheila drawled, "we will."

Arlene's backpack felt strange and heavy on the walk to the village. She could hardly wait to get rid of the letter to Shelley Stewart's relatives, to feel the weight of all of it disappear for good.

But they'd decided to mail it in Mérida, where it would theoretically have a better chance of surviving the Mexican postal system. They'd left the letter as it was first written, including the passage about the ashes being spread in the sea at Playa del Carmen. That way, the family would have a place to come for a pilgrimage. Besides, who'd want to know their daughter's remains were being carted all over Mexico, perhaps snorted off and on by hopeful druggies?

"Did you ask about him and Philippa?" Sheila asked.

"What?"

"Joel. Did you ask him about his and Philippa's, uh, relationship?"

"Yes, as a matter of fact I did. He said she was an incredibly spiritual person; he thinks she's so far above the physical she's a kind of Zen angel." This was true; it was what he had said. "I guess they sort of started off on the wrong foot."

The real truth, though, was that he was so lousy in bed that likely Philippa had tried once or twice and given up. Arlene had led him to a small grove, if you could call anything in the jungle a grove, that she had once noticed on a walk. "Ooh," she breathed, joking around once they were lying in its spongy depths, "it's as good as a bed." With her breasts pressed against his chest, her hand on his hard penis, she considered maybe for starters he could lie on his back, but didn't get a chance to complete the thought. She found herself tipped immediately into the missionary position: he was inside her before she could think how lucky it was she was horny. Pumping away, he gave her a rather sloppy kiss and then, after a cloudburst of violent thrusts, as quick as a rabbit on *The Nature of Things*, he was done. "You're gorgeous Arlene." He kissed her again, not seeming to have a clue, a single qualm about his speedy performance.

"Hmm." She cuddled up to him, her head on his shoulder. She'd thought all the rigorous control needed for Tai Chi would have taught him something. Nostalgically, she remembered

Murdoch boinging into erections two or three times a day, and hoped for the best. The night was still young. They talked for a while in a comfortable, desultory way and after she asked him about Philippa, he said, "I've got to get back." He sounded worried.

She had let him go, and sat there for some time listening to the ocean surf and the jungle twitterings, hoping there weren't any snakes.

"The wrong foot." Sheila looked thoughtful. "So how was he with you?"

"How was he?"

"In the sack, as Lexie would say."

"Oh," Arlene said, "he's a really cool guy, he makes love just like you'd expect." She was thankful for the sunset colouring both their faces a vivid shade of rose, camouflaging her lie. She wanted Sheila to think the prize she'd lost was worth something. "Hey look at us," she said, changing the subject.

"I'm pink therefore I am," said Sheila.

They began to giggle with a kind of helpless inanity. The village was only a few yards past the next palm tree. "Let's stop at the hotel for a beer." Arlene was trying not to dissolve into absolute idiocy.

"I drink therefore I am," Sheila managed to wheeze. Their laughter came in short gasps.

Arlene held her side, in stitches at the thought that now even poor old Shelley's ashes no longer existed. They had magically disappeared. Neither she nor Sheila was responsible for them any more. "Poof," she said. "Gone but not forgotten." Sheila keened with laughter, not missing a beat.

The hotel owner, prosperous in white polyester, walked past them and hissed. Arlene shouted after him, "You're a dink therefore you are." This struck them as the ultimate in wit, and they almost collapsed on the beach. They staggered into the village, wiping their eyes and snorting. They walked for the last time down the sand road leading to the restaurant, stepped up onto the patio, put their backpacks beside some rusty chairs and tried to recover themselves. The place was empty except for a wizened man in a straw hat who didn't bother to look up from his beans and eggs. A young guy in a yellow T-shirt sauntered in for a pack of Fiestas, eyeing the girls as if they were on sale in a shop window. He put the pack of cigarettes in the sleeve of his right shoulder. Someone in the kitchen was whistling "Black Magic Woman" with an expertise that reminded them of Angel the policeman when he'd entertained them so well on the way to Villahermosa.

Nobody came to wait on them. The song changed to "Nights in White Satin" and they sat up, thinking perhaps it really was Angel Delgado. They stood silently, and went in, sneaking like kids playing hide-and-seek, to the kitchen. Arlene half expected to see Angel slouching with his hands in his pockets looking out the window toward the sea, and wondered if it would be a good idea to tell him about the ashes' disappearance. But there was only a skinny cook, stirring something in a frying pan. He quit whistling when he saw them, and waved them away. "*Momentito,*" he said, irritated. "*Momentito.*" He called to the waiter, who had made himself invisible after selling the cigarettes. The girls went back to the patio.

The woman next door came out of her hut to take clothes off the line. Her spotless, intricately embroidered dress seemed to shimmer as if illuminated by black light. Arlene greeted her warmly, nostalgia already colouring her perspective.

"*Buenas noches.*" The Mayan woman smiled and reached up to gather a load of white cotton clothing.

The waiter came slowly onto the patio to take their orders. For a moment, a sort of euphoria lifted Arlene into a realm of new possibilities. A glossy blue fly buzzed with soft thuds against the window beside her.

The woman nodded toward their backpacks. "Go home?" she asked.

181

"*Sí.*" The girls nodded.

"*Vaya con Dios,*" she said. The sun had almost disappeared, but was still bright enough to cast a glow on the clean laundry held in her arms.

PART THREE

2002

15. MAZATLÁN

Arlene is watching her husband and thirteen-year-old son body surf, or at least that's what they say they're doing. In reality they're letting each wave knock them off their feet and tumble them to shore, half-drowned, yelling, whooping at each other as they fight their way back into the churning water for another try. There's quite an undertow, they've told Arlene, though when she carefully waded in yesterday she didn't find it to be very strong. She thinks they just want to pique her concern, to add an edge to her watchfulness.

Although her birthday isn't until summer, this trip is her present. Mazatlán has given her a reprieve from a dark January in Saskatchewan. Being warm outside in the sun is a gift. So is the taste of tortillas and refried beans with hot sauce, the cramped one-way streets, the Latin busy-ness of the market. The ocean. The surf is loud, easily reaching over the noise of traffic to their fifth-floor hotel room. She wakes up in the night thinking it contains some of the same tones as a prairie snowstorm. Sunsets here are quick and spectacular. At home by the lake in summer, they can easily sip several beers, lazily chatting with neighbours while the sun inches its way under the horizon, a backdrop to their evening. Here it's an event: they rush out onto their balcony to watch, the whole show over in a few minutes. The sun drops into the ocean like an orange-red egg into boiling water, steaming pink wisps of cloud for a couple of moments before darkness.

Her husband and son wrestle each other into shallow water. They're coming toward her, each locked in the other's neck-hold. She shakes her head at them, exasperated, thinking, Don't they ever quit. They splash past several people wading into the water, including a woman her age in a bathing suit with a skirt. Arlene feels encouraged to try the water herself, but a small cloud has settled like a hen over the sun, and doesn't seem to be moving. She lies back down on her blanket.

Two figures block Arlene's view of the sky, dripping salt water on her legs. "Mim, we need money for tortilla chips." Imitating a cartoon character named Cartman, her son calls her Mim when he wants something. She hands them the beach bag.

Once they're back with the chips, Murdoch sits beside her dabbing sunscreen on his nose. Murdoch, her husband. If she were writing this all down she could say, "Reader, I married him," though they're no Jane and Rochester.

"That little store across the street charges two pesos more than the one on the corner," he complains, rummaging in the bag for his sunglasses. He's been comparing and contrasting costs and charges ever since they got to Mazatlán, keeping a funereal watch on the Canadian exchange rate and adding up restaurant bills with the fervent eye of a tax inspector. He's always been careful with money, but foreign exchange seems to bring out a particular brand of frugality she notices in other tourists as well. She's seen the odd one with a calculator. She's heard conversations in passing, always the male half, trying to figure out the real cost. "Do you know what she charged us for that avocado? You can get them cheaper at home in Safeway!"

His sunglasses are smudged with oil, and slip halfway down his nose. She gives him a cool glance, and he looks up. "What?" he asks. She shakes her head and pats his shoulder. "Nothing." Jordan sits at her other side eating tortilla chips, looking out to sea with the elegiac expression brought on only by junk food. Arlene thinks he's very handsome, beautiful, really. She refuses to acknowledge how much he looks like his father, her ex-husband. Her fond gaze lasts a bit too long.

"What are you looking at?" he says, annoyed.

"I'm not sure." Keeping a straight face, she considers him. "I'm not quite sure what it is." He sprinkles sand on her leg. "Quit that," she says lethargically.

Murdoch puts down the sunscreen and says, with a slight nervous tic that gives him away, "I booked that charter to Palenque."

"What?"

"Well, you said, uh, you said yes, so I just went ahead and did it." On their first day in Mexico, they'd noticed several travel agencies, one of them advertising a cheap charter tour east to see ruins, Aztec or Mayan, Mexico City or Palenque. They could well afford to take a few days off from their three weeks in Mazatlán. "What an opportunity!" Murdoch was excited. He'd often talked about wanting to go back to Palenque.

Arlene was not so enthusiastic. "I haven't ever wanted to see those ruins again. You know that." But softened up by a couple of *cervezas* yesterday evening, she'd finally said okay. It was after all where they'd first come together. So to speak, she thinks now, not happy but amusing herself for the time being. She'll think about the ramifications of visiting Palenque later.

"Come in swimming, you've hardly even got wet since we've been here. You said you and Aunt Sheila used to body surf." Jordan grins. "Back in the olden days."

"Yeah, us and Wilma Flintstone."

"C'mon, Mim."

"Don't call me Mim." She takes off her glasses and stands up. "I'll go in for a while, but if you splash me you'll be doing the dead man's float for real." He laughs, imitating something maniacal. She walks quickly across the sand, looking straight ahead at the blurred horizon, and splashes into the water until she's submerged to her waist. She looks back at Murdoch, who from her near-sighted vantage point could be anybody, a pale blob looking any-where. He waves, presumably at her, so she waves back. Jordan is a blur barrelling toward her, intent on teasing and splashing, so she dives in.

Along with the cool Pacific, she feels a wash of nostalgia, is reminded of her and Sheila's joy at swimming nude in the ocean, their movements liquid, liberated, part of the sea. The strap of her bathing suit seems to cut into her shoulders; Spandex clings annoy-ingly to her stomach. She feels the sweep of the undertow and stands up, not paying attention to the waves. She is pushed over by a big breaker and tumbled gasping toward shore until she's able to regain her balance. She beckons to her son to come back out with her onto the beach; she's had enough. He imitates a chicken.

Murdoch comes up and touches her arm. "Are you okay?" he asks.

"I'm fine. Here," she motions toward Jordan, and to the water, granting him the use of it, "you're more fun than I am."

The sand here has shell in it that crunches under her feet as she walks back to her beach blanket. The brooding cloud has finally moved on. To Arlene, coming from Saskatchewan in win-ter, the intense brightness of sun on water, the feel of it warming her back and shoulders, is bliss. The only religions she's ever been able to understand are those based on sun worship.

She hasn't set out for Mexico for any purpose other than to relax. She certainly doesn't want to deal with all that a trip to Palenque might unearth. She pictures those memories as ruins, concealed for all these years by jungle growth, threatened again with exposure.

Even Mazatlán, with its high narrow sidewalks, its beaches, the undertow of the Pacific, and especially the quality of the air here, has this effect on her. Where Proust was propelled into the past through the taste of a *petite madeleine*, she is wafted there by Mexican west coast air.

Saskatchewan air is hard, clear. In winter even the sunlight can pierce like icicles, and the cold early darkness is always dismal. Warm summer evenings don't darken until nine or ten o'clock and usually bring hordes of mosquitoes. Here the air is soft, the evenings warm, though every Mexican they've talked to has complained about the coldness of this winter. Pet dogs wear knitted sweaters. Toddlers run around on the windy *malecon* in parkas.

She considers going for a walk along the shore to dry off but rubs on sunscreen instead because a small group of Mexican men are sitting on the cement wall, smoking cigarettes and eyeing the women on the beach. She's wearing a black bathing suit that features a "tummy flattener" which doesn't seem to work very well. She hopes the cellulite on her thighs will be less noticeable once she gets a tan. She quite vividly remembers the moment she noticed, in her bathroom mirror, the first signs of puckered flab. At the time, she was thirty-six. Now she has a theory about that age, about it being an acid test, some sort of turning point. Greta Garbo, Marilyn Monroe, and Princess Diana all put themselves out of the picture at age thirty-six, each in her own way. Arlene figures it was because of cellulite.

She wishes Sheila were here to smile at that little insight. Sheila with her dreamy giddiness, her way of suddenly focusing intelligently on the main point, her theories of various afterlives. For years, Sheila suggested the two of them take a trip here together again, but Arlene never seemed to find the time; she hadn't really wanted to. Her face twists for a moment into grief, and she covers her eyes with one hand, willing herself not to cry.

Then, three months ago, Sheila's sister June called from Winnipeg. "I have some bad news," June said, and Arlene could hear she'd been crying. She didn't have time for dread or panic before June continued. "It's Sheila. I got a phone call in the middle of the night from that friend of hers in England. She came home from a concert, bent over to take off her shoes and died of a heart attack. Just like that. Not exercising or anything. It's so unbelievable."

"What?" Arlene couldn't take it in. "You mean she's in the hospital? In London? A heart attack?" But then she realized. She knew the answer. It came to her then that she'd been waiting for this shoe to drop for thirty years.

"Arlene. Sheila's dead. It's no mistake this time," June added needlessly before she began to cry in earnest.

A section of Arlene's foundation seemed to crumble, leaving her lopsided, even though death itself no longer came as so much of a trauma: Arlene had lost both her parents, too.

But each death since Sheila's mistaken one has been easier in one crucial detail: it has never again been able to shatter Arlene's worldview, her perception of reality. She's never since then felt the titanic bewilderment that comes with the first one, the shock of realizing no one was exempt, that she and those she loved floated in vulnerable chaos along with everyone else.

The prospect of Palenque hangs over her now like a green spectre. Murdoch knew she would change her mind again about booking a flight there, so he grabbed the chance to arrange the tour behind her back. This isn't the first time he's got his way by just going ahead, acting without her real approval, exploiting the fact that she'd waffled back and forth before saying no. Thinking back, she can conjure a long list, ending with her stupid second-hand car with the reliable motor and all the electronic features that have quit working, one by one. She's lucky she can still open her damn window.

She looks back toward the hotel. She wishes the Mexican men would go away so she could go comfortably for a walk. Not that she's the only middle-aged woman around. Many of the tourists staying in their hotel are former hippies nostalgic for the sixties. Instead of bikinis most of the women now wear one-piece bathing suits, often navy or black like Arlene's. Yet none of the men seem to care what they look like; she's seen a couple of horrific sixty-year-old men in Speedos, and her own husband is perfectly happy to gambol along the beach playing Frisbee in the shallow water, his stomach like bread dough rising past the waistband of his boxer swim shorts.

Jordan is still skinny, but beginning to fill out and into a consciousness of self that has only a little to do with self-consciousness. She sees the beginnings of this carefully guarded awareness and wonders what goes on behind his jokes, his passion for video and computer games, his need to hang out with his friends, who have all suddenly expanded so that now when they come to visit, the house seems taken over by a goofy mismatched herd: giraffes and buffalo, all noisy and intense with the need to jostle and entertain each other. This can only get worse as they keep growing. She watches Murdoch dive over a wave and, imitating a whale, spout water onto his stepson.

She closes her book; she hasn't looked at it today. She's been enamoured with the sun and beach, and now she's worrying about the prospect of a trip to the ruins. Usually, though, she reads obsessively; it's as essential to her as breathing. She keeps literary magazines in the bathroom. When she's drinking her morning coffee, if she has nothing else, she reads cereal boxes. Reading a book in a car makes her dizzy, so she reads signs along the road, generally aloud for the annoyed edification of her family.

Because of her interest in literature, for a short time in her twenties she thought she might become an English professor. She couldn't afford, however, to spend all she'd need to acquire a doctorate: time, money, energy, dedication, a certain strength of character. She's always needed to conserve what she has. She eventually became a sessional lecturer. At one-fifth the salary of a professor, she's allowed by the university to teach English 100 classes, a full load each semester if she wants to, since, over the years she's proven relatively reliable. She's not a bad teacher. She points out literary truths which, after forty-three years of avid reading, she finds self-evident, but which are often revelations to students reading literature for the first time.

She wonders why only readers and gardeners are avid. You never hear anyone referred to as an avid hockey player or an avid lover. Her ex-husband was, as a matter of fact, an avid lover. After their son was born, he spread his avidity around too freely. She closed herself off to these betrayals because caring for the baby left her too exhausted to deal properly with anything else.

By the time Jordan turned three, she was almost to the point of contemplating her next move, but hadn't quite let the hurt rise to the top. Then Murdoch moved to town after landing a job teaching computer science at the technical school. Newly single, he decided to look her up. He became part of her life again, funny and reliable, bringing carrot sticks to their potluck suppers and discussing computer programs with her husband.

They started to flirt, making bad jokes straight-faced over the hors d'oeuvres. "Come up and see my, uh, software sometime," she said the first time. He bit into a mushroom cap, narrowing his eyes at her in mock passion. "Only if you let me show you my hard drive."

He started coming over regularly, just for coffee or a drink, sometimes when her husband wasn't home.

One day in particular as she and Jordan were watching *Mr. Dressup* in the rocking chair, he dropped in, helping himself to coffee as he talked about a problem at work. He sat down comfortably on the couch and watched them, Jordan peacefully enthralled with Casey and Finnegan, picking his nose and slightly drooling, Arlene nuzzling the top of his head, and she could see him fall. Or sink, maybe is a better word. She saw Murdoch sink into love, into a morass of tenderness for both of them, his expression one of pained helplessness. And she knew in a vast wave of gratitude that he could be the answer to everything.

And there he is now, ten years later, bobbing in the water next to his stepson: two pin heads dark and nebulous in the distance. She peers at them, thinking they're out way too far. They've tired of body surfing and are now standing up to their necks in the water, judging the exact times to jump so that they're carried over the crests of the waves.

Her ex-husband is now on his third wife, and Jordan has been able to figure things out, and to appreciate his stepdad. And how much does Arlene appreciate him? In retrospect, she can't make up her mind about herself: has she been in love with either of her son's fathers? Does she know what love is? Is she almost fifty and still asking this question?

A little dog, part Chihuahua, with a green and yellow sweater, is zooming around on the beach, hysterically active, enjoying himself playing with every kid he comes across. He doesn't seem to be with anyone, but he must have an indulgent owner somewhere. She thinks his wearing a sweater is silly, although it's true, it does seem cooler here than she remembers. But then memory is a tease.

Over the years, her journey here with Sheila has distilled into impressions of beach and greenery, heat and brightness, the taste of spice, and fits of laughter. Except for Palenque, which seems to have taken on the proportions of a separate country. It all happened so long ago, Arlene can't judge how her ordeal there might have changed her life, affected her courage. The idea of stepping onto a plane and finding herself there again makes her catch her breath for a second, afraid of falling, as if she were looking over a cliff into darkness. She grimaces to herself. A heart of darkness.

She now harbours a desire for safety, for comforting routine, but part of that is middle age. Her favourite poem is Emily Dickinson's "Our lives are Swiss,— / So still so cool." She wants her life to be still and cool. The idea is tantalizing. She dreams of it.

Good things happened at Palenque too, of course. "Those ruins are still the most beautiful in the Americas," Murdoch said last night, trying to convince her, "and I've been reading more about them. It would be really exciting to see them again."

She finally agreed, seduced by his enthusiasm; the romance of returning to their old meeting place; by three Pacifico beer; and by the evening itself with the smell of ocean breeze mixed with Mexican spices and unidentifiable flowers, undermined now and then by a subtle whiff of burning garbage.

In Mazatlán, they have been staying in the old part of town, away from the Golden Zone, the package tour section of expensive high-rises. Although their hotel is basic, with wobbly dangerous fans, an unreliable elevator, and tiles falling off the walls, it's patronized by some actual Mexicans and has an atmosphere of former grandeur. Eavesdropping on a historical tour, they were informed that John Wayne stayed there once, in the 1950s. Besides all this, it's comparatively cheap, they have hot showers, and their own private balcony on the fifth floor overlooking the Pacific.

Though her son doesn't like the Golden Zone as well as *Olas Altas* because the waves aren't as high, when they want to feel superior to other lobster-coloured Canadians, they take a city bus to catch some sun on the long tourist beach. Each bus is privately owned. Their favourite has "El Viagra" printed on a fancy beaded gearshift cover.

Downtown, Arlene has heard hissing for the first time in thirty years. She remembered the sound well, and ignored it; so did Jordan, who knows teasing when he hears it. Murdoch, though, looked around good-naturedly and found the source: young girls, their pretty faces beaming from the second-floor balcony of a square house of earthy pink stucco. He grinned cheekily at them and waved, and they laughed and yelled something like, "No, not you, *him.*"

The girls were hissing at Jordan, and now Arlene has to question all the years she's remembered Mexican men as particularly awful. Maybe it was only this: young people teasing and trying to attract the attention of other young people.

It's an entirely different experience visiting Mexico as a middle-aged matron with her family. No one hisses. She is greeted respectfully as *Señora*, and even the vendors on the beach are comparatively circumspect. Following the advice of a tourist guide, she waves her pointing finger sideways and says, *"No gracias,"* and they melt away.

Murdoch has come out of the water to relax and dry off, and she's relieved to see Jordan back on the beach too, playing with the hyperactive dog who has just stopped in mid-careen and pulled off his own sweater, crouching in the sand and scraping it over his head with his front paws. The sweater lies limp and abandoned near the water's edge and Arlene thinks she should rescue it for the dog's owner, who still hasn't shown up. The dog seems to have come to the beach on his own, like a kid told to go outside and play, able to go home by himself when he's hungry or thirsty.

"Did you see that dog take his sweater off?" Murdoch puts his book down, laughing.

"I hope he's not lost," she says.

"No, he's way too happy. And in good shape. Look at all that energy."

A young couple sitting nearby throws the dog a rubber ball, and he goes into paroxysms of ecstasy. Arlene's son falls over laughing. She has to catch herself before she becomes too enamoured with the whole scene and open to saying yes to a pet dog. She knows who ends up looking after any living thing she allows across their threshold.

Arlene is too old to be a very good mother. She didn't find babies appealing, didn't think of wanting one of her own at all until suddenly, at the end of her twenties and still single, she did. After a Christmas holiday spent with Victor and his toddlers, the desire fell on her: like an avalanche, she wrote to Sheila, like a ton of bricks. She told Sheila that she wanted a baby, that the desire for one seemed as biologically intense as the need for sex, or even for food. She said she craved a baby, she was starving for one, she was even willing to go through childbirth for one.

Sheila was living with someone at the time, and she wrote back that Arlene's letter focused a feeling of vague unease she hadn't been dealing with. She immediately became pregnant. Arlene was livid: it had been her idea in the first place. Soon after their child was born, Sheila and the father, an immigrant from Czechoslovakia, were married, and of course Arlene went to visit them in Winnipeg for the occasion. She found herself thrilled for her friend, happy she could be there to cuddle the baby and talk with Sheila and help neglect the housework. She wasn't jealous. She didn't want Sheila's baby and certainly not her husband. She wanted her own. Within a couple of years, she was married.

In her mid-thirties she finally had Jordan. The memory of her very own fat baby still brings her a sentimental rush. Her inner voice heightens into baby talk as she recalls what a softy tofty, what a cute puddin, what a wriggly little bozo he was, how tasty his fat little feetsies.

She watches him now as he wades into the ocean, slender, his shoulders beginning to widen. When they stand together, his dad looks squat and pear-shaped beside him. His stepdad, of course, but he's been far more of a father to him than her ex. They're a team, whose main joy seems to be irritating Arlene and then examining her reaction, like biologists watching a bug. They seriously try to talk her into going camping with them just to listen to her complain, to watch her deal with smoky fires and crawl grumpily out of a damp sleeping bag. They say it's no fun without her. They rent Arnold Schwartzenegger movies and bribe her to watch them. They tease her about sensitive issues, such as her Master's thesis which should have been done fifteen years ago.

Murdoch, though, knows approximately when to quit. Jordan will retrieve a pop can from the fridge while she's mixing a drink, and shake it up before giving it to her. He calls her reaction "spazzing out." He's taken to messing up her hair as he walks casually past her armchair. He'll recount plots from TV shows until she's cross-eyed with boredom, but won't squeeze out one word about his life at school, especially if she asks. He tries to choreograph her into becoming a cartoon character. "Come on, Mim. Stand in the doorway and say 'Toodle-oo,'" he directed one day as he was off to school. "Just once." She refused. He sends her into orbit by giving her a hug and squeezing her upper-arm flab, saying, "Mmm. Pudding." She has images of hormones, hers menopausal and his adolescent, colliding and attacking each other in a deadly Star Wars scenario.

Sheila's theory was that he's attempting to disarm her. Sons have to convince themselves their mothers aren't all-powerful before they dare try to separate, to break away, she said. Although Sheila raised two sons, Arlene doesn't agree. She thinks boys simply become obnoxious with their adolescent infusion of testosterone.

She is by herself on the beach now, waiting to dry off well enough to wear her denim skirt back to the hotel. She enjoys the feeling of salt water drying on her skin. She looks forward to a hot shower and a meal of spicy shrimp at a downtown restaurant. A Mexican jazz combo is playing tonight in the old opera house, and she'd like to hear it. She admires the old *zócalo* buildings with their white stucco and ornate ceramic tiles. On either side of the plaza, restaurants flourish with tables spilling onto the sidewalks, and coffeehouses and vendors sell pistachios and sugared almonds just around the corner.

She looks up at the hotel, where Jordan waves to her from their balcony and for her benefit pretends to guzzle a bottle of Pacifico. Murdoch grabs the beer away from him and beckons but she pretends she's too preoccupied to notice.

She fastens her skirt and walks to the water's edge, picking up pretty pieces of broken glass ground smooth by sand and waves. She doesn't remember these, thirty years ago. She and Sheila would surely have kept some as souvenirs, since they're free, and easy to carry. She has few actual mementoes of her friend, no presents exchanged over the years except toys and outfits for their kids. Neither of them were gift givers.

She can't get used to the fact of Sheila's non-existence, and wishes she had faith in an afterlife. She would like to continue exchanging e-mail: s.stuart@nirvana.com. Sheila could tell her about her meeting, or reunion, with Shelley Stewart.

It's almost thirty years ago now since she and Sheila made it home from Mexico. They didn't tell their parents much about their trip, certainly no details about Veracruz or Puerto Juarez, and particularly not about what happened in Palenque. They shared a desire to keep their parents in a cocoon of benign serenity: they wanted to be free to live without interference, and part of this included the obligation not to let them know they had been right to worry. So when Vic, thinking enough time had passed, blurted out the Palenque story one Christmas before she got home, she was furious. Her parents spent the entire holiday phoning the Stuarts, visiting back and forth and questioning her and Sheila, who was home for Christmas too. Victor went back to Saskatoon early.

"You didn't get a reply? Three *years* have gone by, and neither of you have tried to find out if that poor girl's family knows what happened to her?" Her mother couldn't get over it.

"We didn't sign our names or addresses to the note with the visa. We thought it would be better not to, at least as long as we still had to cross a couple of borders."

"But you've been home now for three years! You could have written them again. Did you at least copy down the address from the visa?"

They hadn't. They hadn't saved any of Shelley's stuff either, except the dresses and earrings.

Arlene's dad wore his most infuriating expression, not the astonishment of her mother and Sheila's parents, but of calm disappointment, of "I always knew you were capable of this sort of stupidity, and here you are again proving me right." "What can you expect?" he asked Sheila's dad. From these two? From this generation? From Arlene? She can still work up a rage recalling all the instances of his disappointments with her. That time was especially galling because she *had* used her head – they might have inadvertently carried drugs over the border in that tin box. But she couldn't tell him about all that.

Sheila's father went to talk to the local RCMP to see if anything could still be done about finding out who this girl was, if her parents knew anything of what had happened. As it turned out, shamefully for Arlene and Sheila, it was easy to contact Shelley Stewart's family. The RCMP simply consulted Phoenix's Missing Persons and found her name on the list. Even more shamefully, no, the family hadn't had any word at all. They'd never received the girls' letter. They were more grateful than anyone could imagine, they said, to finally know their daughter's fate. They had sent photos and enquiries to police stations all over Mexico. They had gone down there themselves, but hadn't known where to begin to look.

Arlene and Sheila's mothers made them write to the Stewarts, noting down every detail they could recall about what had happened and advising them to contact Angel Delgado in Palenque. They wrote again that they'd buried Shelley's ashes on the beach in Playa del Carmen, and after some discussion, decided to add part of the truth: that the police claimed half the ashes had leaked from the container onto a jungle path near Palenque. Arlene sent a package with her green dress and jade earrings by special delivery, with another note guiltily reiterating the fact that they *had* sent a letter with Shelley's visa three years before. Sheila had managed to shrink her dress in the wash, so it was long gone to the Salvation Army, and she'd apparently lost her earrings.

For a while, their mothers stayed in regular contact with the Stewarts, able to keep Arlene and Sheila annoyingly up-to-date on their activities. The Stewarts went to Playa del Carmen and had a private funeral on the beach, then continued to Palenque for another memorial, and to question officer Delgado. The trip served no purpose, however, except as a pilgrimage, since Angel Delgado had left the police force. No one seemed to know what had happened to him. Many people in the town remembered the incident, recalled some sort of mix-up involving young tourists, but no one knew that the girls had taken Shelley Stewart's ashes, and the police had no record of anything to do with any of it.

Angel's disappearance did nothing to curtail Sheila and Arlene's speculations about the fate of the ashes. Though they didn't reveal this part of the story to their parents or the Stewarts, they were sure the evidence led to a conspiracy, a drug ring: Angel bribing them with Shelley Stewart's backpack so they'd take the blue tin in the first place, the other policeman saving them in Puerto Juarez. If Joel did steal the ashes, he must have tried them out first and got high.

As time went on, whenever the word "ashes" was mentioned, lovers, siblings, old friends all began to flinch and gaze at the ceiling or to drift out of the room. Arlene and Sheila remembered suspicious details and formed various and creative theories until sometime in their thirties, when they lost interest. By then, too much else had happened. Miraculous babies were conceived because of a cold night in October or an old Pink Floyd album; parents and friends ceased to exist because of a first cigarette taken forty years before on a dare or because of a change in plans leading to catastrophe; they met life-transforming people because they decided to take a class or have a drink out on the spur of the moment. Lives were fraught with ordinary mystery, with everyday drama. What was so exceptional about the disappearance of a tin box and its contents? Still, they were never quite able to forget about the Stewarts.

Sheila said sometimes when she was walking alone, especially in a park or out in the country, she felt someone staring at the back of her neck. She thought it had to be Shelley, watching, judging, finding them deficient. Arlene said speak for yourself. Sheila had always believed in some sort of afterlife, one sort of afterlife after another. She and Arlene usually avoided discussing spiritual matters, even when they lived in the same city. But they were good friends for thirty-five years and now Sheila is first again, first over yet another border. Arlene is left standing on the beach, watching the tide inch higher in the late afternoon.

Poetic fragments about borders, lines about the tide, about the sea, come uninvited to her mind, but she resists writing them down. She knows her limitations. She's a reader, not a writer. Besides, lately she's been losing words, or replacing them with wrong ones, and she supposes losing the use of language might be an impediment to creative writing. The other day she was describing the remains of a pigeon killed by a cat on the front sidewalk. "There was nothing left but flowers," she said. When she's finally been given the key to Alzheimer City, she hopes some corner of her brain will still enable her to garner some joy from the few poems she's memorized.

One summer while visiting her brother's farm, she wandered lonely along the grid road past fields of golden canola memorizing, *Our lives are Swiss,– / So still so cool, / Till, some odd afternoon, / The Alps neglect their curtains, / And we look farther on.* She was interrupted, however, by the theme from *The Beverly Hillbillies*, which ran so insistently through her mind that the two pieces became inextricably connected. Now she considers this a metaphor for her life. Any attempt to attain a vision of truth or beauty is invariably haunted by the inane, by silliness. But looking out over the water, she remembers the second verse: *Italy stands the other side, / While like a guard between, / The solemn Alps, / The siren Alps. / Forever intervene!* It's the word *siren* that transforms the poem into something wonderful. Dickinson could have written "silent" or "stalwart" and it would still be great in its way. But *siren*. It's as if she'd written the poem just for Arlene.

She always envied Sheila's courage, her insistence on not compromising. She thought she chose to have it all, to have everything within reason and more. But where is she now? Arlene can't help but give her ghost, somewhere off in the distance, a jaundiced look.

She makes her way to the *malecon* to pull on her sandals. Why not try to make the most of a trip to Palenque? First experiences with sex and death, recalled in tranquillity. She could make a pilgrimage to the jungle, maybe have her own memorial service for both Sheila and Shelley. She examines a perfect black oval among her handful of coloured glass, and realizes it's petrified beach tar. *Oil that is. Black gold. Texas tea.*

Joel always had beach tar on his feet. She remembers him, with his Tai Chi and Zen kōans, his search for peanut butter and a higher level of existence, asking her and Sheila a riddle. "What did the Buddhist monk say to the hot dog vendor?"

They looked up at him from sorting beans, his shadow blocking their light. "What?" they asked.

"Make me one with everything."

16. PALENQUE

Arlene is standing on their small third-floor balcony looking down at the street. Things have changed. Palenque is still a small town but has lost its quiet rural quality. The streets are all paved, and she doesn't remember all these cables and power lines criss-crossing the horizon. Not that she can remember many details. But the damp heat greeted her like a familiar acquaintance as she stepped off the plane, robbing her of energy. She was afraid for a moment that it would send her into the tailspin the small charter plane had threatened throughout the flight, but that hasn't happened.

The building across from their hotel is an unusual chartreuse colour, the second storey hanging over a *zapateria*. A truck carrying giant glass jugs of water rumbles by, clinking. People and cars come and go, the noise of the traffic punctuated by dogs barking, a rooster crowing in the distance. Normal, everyday sounds. She can feel the knot in her stomach start to unwind.

She can't recall where her old hotel was, can't even remember its name. Maybe Murdoch will find it on his walk. She would like to visit the *Señora*, show her that in spite of her skepticism, she has at least partly grown up. But Louisa would be retired, that is if she's still alive.

Jordan is sleeping, exhausted after being so sick on the plane he'd had to use the scanty barf bags. Once they'd changed planes in Mexico City, the flight was so awful that Arlene said only one sentence to Murdoch the whole time: "You and your bright ideas." Both she and Jordan were nauseated and miserable, though at least she hadn't thrown up. By the time they reached their hotel, Murdoch was forced to get away to escape her deadly rays of resentment. She closes the balcony doors, startling two geckoes who scamper up the wall, becoming still as ornaments when they reach the ceiling. She puts her hand on Jordan's forehead. He wakes up, asking for a drink of Coke. "Coke? Do you want to get sick again? Here's some water." She hands him a new bottle.

"Where's Dad?"

"Gone for a walk."

"I'm hungry."

"How can you possibly be hungry?" But it's true. He has his colour back; he's already recovered. After standing on the bed to examine the geckoes, he settles back against his pillow and finds *Mexico's Funniest Home Videos* on the television.

The hum of the air conditioner seems louder, intensified by the insanely enthusiastic Spanish blaring from the TV. She's hit by another rush of annoyance. "I'm going out to find some tortillas and cheese for supper. I don't feel like going to a café, and you should wait before eating much."

"What?" He surfaces for a moment from TV underworld.

"Going. To find. Food."

He grins at her and waves as if she were already a block away. She escapes back into the heat. Descending cement stairs with an intricate wrought iron railing, she wonders if this hotel was here thirty years ago. She really can't remember a thing about the town. Just her concrete hotel room, the spectacular ruins, a vague impression of the campground and waterfall. Halfway down the street a group of young men watch as she passes. There's no hissing but one of them reaches down to put his hand on his crotch, a gesture of contempt for a woman alone. She feels the old familiar rage mixed with vulnerability and decides not to search for the market after all. She stops by a corner store to be over-charged for warm cheese and day-old tortillas. As the girl at the counter hands her the bag, a voice from a dark corner hisses, "*Mamacita!*" Arlene looks around; she is the only customer in the store. She stifles an urge to look for a mirror.

The girl smirks apologetically. "Carlos," she nods reprovingly at the corner and he says it again. She turns on a light, illuminat-ing not only her own gold earrings and shiny hair, but a brilliant green and yellow parrot perched in the corner.

Arlene laughs. "Carlos! You bad bird." He bobs his head up and down and hops sideways, squawking. The girl's smirk turns into a smile. Her warm eyes and grace are like a homecoming for Arlene: that remembered exquisite competence, the gracious aura of certainty Mexican women have.

And Mexican men are still *macho*. She walks past the young men again on the way back and nods this time, giving them the fish-eye. Surprisingly, they nod back. She could be their mother, she thinks, although then again, she hopes no son of hers would ever rearrange his balls in public.

The hotel is quite beautiful, high and narrow with three floors of ceramic-tiled rooms leading to outside hallways, more like com-mon balconies surrounding a courtyard of trees and lush greenery shading a rather soupy-looking swimming pool.

"Oh there you are!" Murdoch is back, and he and Jordan look at her together as she comes in, the TV flickering on their faces.

The coolness of the room, their expressions of welcome and slight worry give her a sense of well-being, if only for a moment. "Can we at least eat in peace without that damn TV on? You can't understand what they're saying anyway."

"I know what's happening," Jordan says. "It's a repeat." Homer Simpson is examining the contents of his fridge, speaking Spanish in a deep, profoundly unsuitable voice.

Murdoch turns down the sound. "What did you buy?" He asks this hopefully, recognizing that she's in a better mood.

"Tortillas and cheese, an avocado, something to drink."

"Tortillas and cheese." He smiles at her across the room, and she remembers their first picnic outside his little orange tent.

"Déjà vu all over again," she says, grinning back at him.

Feeling left out, Jordan turns his attention away from *The Simpsons* and grabs the remote control from Murdoch.

"So romantic," Murdoch says. "Back to our old stomping grounds, just us three."

"I'll cut the cheese," Jordan offers. This is an old joke.

"You'd better not. And give me that remote." Murdoch grabs it back and cuffs Jordan, who immediately attacks, trying to push him face first into the pillow. "Hey, watch out for my glasses!"

As Arlene spreads the food out on plastic bags, she is surprised to find her face wet with tears. "I'll eat later," she says and heads into the bathroom for a shower.

Of course she'd be upset, finding herself back in Palenque after all these years, with Sheila dead now for real. But this isn't grief; she can tell the difference. Nor is it the memory of trauma. This is something else.

Maybe she's simply been pushed too far, maybe she's become hysterically annoyed at having to travel with two of the Three Stooges. Maybe she wants more attention paid, from Murdoch at least.

But no. She stands under the shower, trying to sort out her feelings. Sadness. The word flows over her along with the lukewarm water. An unsuspected spring of sadness has welled up with no warning. A deep spring.

It comes upon her again the next day as she's riding in the *collectivo*, the taxi van to the ruins. Clouds hang low and misty, the day is dull with suspense. They're passing by a giant white reproduction of a Mayan head just outside of town, when she's aware again of tears on her cheeks. Reflected in her compact mirror, her eyes are only slightly swollen, her nose isn't red at all. Tears are just there, coming as easily as they do for a movie star, no sobbing, no wretched twisting of her mouth in hurt or anger. Nothing. Just tears rolling down her cheeks as if her eyes have sprung leaks. When Murdoch and Jordan finally notice, a look passes between them. They think she's crying for Sheila.

Then, as suddenly as they've begun, the tears stop, luckily before the van arrives at the ruins. When they get out, Murdoch pays the driver quickly, too excited to count *pesos*. They follow a tour group of Germans.

The weather continues to threaten rain. In the grip of his old enthusiasm for the Mayans, Murdoch reels off newly discovered facts as they make their way past a *palapa* restaurant advertising American food, past a few shops and vendors selling carvings and Mayan artwork, and through the entrance to the lush grounds.

She sees the Temple of the Sun and remembers walking here in this very spot with Sheila just before they met Manrike. She rubs her own temple for a moment, warding off the foreshadow of a headache.

"Did you know," she says quickly, "that even though they rarely sacrificed people, the Mayans sacrificed human blood to the gods?" Murdoch interrupts himself long enough to give her an absent assent. She's struck for a moment with a queasy weightless feeling, recalling herself bleeding, here alone in her hotel room. She found out years later it wasn't caused by the shock of think-ing Sheila was dead, but by her exhausting hike in the sun after-ward. It happened again, in her late twenties, one hot summer after she'd gone picking strawberries for several hours without a hat. The doctor who stopped the hemorrhage with a D. and C. said he didn't know what drugs the Mexican doctor would have given her, and in fact didn't believe sunstroke could cause such bleeding. But she knows better. She spent most of the summer she was pregnant indoors with the air conditioner on.

"They'd puncture their tongues," she continues matter-of-factly, "or their penises, in order to get lots of blood from a relatively small wound."

This gets Jordan's attention. "Ugh. Is that true?" He stops and looks at her suspiciously. "How do you know that?"

"I met somebody once whose grandmother was Mayan. Well, it was that guy from here Sheila talked about. Manrike, her old boyfriend. He knew lots of things about the ancient ones." She tries to remember what else he said. "He told us that all the blood loss used to make them have visions."

Jordan makes a ghoulish face and sidles up to her. "Bluuuud," he mimics something between a vampire and Frankenstein's Igor. "I vant to haff bluuu-ud." She plays her role and gives him a disgusted look.

Sheila's affair with Manrike left her with a lifelong addiction to foreigners. She claimed that just about any accent could do her in. "Some guy will say his version of 'Meet me at zee casbah,' and I'm there like a dirty shirt, waiting." She spent years travelling and living with foreign men, sometimes in their home countries, even marrying two of them. The cold war was still on when she was married to the Czech, so she never went to his country, never learned more than a few words of his language, but she eventually became fluent, perfectly at home in French, Spanish, and Italian. She could even go shopping and exchange small talk in Dutch and German.

After they got home from Mexico, Sheila went back to university and became an ESL teacher. Teaching English, she was able to find work just about anywhere. "It's not all because of the men, you know," she said. "It's because I feel most alive when I'm in a strange country. I don't know how to explain it. I feel more at home when I'm travelling."

What caused her heart attack? No one knows exactly. She was a few pounds overweight and she'd never quit smoking. Though she was pushing fifty, she was still on the pill. Her older son, who'd been staying with her, said she'd been feeling tired lately. But still.

After Sheila's memorial service, Arlene began to be conscious of feeling tired too. She became aware of her heart beating; it fluttered sporadically, she thought. It was feeble. She couldn't sleep. During the day she would feel a tightness, a pressure around her chest and wonder if it was a sign of something dangerous, until she'd realize it was her bra band.

Somewhat surprisingly, her doctor agreed her heartbeat sounded a bit irregular, though all she recommended was to cut down on caffeine. To be on the safe side, she sent Arlene for tests. For twenty-four hours, she had to wear a heart-monitoring device and record each of her activities. She spent that day cleaning the house, so she'd have something to write down.

She had an EKG, was able to watch the pencilled mountains and valleys, speed bumps and dips of her heart's rhythm printing out on a page. She went for an echocardiogram, which turned out to be an ultrasound of the heart. She lay on her side resting on her raised left arm with her hand touching the back of her head in a bathing beauty pose, her breasts flopping to one side while a technician slipped a cool gelled instrument around on her chest. There, on a TV monitor, was her heart, a pulpy grey mass beating inside a cut-off triangle shaped something like a one-dimensional Mayan pyramid, she thinks now. What made Arlene squeamish wasn't the picture, but the sound. The technician turned up the volume so she could clearly hear the liquid whooshing of her blood, the loud pop of her arteries opening and closing. She couldn't quite believe that was all that kept her going. Once she cut back to two cups of coffee a day, the fluttering went away.

By that time, Sheila's sons and lover had sprinkled her ashes somewhere in England's Lake District. Arlene has never been there, but has the impression it wouldn't be suitable for Sheila: too tame, too pastoral. Better to have let them seep out in a thin snake along the jungle floor.

But then, Arlene may have it wrong this time, too.

Murdoch points to the Temple of the Inscriptions. "There's the tallest one." Figures dot the side of the pyramid, people walking stolidly up the steps. She notices Pacal's tomb is now closed to the public, for today or for good, it doesn't say.

Jordan runs on ahead of them. He's been mildly interested in the pyramids and in sightseeing, but the idea of climbing to the top of the highest one has sparked real enthusiasm. "Come on!"

"Do you have your water bottle?" Arlene calls. She knows he has it in his small backpack, but has to ask. It's a compulsion she never bothers to resist: do you have your bike helmet, your lunch, your gloves, jacket, toque, scarf, sunscreen, an extra sweater? He ignores her.

"Yes, yes," Murdoch waves him on. "Go ahead. We'll meet you up there."

Arlene takes off her fake Tilley hat and fans herself with it. The heat is weighing her down. They watch Jordan scramble a quarter of the way in no time.

A Mexican couple, both grey-haired and solid and in their seventies, pass them. They're on their way up although they don't look particularly fit for their age. The woman wears a dark, old-lady print dress, the man has a light blue shirt tucked in neatly around his thick waist.

Murdoch grins at Arlene. "We'll follow those two."

She stands at the base looking up. The old couple stop every few steps to rest. Ridiculously, this calls up a memory of Angel the policeman whistling in his car on the way to Villahermosa. "'Stairway to Heaven,'" she says.

Murdoch nudges her, ready to start climbing. "Ooo it makes you wonder," he says, deadpan. Jordan is halfway up now, waving at them disdainfully.

The three of them sit on the edge, the view as lush and spectacular as she remembers. "I met your dad right down there," she says.

"You mean Murdoch."

"Yes."

"No you didn't, we met on the west coast!" Murdoch is astounded she could forget that.

"Well of course, I mean this place is where I got to know you. In fact you were on top of this very pyramid when I first noticed you. You looked like an ant."

"Yes. I climbed down and there you were."

"But you were just friends for a long time." Jordan knows their history. Or thinks he knows.

"Good thing we didn't start living together right away or you'd never have existed." Murdoch grins at him.

This concept strikes him silent. After a moment, he stands up and moves to the other side.

Like Jordan she is struck silent, but with the thought of the alternative lives she could have led. A life without her son is incomprehensible. What about a whole lifetime with Murdoch? Or a whole life without Murdoch? She takes his arm for a moment. After all he could have ended up with someone else as pretty and exotic, as flaky as that flame-haired Jeanette. Instead he'd chosen her. If he hadn't, how would she have managed alone as a single mother?

Sheila had, now and then, with two kids. She insisted on passion, and when it fizzled out, she always moved on. Arlene resents her for getting off scot free, for travelling the world with or without her boys, solo or with her latest lover, eased by her tolerant Czech ex-husband and by her own insouciance.

The last time she came to visit, Sheila was beginning to flirt with the Christianity they'd both grown up with. She had started to attend interdenominational services in London, where she'd been living for the past two years with a Cockney songwriter. "It's the sense of community," she said. "Shared spiritual beliefs."

Arlene said, well, in the midst of a typical baby boomer midlife crisis, it was likely more sensible to find Jesus than to have another affair. Sheila gave her a look and said of course she'd tried that, too. They moved into the verandah with their wine, and settled in for a long talk. Becoming giddy, they spent the entire afternoon discussing old boyfriends, exchanging salacious details they'd previously considered themselves too discreet to talk about. They wept with laughter, they held their sides, they were in stitches, they fell out of their chairs.

"Remember Joel at Playa del Carmen?" Sheila asked, wiping her eyes.

"Of course I do."

"Was he really a good lay? Tell the truth now, Arlene."

Arlene remembered of course that he hadn't been, but had to think before she could recall anything specific about that night. "No. He wasn't. It was all sort of a wham bam thank you I've got to get back to Philippa type of thing. Maybe five minutes. I mean we talked for a while and all that, but the sex itself, well." She laughed and made a raspberry sound.

"Huh. He was the same with me."

"What?" Arlene spilled some of her wine. "You're joking. I would have known."

"Arlene. Remember that night on the beach near Puerto Juarez? Did you really think we were just turning over a turtle?"

God, she misses her. It's not only that Sheila was her oldest friend, that they'd known each other as girls, but that each of them had come through her life to middle age with the other intact, somehow. Old rivalries, even recent years of neglect when they rarely saw each other, meant nothing.

The longer she sits on the ledge, the harder it is to move. She recalls this inertia, sitting up here – was it here or one of the other pyramids? – with Murdoch thirty years ago. But back then it was mostly what they'd been smoking. Now it was nothing but age and this heat. Swamp ass. That's what Ian and Molly used to call it, the paralyzing lethargy induced by hot damp weather. But in Playa del Carmen there was, at least, the breeze off the sea.

Last night, she dreamed she and Sheila were again hitchhiking in Mexico, though it seemed to be a universal place; it could have been anywhere with a seacoast. They were picked up by two guys in a van. Arlene was aware that they were Mexican but they, too, seemed strangely generic: they seemed to be somehow from her own culture. The driver was big, like a football player, with puffy eighties-style hair, the other was skinny with greased-back hair. She recognized him later as Pedro, the street kid from Veracruz, grown up. Once in the vehicle, she was hit by a powerful sense of doom, which was heightened to terror when the driver began to speed backwards down the coastal road. He drove backwards for miles, faster and faster, while they sobbed, begging him to stop. They were still accelerating when she woke up, panting but tearless, as if in the dream she'd been running instead of weeping.

Jordan is older now than Pedro was when she met him in Veracruz. If she could pray, could believe in anything other than nature and the anarchy of chance, she would offer something up to the gods for Pedro's well-being. If he's alive, he'd be about forty now, set in a life of crime. Maybe he has a small business. Maybe he's a vendor selling Indian-made turtles or beaded bracelets. Or maybe he made it over the border, is doing all right in the USA. She'll never know what happened to him, any more than she knows whether Tex's chest pains were heart disease or heartburn, or whether El Kafkasito really had been arrested as a student dissident, or was simply a common thief. But student or thief, he had those scars. She shivers in spite of the quilt of muggy heat.

She's led a sheltered life. She never has come to terms with seeing physical evidence of torture. She can't bear to think of it. She herself barely survives discomfort at the hands of someone else for the good of her own health. A trip to the dentist unnerves her.

She doesn't belong to Amnesty International. She never walks in protest marches. She does donate money to women's shelters and, during graphic publicity drives, to starving Africans. Whenever she's on the Internet, she clicks the Hunger Site, which is set up so every visit donates a cup of food to the third world. Sponsoring advertisers often feature gourmet cooking recipes, or ads promising ways to lose twenty pounds in a month.

She feels a remote and cynical self-contempt: about her inaction, her deliberate turning away, her feeling helpless and lucky. But how else, she wonders, can you survive in the world the way it is, and stay sane?

The rain comes now, and Murdoch stands, holding out his hand for her to join him and Jordan under an overhanging piece of stone from the temple. Some of the other tourists crowd into the enclosure, some stay out in the downpour, their faces raised in relief. Arlene finds she still can't move and waves Murdoch away. The rain is lovely. She unfolds a little plastic package she bought at the dollar store before she left home, a rain poncho, which she waves smugly at Jordan who mocked her for bringing something that looked so cheap and useless. Jordan.

After they had children of their own, Arlene and Sheila realized, admitted to each other, how extreme their negligence had been in not trying to contact Shelley Stewart's parents. Their own parents, in the meantime, had sent Christmas cards back and forth to Arizona for years. Until finally, in their mid-sixties after several years of being invited, the four of them went to Phoenix for a month one January to stay as guests in one of the Stewarts' condominiums.

"We were treated like royalty," Arlene's dad said.

"Yes, but it got to be a bit much." Her mother was relieved to be home. "They insisted on paying for everything, and there was always their great loss to think about."

Arlene looks back at her small family, and is stabbed by a moment of fear as she thinks only a few more years and it could be

Jordan out in the world, travelling, living dangerously. She has a clear picture of herself and Sheila falling asleep on each other's shoulders on buses, and feels an obscure affection for the children they were.

Her own mother said that while they were in Mexico she worried so constantly, her life seemed to be unravelling, until one night she dreamed Arlene was eaten by an alligator. She woke up and said, "That's it. I've had enough." From then on she refused to let herself dwell on anything to do with her daughter until she was home, safe. Arlene supposes she's inherited that ability. She was able, for instance, to put Jordan's father's philandering out of her conscious mind until she was ready to deal with it. And for three years, she pretended nothing had happened here in Palenque. She turned her back entirely on Shelley Stewart. She flinches. That might have been the worst thing she's done in her life.

But no. She and Sheila were young. They were stupid and irresponsible; they didn't know any better.

But how did Shelley's parents keep their sanity? For three years, they hadn't known if their daughter had been raped and murdered or what. The possibility that she was still alive must have been the worst. The excruciating hope, thinking maybe she'd been brainwashed by a cult; maybe she'd become addicted to drugs. The fear that maybe she was living in unspeakable circumstances, none of them unimaginable in the small hours. Mrs. Stewart confided to Arlene's mother that once they learned Shelley was dead, it was a great relief to know she'd been killed by mindless chance, a force of nature. A car accident, an earthquake, a fall off a cliff, a drowning, the actual snakebite, all seemed merciful compared to any human act of violence, or violation.

The Stewarts seized on Arlene and Sheila's version of what happened to their daughter as the absolute truth because they needed to. Yet, anything could have happened to Shelley out there in the jungle. Anything. Who would ever know? Arlene and Sheila had talked themselves into believing what the *policía* told them, too. Even back then they knew that some mysteries are better left alone. And back then, she resented Sheila for having the time of her life while she, Arlene, was devastated, traumatized. Much later, she understood that Sheila had been marked for life too.

One afternoon when Arlene was pregnant, she excused herself for pigging out on Sheila's baking with the old saw that she was eating for two. Sheila became pensive, uncharacteristically subdued. She finally confessed that sometimes she thought she was living for two. Sometimes she felt Shelley Stewart had been sacrificed for her: almost obliging her to throw herself into life and love headlong, to live a sort of heightened existence. She couldn't explain this logically. She didn't even know whether it was true, whether her life would have been different without Shelley and her ashes. But once this idea had gripped her she was never able to shake it off.

Sheila went into her bedroom then and came out with Shelley's opal teardrop earrings. Arlene was speechless. "I didn't exactly lie," Sheila said, blushing. "I couldn't find them when you sent yours back, but then when I did, I couldn't bear to part with them."

Arlene understood. She'd felt that way about the green linen dress. Whenever she slipped it over her head, she felt as if she were putting on beauty. She's always regretted giving it back. She felt Shelley would have wanted her to have it: it was rightfully hers. Returning the jade earrings would have been enough. At the time, Shelley's parents no doubt had lots of her dresses still hanging in her closet. They likely gave them all away, to strangers.

"Mim! Come in out of the rain." The rain has cooled her, restored her energy. Arlene considers getting up and joining Murdoch and Jordan by the temple. But she stays where she is; the downpour has almost stopped and a mist hangs over the ruins, making them look like something from the legends of King Arthur.

She never did try to meet the guy from the Mazatlán bus depot. She never took that detour to San Cristóbal. Once they started the trip home, she and Sheila both became intent on getting there. They felt as if their trip were over and they needed to keep moving until they were back in Saskatchewan. But that was only part of the reason, she thinks now. Sheila would have gone with her to San Cristóbal if she'd wanted to stop. But Arlene was afraid to.

Not because she thought his old girlfriend might have been Shelley Stewart, or because she'd lost all her courage at Palenque, as she used to rationalize, but because she'd never really wanted to meet him in the first place. She simply knew he was out of her league. She would not be able to interest him. Even if she had, she thinks now, it wouldn't have worked out. Not for long. She was the type of person who escaped from Saskatoon in January to the heat of exotic Mexico, looking for adventure and romance, only to have her first affair with a guy from Swift Current. And ended up marrying him.

She glances back at Murdoch, who is peering at the disintegrating plaster of the temple with a magnifying glass. Maybe Heidegger was only partly right. It isn't just knowing *that* you are. It's knowing *who* you are.

In the distance, she can just make out a waterfall where the campground might be. She sees herself and Murdoch diving into clear water, kneeling in the cave under the falls, eating pineapple.

The clouds have thinned, shedding a delicate silver light that sharpens the details of the panorama beneath her, transforming the ruins into the image that has crystalized in her memory of this place: stone and ivory miniatures set in moss and broccoli. Somewhere in the encircling jungle is the undergrowth Sheila and Manrike slipped through, being jaguars. Somewhere in the heart of that greenery, a young girl's ashes.

ACKNOWLEDGEMENTS

I wish to thank Connie Gault, Dianne Warren, Joan Givner, and David Carpenter for their critical advice and encouragement; the Saskatchewan Arts Board for funding part of this novel; and Joanne Gerber for her meticulous editing. Thanks also to Melissa Nordin and Brenda Roberston for writing down their impressions and memories of their own trips to Palenque. Finally, as always, I want to thank my husband, Lutz Wesseler, for his support, not only in his role as a one man funding agency, but as an astute reader.

Grateful acknowledgement is made to Kazuaki Tanahashi for permission to use his translation of Hakuin Ekaku's kōan, "Monkey."

ABOUT THE AUTHOR

Marlis Wesseler is the author of two Coteau short story collections, *Life Skills* and *Imitating Art*, and the novel *Elvis Unplugged*. Both *Elvis Unplugged* and *Life Skills* were finalists in the Saskatchewan Book Awards. She is a former fiction editor of *Grain* magazine, and has taught at the Sage Hill Writing Experience Youth Camp.

Marlis Wesseler was born and raised in north central Saskatchewan and received her English degree at the University of Regina. She lives in Regina with her family.

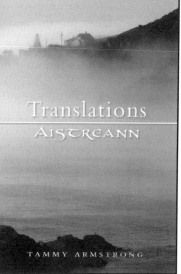